BOROUGH

D0487485

Edith's cheeks took on the colour of a spring dawn and her pale blue eyes began to sparkle, turning her face from pleasant to truly beautiful and desirable.

Brand's body responded anew to her nearness and her delicate scent. He tapped a finger against his mouth as a glimmer of an idea came to him. The perfect lesson for a proud lady. She needed to learn her new status and he needed to learn the secrets of this estate.

'The estate is indeed productive. You appear well-versed in all aspects of it. A surprising pastime for a lady.'

'You see the value of keeping me as a steward?'

Her nostrils quivered slightly with tension, much as a high-strung horse might quiver before battle. She wanted to run the estate. Why was it so important to her? What game was she playing?

'Not as a steward.' He paused, beginning to enjoy himself. 'But I do wish you to remain on in this hall. You are an unexpected addition to the estate.'

She licked her lips, turning them a deeper red. 'As what? I'm no maidservant for your wife. I have my pride.'

He waited a heartbeat and leant forward so that his breath interlaced with hers. She did know the game. The pretence ended here.

'As my concubine.'

AUTHOR NOTE

On 1st November 866, taking advantage of a Northumbrian civil war, part of the Great Viking Army led by Halfdan captured the Northumbrian capital of York. The capture was relatively bloodless as all the nobles were at York Minster, attending the All Saints service. By March 867 the Northumbrians had settled their differences and tried to retake the town. The town was sacked and the Northumbrians comprehensively defeated. Aella, one of the Northumbrian leaders, suffered a particularly horrific death—being made a blood eagle. However, he had slowly poisoned Halfdan's father, if the saga is to be believed.

Halfdan and his warriors then left Northumbria to its own devices. In 876, after some unspecified disturbance, Halfdan decided to settle his warriors in the Yorkshire countryside. Up until this time the Vikings had mainly stuck to York. They settled as far north as the North Riding, rather than going up to what is now the county of Northumberland. There is a singular lack of Norse place names in Northumberland and Durham, so the conclusion is that they did not maintain permanent settlements.

The Vikings were not a literate people and left few written records—thus things can change as new evidence is uncovered. Late in 2011 a hoard of silver coins from the era was uncovered in Lancashire and revealed the existence of several Viking Northumbrian kings missing from the historical record. The Jorvik museum in York is well worth a visit. It is designed to be accessible to anyone from the age of five and up, and is dedicated to researching this highly interesting era.

PAYING THE VIKING'S PRICE

Michelle Styles

MILLS & BOON

First published in Great Britain 2013
by Mills & Boon, an imprint of Harlequin (UK) Limited,
Large Print edition 2014
Harlequin (UK) Limited, Eton House, 18-24 Paradise Road,
Richmond, Surrey TW9 1SR

© 2013 Michelle Styles

ISBN: 978 0 263 23957 7

Born and raised near San Francisco, California, **Michelle Styles** currently lives a few miles south of Hadrian's Wall, with her husband, three children, two dogs, cats, assorted ducks, hens and beehives.

An avid reader, she became hooked on historical romance when she discovered Georgette Heyer, Anya Seton and Victoria Holt one rainy lunchtime at school. And, for her, a historical romance still represents the perfect way to escape.

Although Michelle loves reading about history, she also enjoys a more hands-on approach to her research. She has experimented with a variety of old recipes and cookery methods (some more successfully than others), climbed down Roman sewers, and fallen off horses in Iceland—all in the name of discovering more about how people went about their daily lives. When she is not writing, reading or doing research, Michelle tends her rather overgrown garden or does needlework—in particular counted cross-stitch.

Michelle maintains a website, www.michellestyles.co.uk, and a blog: www.michellestyles.blogspot.com. She would be delighted to hear from you.

Previous novels by the same author:

THE GLADIATOR'S HONOUR
A NOBLE CAPTIVE
SOLD AND SEDUCED
THE ROMAN'S VIRGIN MISTRESS
TAKEN BY THE VIKING
A CHRISTMAS WEDDING WAGER
  (part of *Christmas By Candlelight*)
VIKING WARRIOR, UNWILLING WIFE
AN IMPULSIVE DEBUTANTE
A QUESTION OF IMPROPRIETY
IMPOVERISHED MISS, CONVENIENT WIFE
COMPROMISING MISS MILTON*
THE VIKING'S CAPTIVE PRINCESS
BREAKING THE GOVERNESS'S RULES*
TO MARRY A MATCHMAKER
HIS UNSUITABLE VISCOUNTESS
HATTIE WILKINSON MEETS HER MATCH
AN IDEAL HUSBAND?

*linked by character

And in Mills & Boon Historical *Undone!* eBooks:

THE PERFECT CONCUBINE

**Did you know that some of these novels
are also available as eBooks?
Visit www.millsandboon.co.uk**

For exercise trainer Tracy Anderson and her online Metamorphosis community, particularly Leah, Patrizia, Tracy, Shaunna, Jenn, Katie and Kathy, in grateful thanks for showing me that exercise is something to be embraced and enjoyed rather than feared. The only fairy dust is truly sweat and you have to be persistent.

If you are interested in reading more about the Vikings in England I would suggest:

Ferguson, Robert, *The Hammer and the Cross: A New History of the Vikings* (2010 Penguin Books, London)

Haywood, John, *The Penguin Historical Atlas of the Vikings* (1995 Penguin Books, London)

Jesch, Judith, *Women in the Viking Age* (1991 The Boydell Press, Woodbridge Suffolk)

O'Brien, Harriet, *Queen Emma and The Vikings— The Woman who shaped the events of 1066* (2005 Bloomsbury, London)

Magnusson, Magnus KBE, *The Vikings* (2003 Tempus Publishing Stroud, Gloucestershire)

Rosedahl, Else, *The Vikings revised edition*, translated by Susan Margeson and Kirsten Williams (1998 Penguin Books, London)

Wood, Michael, *In Search of the Dark Ages* 2nd edition (2005 BBC Books, London)

Chapter One

Early March 876—North Yorkshire

His land. His and no one else's, won by his sword arm and given by the grace of his king.

Brand Bjornson knelt down in the dark soil and gathered a handful of sun-warmed dirt. He squeezed it, feeling the richness of the earth between his fingers. After more than a decade of war and fighting, this, this was all he dreamt about—land to put down roots and to create his own piece of paradise on earth.

Finally. Instead of a landless mercenary whose only future was a quick death, he was now a jaarl with a large estate to prove it. Halfdan, once the leader of the felag to conquer Northumbria and now his king, had kept his word and given him worthwhile land, one of the finest estates in all of Northumbria.

Brand gave a wry smile as the rich loam coated his hand. Honouring a long-ago promise was a rare thing in Viking politics where allegiance and alliance shifted on the point of a sword or the jangle of a money bag.

He stood and surveyed the gently rolling hills where the new spring grass had started to push through the dry hassocks of winter. A river meandered. And it was all his as far as the eye could see. He'd fought hard enough for it, from Byzantium to the wilds of Northumbria. He'd earned it and he would be a good overlord. He'd encountered enough poor ones to last a lifetime.

'Do we burn the empty barns and teach them a lesson?' Hrearek, his comrade-in-arms and sworn sokman asked, nodding towards where the various ramshackle buildings stood. 'There are rich pickings here which they are trying to hide from us with their lack of cattle, sheep and horses. Always the same, these Northumbrians. Same tricks and attempts at deception. They think we're stupid because we don't worship the same god as they do or have the same customs but I can sniff out stores and gold from ten paces. And this place has them, despite what they claimed.'

'We've come to settle, not to raid. My sword

time is over.' Brand stood and wiped his filthy hand against his trousers. There was more than a faint hint of spring in the chilly March breeze. His face was towards the future, rather than his blood-soaked past. Reborn and renewed, he would remake this land to suit his needs. 'It is time to plant and grow crops. They will learn it is wise to be on the right side of their overlord. Once they know me, they will be glad to have me as their jaarl.'

'And you think they will give in like that?' Hrearek snapped his fingers. 'This was the heartland of the rebellion. They need to be taught a lesson which they will not soon forget.'

'They have no choice. The rebels lost. My sword dispatched their leader and saved your life.' Brand shrugged. War, when it came down to it, was merely a game. Afterwards, the winner had everything. It was the way of the world and the Northumbrians knew it. It was why they'd rebelled rather than accepting that they had lost all of their power when the Norsemen defeated their fathers and brothers in Jorvik ten years ago. 'Halfdan is their king. Any rebel will be punished and their land taken.'

'And will you marry? Send back home for the

lovely Lady Sigfrieda? You have spoken so much about her.'

Brand looked up in the clear blue sky. Once the thought of winning Sigfrieda's hand had driven his every move, now he had not thought about her in months. He'd been too busy helping to put down the rebellion and finally winning his land. He struggled to remember her face, beyond the dazzle her golden hair had given in the candle-light, and how regular her features were. She would be the perfect demure wife for him. To-gether they would breed strong sons.

'That is the plan.' He fingered the scar on his neck, remembering how he'd been turned away, bloody and beaten from his father's house as his father lay dying. Then he'd been known as the bastard son of a cast-off mistress who dared speak his mind. 'Once I'm settled, I will send word to her father. If fortune favours me, the lovely lady will be here before the autumn makes the passage difficult. I need sons to make sure what I have done is not written on the wind.'

His sokman nodded, accepting the statement at face value. Hrearek was not a friend, but rather a companion-in-arms and didn't need to know the full history. 'I'm impressed. You never falter or waver in your schemes. You are an inspiration, Brand Bjornson. I can only hope that fortune will favour me in the same way. By Frieda's bower, I too would like a woman to open her thighs and bear me sons.'

'My dream kept me alive on the blackest of days. Now it is time to live it.' Brand gestured towards where the Anglo-Saxon hall stood, proud and defiant. The occupants were to learn a powerful lesson about who controlled this land.

'Time to claim my land and see precisely how impoverished this Lord Egbert truly was.'

'The Norsemen! The Norsemen are here!'

The cry went up and echoed around the hall. Lady Edith stilled, her spindle falling into her lap.

She had expected this for weeks, ever since she'd heard the news of her husband's death in the rebellion against the so-called King of Jorvik and leader of the Norsemen. Her counsel against the rebellion had fallen on deaf ears.

Now Egbert was slain in battle and she had to contend with the consequences of his actions. Silently she thanked God that most of the stores were stowed safely and the land showed its usual before-the-spring barrenness, nothing to alert the Norsemen to its true worth and productivity.

'What will we do, cousin? The Norsemen are here! There is no one left to defend us. We're doomed,' Hilda asked, jumping up and spilling wool and spinning whorls all over the stone floor. 'Doomed, I say!'

'We must hope the Norsemen go as quickly as they came with the minimal amount of fuss.' Edith carefully placed her spindle down on the wooden trunk. She gathered up the wool and the three spinning whorls that she could find. One, she noticed with a sigh, now had a crack running through it. Hilda didn't bother to help, but instead stood wringing her hands and repeating her words. There was little point in panicking when her distant cousin did it well enough for the both of them.

'Will they go?' Hilda asked when Edith had picked up the final whorl.

'Always.' Edith tightened her fingers about the whorl. 'The Norsemen never settle. They take what they can grab and go.'

The one thing she was certain of despite their conquest of Eoferwic, which the Norsemen now called Jorvik, ten years ago—the Norsemen did not settle inland. Instead they used the land for raiding, their own private larder of cattle, sheep and women, one of the main reasons why Egbert found so many recruits for his rebellion.

Edith wrinkled her nose in distaste. The Norsemen were barbarians with no thought for the lives they destroyed.

Against her husband's direct order, she had made sure all the essential stores were carefully hidden, including moving all the silver and her mother's jewels into the hidden cavity in the lord's bedchamber. Unlike Egbert, she had been in Eoferwic the day the Norsemen first took that city and had seen how well they could fight. Despite Egbert's words and posturing, she'd doubted that he could retake it with his ragtag army when so many others had failed. When they were first married, Egbert had won a few bouts with his sword, but he'd long since run to fat.

Her people would make it through until the late spring when food became plentiful again. She refused to allow any Norseman to starve them simply to increase his own bloated belly.

'What will you do? They are bound to know about Eg...Lord Egbert and his part in the struggle. We will all be punished for it, just like you warned him!'

'It gives me no pleasure to be right, cousin. You must believe that.'

'But you know what they will do. They'll burn, rape and pillage.' Hilda's eyes bulged with fear and her body shook.

Edith pressed her lips together. If she didn't do something, her cousin would collapse in a heap on the floor, insensible to reason, one more problem to be sorted before the Norsemen arrived. Edith concentrated and searched for a soothing phrase, rather than screaming at Hilda to pull herself together.

She could never stoop so low as to scream at Hilda. She knew whose bed her husband had shared the last time he was here. Everyone knew it. The whispers had flown around the hall until she thought everyone had looked at her with pity. Edith despised pity. It did not mean she approved of her cousin's affair with her husband. Far from it, but she knew what Egbert was like underneath the good humour he showed to visitors and people who might have been able to assist him. If Hilda had objected to his advances, he'd have raped her. Sending her away hadn't been an option while

Egbert was alive. And now there were the Norsemen at the door.

'I will mouth the words of fealty if it comes down to it,' Edith said in her firmest voice. 'You will see, Hilda. All will be well once I do.'

'You?' Hilda put her hand to her throat and the hysterics instantly stopped. 'But will this Norseman jaarl accept your word?'

Edith clenched her fists. Hilda should trust her. Hadn't she looked after the estate, making certain it prospered while Egbert indulged his passion for hunting and whoring? 'He will have to. This land has belonged to our family since time began. And I will not be the one to lose it.'

'You mean you expect him to marry you.' Hilda tapped her nose. 'Clever. I wish I'd a dowry like that instead of my looks. You'll be dressed in silks and ribbons and forget about us.'

'I've no expectations,' Edith said carefully. Marriage to a Norseman was the logical solution, even if she hated the thought of being married again. An unmarried widow with a large estate was too great of a prize. 'But you're wrong if you think I could ever forget this estate and its inhabitants. They are my people. Every single one of them.'

'Your husband will be turning in his grave,

cousin, to think that you of all people should swear allegiance to the Norse king.'

'My father swore fealty to Halfdan in Eoferwic, ten years ago. Egbert broke that promise, not me.'

Hilda shook her carefully coiffured head and her bee-stung lips gave a little pout. 'I expected more somehow. You were his wife for seven years. Are you sure the king won't worry about that? You must have shared some of the same views.'

Edith raised her chin. How dare Hilda question her as if she was a common servant? Her entire being trembled with anger and she longed to tell a few home truths to Hilda. Instead Edith gulped air and concentrated on controlling her temper.

'When did Egbert and I ever agree on any-thing?' she said as steadily as she dared. 'Lord Egbert is no longer the master here. He ceased to be when he breathed his last. The hall and its land were never fully his. We shared responsibility. I know the marriage terms my father negotiated. The hall and its lands were to be returned to me should anything happen to Egbert. And I intend to keep them safe.'

'Cousin, this is no time for jesting.' Hilda widened her pale blue eyes. 'You know little of the art of war. Egbert always used to say—'

'It's the people of this land I must consider.' Edith glared at Hilda. The last thing she wanted to hear was her late husband's opinion on her many failings. 'The Norsemen should accept my assurance and my gift. They should move on to the next estate, hopefully without burning our hall or forcing a marriage. We survive whatever happens. Survival is important.'

Edith wasn't sure who she wanted to convince more—her cousin or herself.

'They will take everything that is not nailed down, even if you don't have to marry.' Hilda turned pale. 'You know what the Norsemen are like! Two years ago in the south before I journeyed to you, all the farms were ablaze and the women… Promise me that you won't allow that to happen to me. I saw unspeakable things. You must protect me. Lord Egbert would expect it.'

'I have taken precautions. My parents taught me well. The Norsemen have been a danger for years.' Edith gave Hilda a hard look. 'We survived before. My parents even entertained Halfdan in the early years.'

'What should I do?' Hilda wrung her hands. 'Lord Egbert always made sure I had a special task in times of emergency. On second thought,

I should be the one to speak first. Soften their hearts with a gentle word. You can be abrupt, cousin. Allow me to win their regard with a smile.'

Edith stared at Hilda in disbelief. Was she serious in her offer? Her entire being recoiled at the thought of Hilda greeting the Norsemen in her stead. And she'd been the one to think of employing Hilda in some task to save her from Egbert's ire. Egbert could only be bothered with Hilda and her demands when it suited him.

Even now, Hilda had started to prance about the hall, practising the gestures she'd make as if she was the one in charge.

'You see, cousin, how much better I'd do it?'

'Hilda, I need you to go to the stew pond and make sure the various dams are closed. I've no wish to lose fish because the men are slack,' Edith said, retaking control of the situation.

'You mean…'

'I will greet the Norsemen, dressed simply, and explain about our meagre circumstances. We have avoided being burnt out before. We may do so again. Trust me.'

'You mean I might avoid the Norsemen? Altogether?' Hilda stopped.

'There is that possibility.' Edith held out her

hand. 'You would be doing me this small favour, cousin. It would put my mind at ease to know this task was properly done.'

'As you wish, cousin, *you* are the lord here now.' Hilda made a curtsy which bordered on discourteous and left the main hall with her skirts swishing.

Edith sighed. There had to be some decent farmer that Edith could marry her off to. She'd provide a reasonable dowry so the man would take her. The question was who, given the common knowledge about her relationship with Egbert. Edith tapped her finger against her mouth. All that could wait until the current crisis was solved. She had to concentrate on the matter at hand and ensure that everything had been done. No mistakes made.

She adjusted her wimple so that her black hair was completely covered as she cast an eye about the hall, searching for things left undone.

The majority of the silver and gold were safe in the cavity. There was no need to check that. She was the only one who knew about it.

The pagan Norsemen were no respecters of churches or monasteries. If anything their wealth attracted the raiders. When her father showed her the hiding place, he recounted the story about the Lindisfarne raid and the countless other raids. However, he boasted about his alliance with Halfdan and confidently predicted she'd never need it.

She had kept a few trinkets to appease the Norsemen, but they had to believe that they were poor and the farm was not well managed so that they would not demand an enormous payment. Her father had drilled that notion into her head since she had first toddled about the yard.

'The Norsemen never stay long. Raiders rather than settlers. They move swiftly and overlook the well hidden,' she whispered over and over as she tried to decide where she'd stand. She practised her gestures and decided against kneeling with hands raised in supplication. A bowed head would suffice. Welcoming, but far from subservient.

She could do this. She had to. Everyone in the steading was counting on her to save them from the Norsemen. There were no warriors to fight. No one but a barely bearded boy had returned from the rebellion. And he'd been burning with fever and had only survived a day or two after telling his story of the Norsemen treachery and Egbert's final heroic stand. He had found his courage far too late, but she was glad that he had found it.

Heavy boots resounded on the stones outside. Edith pressed her fist to her stomach and willed the sick feeling to be gone. Far too soon. She hadn't even had the chance to move the spindles or the whorls.

Why hadn't there been more warning? Why hadn't someone seen the fires that surely must be burning as the Viking horde swept through the countryside? Silently she cursed Egbert for taking every able-bodied man to fight in the rebellion. A pain tugged behind her eyes. Later, she'd investigate ways of improving the warning system.

She motioned towards one of her few remaining manservants to unbar the door. The elderly man shuffled forwards.

Before he could get there, the door fell to the ground. In the doorway stood one of the tallest men Edith had ever seen. Clean-shaven, but with dark blond hair flowing over his shoulders. The very epitome of a Viking warrior, he was dressed in a fur cloak and skin trousers. In his hand he carried a double-headed axe, but it was his piercing blue eyes which drew her attention, swiftly followed by the angry red mark about his neck. A barbarian warrior if ever there was one. A true pagan.

Edith wet her lips, but no sound beyond a shocked gasp rose from her throat. She tried again to mouth the welcome, but her voice refused to work. A sharp stab of fear went through her. Her hands shook as she lifted them.

In her mind's eye she saw the hall blazing and its people killed with her unable to do anything to prevent the carnage. If she'd been born a man like her parents prayed she'd be, none of this would have happened. All she had were her wits and her tongue and both appeared to have deserted her. Silently Edith prayed for a miracle.

The barbarian advanced forwards, and his men streamed in behind him, filling the hall.

Edith retreated backwards. Her leg hit the wooden trunk, causing the spindle to tumble to the ground. The whorl rolled across the rushes, disappearing. Her favourite one. Worrying about a worthless whorl when her entire life hung in the balance! Typical. She gave a hiccupping laugh.

The sound cut through her panic. She stopped and squared her shoulders. She had an intellect equal to any man and that included this enormous Norseman who glowered at her, fingering his axe.

'It is customary to wait for an answer before knocking the door down,' she said. The steadiness of her voice gave her courage. She was this mountain of a Norseman's equal, not his slave.

'It is customary for people to greet their new lord with civility and speed. I thought the hall long deserted from my welcome.' The Norseman's rich voice thundered through the hall. It surprised Edith that he could speak her language so well. The Norsemen she'd encountered in Eoferwic, if they could speak it at all, spoke with accents so thick that she'd almost considered them to be speaking another language. But this one was different. His voice held only the faintest lilt of Norseman's accent.

'We had little warning of your arrival.' Edith met his fierce gaze. 'A proper greeting requires proper warning.'

'It fails to alter the fact. Your new lord has arrived. I deserved a better welcome than having my door barred against me.'

New lord? Edith's insides clenched as his words sank in. What did he mean? Had the Norseman king decided to marry her to him, then? A faint shiver went down her back. Despite her earlier conversation with Hilda, she had no wish to marry again. And certainly not to someone who looked like he could crush her with one hand. She wanted someone cultured who loved learning and music and who would respect her intelligence. She'd had enough of the brute with her first husband. Edith pushed the thought aside. Her feelings were unimportant. It was the estate which mattered.

'You are the new lord?'

He inclined his head, but his eyes flashed with fire. 'The king has decreed it.'

'I am the Lady Edith, mistress of this hall as my father was lord before me. The Norseman King Halfdan has sent me no decree.' She raised her chin defiantly. Thankfully, her father had had the foresight to bend his knee and kiss Halfdan's ring ten years ago. 'My father and your king were friends. He stayed here early in his reign after Eoferwic was burnt.'

The barbarian lifted an arrogant eyebrow. 'You deny this hall belonged to the rebel Egbert of Breckon?'

Edith pursed her lips. 'My late husband.'

'He died rebelling against his king, in the foulest act of treachery I have seen in many years.'

'The hall has always belonged to me and my family, going back as far as anyone can remember. My husband and I shared custody. When Egbert of Breckon breathed his last, the lands immediately reverted to my name and custody as there was no heir from my body.'

'Is that so?'

'When I married Egbert of Breckon, Halfdan promised to honour the agreement. I've a parchment with his seal.' She kept her head up and knew she had to ask the question. She had to find out what Halfdan intended with this barbarian or she'd collapse in a gibbering heap. She had to know her fate. She had survived Egbert; she could survive this Norseman. 'Do you mean the king intends that we marry?'

The Norseman's mouth curled downwards and his gaze raked her form. Edith forced her hands to stay at her sides, but she was aware of her gawky frame and big hips. She wished that she was tiny with curves like Hilda, the sort of woman that men would marry in an instant, and not just to gain a fortune or lands.

'Your husband broke fealty with my king. Why should he honour his promise to your father?' he said finally. 'Halfdan gave all of Egbert of Breckon's land to me as a reward for my services.'

Had the mountain actually killed Egbert in battle? The boy had whispered of an ambush and a truce broken where all the true Northumbrians were slain. Edith put the thought from her mind and concentrated. This was far worse than she'd considered possible. Her entire life hung in the balance.

'My husband acted against my counsel. We who are left never broke fealty. In the interests of peace and love he bore for my father, I'm certain Half-dan will have ordered some form of marriage.' Edith held out her hand. 'Show me his parchment.'

His blue gaze raked her a second time, more slowly, but leaving her in little doubt of her own inadequacies as a desirable woman—her fig-ure was far too thin and angular, her chin too masculine and even her hands were stained with ink rather than lily white as a lady's should be. Edith fought against the rising tide of heat which flooded her cheeks. It was bad enough that Eg-bert had taken great delight in telling her how few feminine charms she possessed, but enduring the Norseman's gaze was far more humiliating.

'There were no conditions to the gift, lady,' he said, his voice thundering so all could hear. 'The lands and all its possessions were in Halfdan's gift. My need for a wife is not pressing. Halfdan knows my feelings about marriage and the sort of woman I wish for a bride.'

'My mistake,' she whispered and forced her legs to curtsy. Bile rose in her throat. One solitary look and he'd rejected her as marriage material.

'Yes, it was. I trust the matter is now closed. I claim overlordship to this estate.' He stepped forwards and brought the axe down on the stone flagging. The noise thundered through the hall.

Edith thought quickly. An overlord? There was always an overlord. It might be the best of possible worlds, the miracle she'd prayed for. She had been far too hasty in assuming marriage. 'We will be happy to pay a tithe to you if you show me that your word is true. Forgive me, Norseman, but my experience with other Norsemen has been limited and sometimes the language has caused confusion. Do you have some sign, a scroll perhaps, which tells the amount we must pay?'

'You wilfully misunderstand me, Lady.' The Norseman fingered his axe. 'Egbert of Breckon's lands are forfeit. He rebelled against his rightful king. You have no rights here, but I bear no malice towards you. You may depart without molestation if you leave immediately.'

Edith heard the shocked gasps from the servants ranged behind her. Tears pricked her eyelids. This was her home, her land and her people.

She'd never asked Egbert to rebel for all the good it had done her. This was absolutely wrong.

She bit back the words. Tact, not hollow words of protest, was needed here. Egbert had led the rebellion, until the bitter end. From what she understood, he'd been one of the last to fall. An honourable death, the boy had whispered.

'The lands are in my name. I did not rebel. They remain mine until the king sends a scroll to tell me otherwise. I understand Halfdan is an honourable man.' She crossed her arms. She had to play for time. 'I don't know how things are done where you come from, but here in Northumbria we do ask for more proof than a double axe and a broken door.'

She stared defiantly at the Norseman, trying not to notice his axe and the way he fingered the hilt. One stroke and her head would be rolling across the floor, like the rumours said the Norsemen had done to so many other people.

Her heart pounded in her ears as she waited for the Norseman to respond.

A rumble of laughter resounded behind the Norseman, breaking the silence.

'She has spirit, this Northumbrian lady, I'll give

her that,' one of them called out. 'There are not many who would stand before Brand Bjornson and argue.'

'Maybe they should,' Edith answered as steadily as she could even as her legs threatened to crumple under her.

Her luck had truly run out. Brand Bjornson claimed her land. He was reputed to be one of the fiercest Norseman warriors, a name that nurses whispered to frighten children. She waited, hardly daring to breathe. Her next heartbeat was sure to be her last, once he lifted that axe.

The Norseman regarded her with those fierce eyes, unmoving but speculative. She forced her gaze to match his.

His hand loosened on the axe and his shoulders relaxed. Edith released a breath. She was going to live. The thought filled her with giddy excitement.

'I regret, my lady, but you're wrong. This hall and land belongs to me.' He reached into his belt and pulled out a piece of vellum. 'The king did anticipate that some may be prepared to doubt my word. Everything is in order. His seal is set with the date. Call for your priest to read it out loud.'

'There is no need. My father ensured I could

read.' At his questioning glance, she added, 'He'd little love for our priest.'

'Wise man.'

Edith stared at the parchment. The words swam before her eyes. All of Egbert's lands were forfeit to Brand Bjornson, including the hall and its property. They were specifically named, but it was a general proclamation. The king hadn't even bothered to address her. She truly meant nothing to him.

Tears stung at the back of her throat. Everything gone, just like that. She wished she could wring Egbert's fat neck. Her father had been wrong for so many reasons when he forced the marriage because he'd thought she needed a strong warrior. She could have held the lands on her own.

'You may have the estate, but will you have the hearts of its people? I have never seen a Viking warrior stay in one place for long. Undoubtedly your king will have call for your services,' Edith said before she could give herself time to think and be scared. 'After seeing your parchment, I'm happy to pay a reasonable tithe to you and promise to keep good order. I know these people and this land.'

'And you have their hearts, now that their menfolk are dead? You can guarantee that they will no longer rebel against Halfdan or his chosen successors?'

'I like to think so.' Edith tilted her chin upwards. 'My family has cared for this land since before the Romans left. The folk here are honest and loyal. Those who rebelled left with my late husband. Never to return.'

A sardonic smile crossed his lips. 'I find a full belly guarantees loyalty far more than blood or tradition.'

A snigger came from the ranks of the Vikings. 'What sort of man obeys a woman?'

Edith clenched her jaw and ignored the remark which reminded her of Egbert's attitude. She had proved him wrong and, given half a chance, she'd prove the unknown Viking wrong as well.

She motioned for her servants to be still.

Where else could she go? Some convent? To work like a thrall? It was what would happen to her if she appeared without any money. Goodness knew Egbert had threatened it often enough. Death by a Norseman's axe was preferable to death by slow starvation. She had one last chance.

'You must give me a chance to prove my words.

I could be useful here. You are a warrior. Do you know how to run a large estate? I do. Put me to the test!'

Chapter Two

Edith waited as her plea echoed around the hall. Her entire life hung in the balance.

'There is no need for someone else to run it. I shall be here.' Brand Bjornson's lips quirked upwards as if she amused him. A loud laugh escaped his throat, swiftly followed by the other warriors' laughter.

Edith frowned. Amusement was precisely the wrong reaction. 'My offer is serious.'

'My days of fighting are at an end. My king has another use for me. For too long this part of the North Riding has harboured a nest of vipers. It is my task to ensure peace. With force if necessary, Lady. I'll allow you safe passage to the nearest nunnery as a token of the *loyalty* you and your father showed my king.'

'And you know everything there is to know

about this hall and its farms? How to run it most efficiently?'

The blue in his eyes deepened. 'From what I have seen, it will not be hard to run it better… unless there is some reason to think differently.'

Edith winced. He knew about her deception and was giving her the opportunity to confess. The Norseman was sharper than he first appeared.

'My father trained me after my brothers died in infancy. I served first as his steward and then my late husband's.'

'Then they were both fools. This hall and its farms look miserable. A child could run them better.' Brand Bjornson waved an impatient hand. 'Save the stories for the children, Lady Edith. I'm in a generous mood, but that may change.'

'Lady Edith speaks true, my lord!' one of the servants burst out. 'My Lady Edith runs this hall better than anyone. It is why the storage barns are overfull this year and our sheep are…'

At Edith's look, the servant's voice trailed away. Edith bit her lip. Now the Norsemen knew they were not poor. How much chance did the food have of getting to the people who needed it the most? These Norsemen warriors would more than eat their fill and leave everyone else to starve, just as Egbert had once attempted to do.

'The hall is more prosperous than it looks? Show me. Now. While you have a chance to undo your deception.' Brand Bjornson took a step closer to her. She became aware of the power in his shoulders and forearms. He was definitely not a man to be trifled with.

Edith shifted in her shoes, torn between a desire to protect what was rightfully hers and the knowledge that her unwomanly success might be the only thing to save her and her home. If she left now, she'd never be able to return. She'd seen enough refugees after the fall of Eoferwic ten years earlier to know her chances of survival. Who would give her shelter like she'd given shelter to Hilda? Anyone who might have helped her was dead or had lost their lands and had fled to the south. Edith curled her hand into a fist. She had no choice but to reveal some of her secrets.

She had to show him the ledgers and the storage areas and hope that he'd understand what a huge undertaking this hall and lands were. He had to understand that she was essential and why they needed the food to stay here.

Later, she'd figure out how to get rid of him.

Vikings never stayed long. As long as she was here, there was a chance her lands would be restored to her.

Edith raised her chin so she stared directly into his startling blue eyes. An awareness of him and the power in his shoulders filled her. 'Yes, it is true, Brand Bjornson. I had no wish to give more than I had to. Can you blame me after the ravages that the Norsemen have wrought on the countryside?'

'Show me!' Brand ground out, regarding Lady Edith with her very Anglo-Saxon wimple, figure-skimming dress and proud tilt to her nose. He struggled to remember when a woman had affected him this much.

Her figure was not overly curvy, but pleasing enough, her features were regular and even, but it was her long neck and the way she held her slender hands which held his attention. And she was tall, coming up to his nose rather than forcing him to stoop.

Everything about her screamed arrogance and inclined to overestimate her own intelligence in relation to his. She was about to learn an important lesson in humility. She'd assumed that he should be kissing her feet in gratitude earlier when she offered to marry him. No, they did this his way. He had made his plans.

'I am happy to show you the stores, but you must know they are depleted after the winter. You may inspect the ledgers and they will show you that they are in my hand.' Her full lips turned up even more insolently. 'Can you read Latin? Or do you wish to call your scribe?'

'That is my concern.' Brand retained a narrow leash on his temper. 'I very much wish to inspect the entirety of my new lands.'

He did not believe for one heartbeat that she could read or write. What sort of woman did? She merely wanted to show him up and gain time to remove whatever treasure she had hidden, treasure which now belonged to him. Egbert of Breckon had cut down Brand's best friend, Sven, while crying for peace. Hrearek had reached him first and cut him down but Sven had been the closest thing he had had to a brother. He could never forgive the treachery that had cost him the one person he held dear.

'I've nothing to fear from the truth.'

He leant forwards so that their breath touched. 'We start with the ledgers.'

Her colour heightened, infusing her cheeks with

a dusky pink. If she shed the wimple, she'd be beautiful, Brand realised with a start as his body responded anew to her nearness.

Was there a reason she had deliberately wanted him to overlook her feminine charms? He wanted a willing bed partner, rather than one he'd forced. But then seeing how her breath quickened, she was not entirely immune to him either. Suddenly the possibilities became much more intriguing.

He raised an eyebrow and the flush deepened. She dipped her head, breaking the contact.

'Very well, the ledgers.' She motioned to one of the servants and spoke to him in a low voice. The man bowed and hurried off. 'It may take a little time, Lord Bjornson.'

'I've time.'

'Would you like to sit? I'm sure you and your men are thirsty. My late husband was always thirsty whenever he returned to the hall.' She gestured towards a stool with a little wave of her hand before ordering one of her elderly servants to fetch some mead. 'Please give us a chance to welcome your lordship properly. Now that we know who you are.'

The gesture and the words reminded him of his father's wife and the way she ruled his father's steading, always making him feel like an outsider with no real right to be there. He'd left that past long ago. He was the lord and master here, rather than the son of a thrall who had no right to be in the hall. He'd earned the right to respect with his sword arm. Brand gave his head a little shake to rid his mind of the memory.

'I have no problems with standing, but my men require some refreshment. The road brings a thirst and hunger. We must have meat.'

'A good leader looks after his men first.' Her smile did not reach her grey eyes. 'Meat takes time. We live simply here and it is Lent. Nothing has been slaughtered since Michaelmas.'

'Time we have.' Brand inclined his head. 'In due course after I have assessed the supplies, I will arrange for several animals to be slaughtered. My men need to celebrate my good fortune. They expect to feast well.'

'The considerations of Lent mean nothing?'

Brand considered the question. 'Should they? My men do not share your religion.'

'As you wish.' She strode over to where a leather stool rested and sat. A queen or his father's wife could not have done it better. 'There appears to be little point standing on ceremony. My late husband used to enjoy sitting.'

'I'm not your late husband.'

Her neat white teeth worried her bottom lip and for the first time, he saw the shadows in her eyes. 'No, you're not. We must all consider you fortunate then.'

'Meaning?' Brand tried to remember what he knew of the man. Lord Egbert had obviously inspired men to follow him. The men left in the hall were the ones who were either too old or too young to fight. But he knew little of the measure of the man or how he'd dealt with his wife. He had been the one to break the truce. Hrearek was quite clear on that.

'My husband died and you are alive. The hall now is under your rule.' Her hands clenched together so tightly that the white knuckles stood out. 'What did you think I meant?'

'Thank you for the explanation.' He'd allow the explanation to stand for now. But it was clear Lady Edith was no grieving widow. Were her earlier words about not supporting the rebellion true? Lately Halfdan had used marriage between the Vikings and the Northumbrians as a way of ensuring peace, but he'd kept her existence from him.

Had Halfdan actually remembered about Brand's plans for the future? How he hoped to marry Sigfrieda? Brand narrowed his eyes. Or was there something else? Something that Halfdan knew about this woman that he had chosen to keep to himself?

Lady Edith picked up a spindle, looking for all the world like a woman who had plenty of time and fewer cares. However, a thin sheen of sweat on her forehead betrayed her nerves. Brand smiled inwardly. Her play-acting skills were no rival for the courtiers at the Byzantium court.

'Shall we speak about the changes to Eoferwic…I mean Jorvik?' She gave her spindle a fierce twist. 'I understand King Halfdan has completely remade the city after the Norsemen burnt it to the ground.'

'There we must agree to differ. It was the Northumbrians who burnt the city when they attempted to take it. I was there on the walls, my lady.'

Her eyes flashed, betraying her annoyance. 'It was our city. The Norsemen attacked on All Saints' Day when we were at church. I was there with my mother and father. No civilised person attacks on such a holy day.'

'Your god is not Halfdan's. Do you respect Thor's feast days?'

'That is beside the point.' She gave the spindle a vicious twist and the thread broke, sending it bouncing across the floor. A small cry escaped her lips.

Brand bent and retrieved it, holding the neatly spun wool in his hand. It was unusual for any woman to speak so boldly to him, but Lady Edith was refreshing. All too often women uttered inanities and deferred to him. Spineless, but calculating. He learnt that lesson well in Constantinople. Lady Edith had already revealed the steel she had as a spine. She was forged from the same metal as his father's wife and he should never forget that.

Lady Edith needed to learn that she no longer held any power in this hall. Her intelligence about the halls and its lands being more prosperous than it appeared failed to surprise him. He had seen the richness of the soil and suspected that the sheep grew thick fleeces. The very air breathed fertility.

For how much was this woman responsible? And how much did she want to unjustly claim?

Brand had met many capable women in Byzantium who were involved up to their pretty necks in palace intrigue, but he had never heard of a Northumbrian woman doing such a thing. Their priests frowned on it or so he understood. It was a mystery and he disliked mysteries, particularly ones which included beautiful women. Invariably they attempted to use their looks to gain what they wanted. Given the way the spindle bounced and the thread tangled, he doubted if Lady Edith spent much time spinning.

'I wish to learn everything about my new estate,' he said with a bow. 'Perhaps we should converse about that while we wait rather than long-ago history which neither of us can change.'

'Yes, of course.' Her pale pink lips curved up into a superior smile. 'Here comes John with the latest ledger.'

The servant handed her the book. Lady Edith placed it on the trunk with a thump. With a slight tremor in her hand, she opened the pages and ran her finger down the neat figures.

'Shall I explain what it all means?' she asked with a honey-sweetened voice. 'Or do you require me to demonstrate that it is my writing?'

Brand carefully schooled his features. He could tell by the way Lady Edith arrogantly raised her eyebrow that she expected him not to be able to read Latin. The time he'd spent serving the Emperor in Byzantium had taught him both the value of an education as well as the value of keeping such knowledge to himself.

'Both.'

Lady Edith launched into lengthy but simplistic explanation, pointing to various notations and numbers. Her cheeks took on the colour of a spring dawn and her grey eyes began to sparkle, turning her face from pleasant to truly beautiful and desirable.

Brand's body responded anew to her nearness and her delicate scent. He tapped a finger against his mouth as a glimmer of an idea came to him. The perfect lesson for a proud lady. She needed to learn her new status and he needed to learn the secrets of this estate. This estate would belong to his descendants for all of time. It meant all of his struggles were worthwhile. He would succeed and prove his father's wife's words wrong. He was not worthless and fit only for the pigsty. This estate proved his worth, and he needed the right sort of woman to be his wife, someone who understood what it was like to be from the North.

'The estate is indeed productive,' he said at the end of Lady Edith's lengthy recital about what she had done to improve the estate this year. 'You appear well versed in all aspects of it. A surprising pastime for a lady.'

'You see the value of keeping me as a steward?' Her nostrils quivered slightly with tension, much as a high-strung horse might quiver before battle. She wanted to run the estate. Why was it so important to her? Running an estate was a thankless task. What did she want out of this? What game was she playing? His father's wife had always played games.

The saying he learnt in Byzantium—to keep your friends close, but your enemies closer—flashed in his mind.

'Not as a steward.' He paused, beginning to enjoy himself. 'But I do wish you to remain on in this hall. You are an unexpected addition to the estate.'

She licked her lips, turning them a deeper red. 'As what? I'm no maidservant for your wife. I've my pride.'

He waited a heartbeat and leant forwards so that his breath interlaced with hers. She did know the game. The pretence ended here. 'As my concubine.'

She drew back, her eyes widening as the colour drained from her face. 'Your…your concubine?'

'I have no need of a wife, but there is a current that runs between us. You can feel it as well as I.' He stroked a line down her face. Her flesh quivered deliciously under his fingertips. 'One year will be enough to satisfy my desire.'

'And after the year?'

'I will provide you safe passage to wherever you wish to go. You will be handsomely compensated for your time. I'm a generous master. None of my women have ever complained.'

A shocked gasp ran through the hall and he heard the soft swish of his men drawing swords. He ignored the sounds and concentrated on Lady Edith. Everything depended on her answer.

'You are asking me to forsake my honour and become your whore for the promise of an unspecified payment?' She swallowed hard and kept her body rigid, far too rigid.

Brand narrowed his gaze. Had he misjudged her earlier expression? Impossible. But as her cheek continued to be pale, he relented slightly and gestured towards the door.

'You are welcome to go to the nearest nunnery if the terms do not suit you. My men will ensure your safe passage, but you leave immediately with only the clothes on your back. If you meet my terms, you will be able to choose where you go. My men will even escort you to Wessex if you so desire, but only after our bargain is complete.'

Her gaze narrowed. 'With baggage? And any of my people who wish to go?'

'With whatever belongs to you at that time.'

Emotions warred on her face. Was her love of treasure greater than her honour?

She glanced over her shoulder at her servants who now wore furious faces and gave a quick shake of her head. Her lips curved up in a false smile. 'When you make an offer like that with such grace and tact, how can I refuse, Lord Bjornson?'

'You can't, mistress!' someone shouted. 'We will fight for your honour. Allow me to be your champion!'

The entire hall broke out in an uproar. Brand slammed his axe down on the stone flagging. The ringing sound silenced everyone.

'I can and I will!' Lady Edith retorted. 'This Norseman has left me with no other choice. There will be no blood spilled in defence of my honour. I forbid it. It is a pale and worthless thing compared to one of your lives. Each of you is precious to me.'

Instantly the shouting stopped. Lady Edith stood, proud and alone, with more than a hint of vulnerability to her mouth. She held out her trembling hands.

'And what will you do, Lady Edith? I want the words,' Brand said. 'For all to hear. I will not have it whispered that you were forced.'

'I will be your concubine, Brand Bjornson. I do this of my own free will and at your asking.'

'For an entire year?'

'You will have me for a year and no longer.' Her voice was colder than a Norwegian winter. 'Then I leave for a place of my choosing with those things which belong to me and those people who wish to join me in exile.'

'You have chosen, my lady,' Brand said softly, not taking her outstretched fingers. There would be time enough to seal their bargain properly later. Without the benefit of onlookers.

He refused to feel sorry for her. Whatever was hidden here meant more to her than her body or her so-called honour and virtue. Sending for a wife could wait until he concluded his business with Lady Edith. It would be short, sweet and ultimately pleasurable for the both of them, but such dalliances never lasted long. After the passion was spent, women ceased to intrigue him.

'Then it is done?' Her grey eyes appeared troubled. 'Settled?'

'It is done.' He raised her hand to his lips. 'I will hold you to your word. What is mine stays mine. And you are mine for an entire year.'

His concubine. For an entire year. The enormity of what she had done, in front of everyone, thudded through Edith. She leant against the kitchen's outside wall, trying to get her racing heart to slow down.

She'd agreed to be Brand Bjornson's mistress. Not even his wife, but his mistress. Hilda could have made a better fist of it. Shackled to him as little better than a bed slave!

The scared faces of her household had made the decision simple. She couldn't abandon them to life under Norseman rule while she made her way to the relative safety of a nunnery.

Who knew what Brand Bjornson might do to some of them—people who had given their lives to ensure she and her family lived in comfort? What good would her honour be if she abandoned those who were ready to lay their lives down for her?

It wasn't the future she'd envisioned this morning, but she had to do it. She had to be able to speak for those who couldn't. In a year's time, she could leave and even go to the relative safety of Wessex with a baggage train. If all went well, she could take those people who wanted to go with her. She wrapped her arms about her waist and tried to control her shaking.

She'd have to share his bed and keep him entertained. Something that in the past she'd singularly failed to do for a man. Egbert's many accusations and taunts echoed in her mind—she possessed not one feminine attribute, was confrontational at the wrong times and the only thing about her which even remotely interested a man was her dowry.

She must've been mad. This little adventure would end the instant Brand Bjornson took her to bed. The entire world tilted. She put her hand out to steady herself. What had she done?

'Cousin? Is anything the matter?' Hilda asked, catching her arm. 'At last I find you. I have been hiding, but heard no sound of battle so decided to come and find you. Have the Norsemen left? Is everything as it was? Your scheme worked, didn't it?'

'I...I...' Edith struggled to find the right words.

Edith allowed Hilda to lead her to an alcove where they both sat. Hilda patted Edith's hand.

'You rest. You've done enough getting rid of the Norsemen and having everything hidden. You're close to collapse, Edith.'

Hilda's appearance served to emphasise Edith's problem. Every movement Hilda made seemed designed to entice or make her more attractive. Around her, Edith always considered herself gawky and awkward.

If Hilda had been there, would Brand Bjornson have been so quick to make her his concubine? She dug her nails into her palm. She should be grateful for small mercies.

Hilda only thought of herself. She had no feeling for the land or its people. All Edith could do was to try to survive and play whatever game this Norseman was playing to the end.

'Not yet. They haven't left yet.' Edith smoothed her skirt. The action calmed her jangled nerves. She'd go mad if she tried to think about what ifs and how the past could have been different. 'But don't worry, Hilda. I have a scheme. They will go in time and all will return to how it was. I have to believe that.'

'Oh, no!' Hilda stuffed her hand in her mouth

and she began to rock back and forth. 'A scheme? And time is something we don't have.'

'They will go eventually.' Edith didn't know whom she was trying to convince. 'The Norsemen never stay long. War and the open sea call. Everything will go back to how it was. You see I still have the keys to all the stores? Trust me to make it right. We simply need to keep our nerve.'

She jangled the circlet of keys which hung from her waist. They'd belonged to her mother and every other lady who had ruled this house.

Hilda drew a deep shuddering breath and her eyes became marginally less wild. 'If I must. Where will they stay? Will I have to encounter them and their barbaric ways?'

How their way could be more barbaric than Egbert and his men, Edith couldn't say. She shuddered, remembering how powerless she'd felt in those few weeks before he departed. How hard she'd worked to shield various children from his abuses and what limited success she had had. Unlike Hilda, she hadn't wept when she'd heard of Egbert's death. She only wished it had happened before he had ruined everyone. All those countless lives lost and all the beatings she and others had suffered, simply because Egbert's temper was uncertain. But he'd been unable to take the gold, silver and jewels. Some day she'd retrieve them from the lord's bedchamber, but for now they were safe, stored right under the Norseman's nose. The thought buoyed her spirits no end.

'You'll have to be civil, Hilda. There is little point in antagonising them. One must be practical about such things,' she said carefully.

'Will you marry the new earl? Did it happen like you predicted?' Hilda watched her with narrowed eyes. 'Is that what is going on? You can tell me, cousin. I can imagine the Norseman's king doing that, not giving you time to properly mourn and seeking to secure peace on the land that way.'

'No, my fate is something else.' She paused and gazed directly at Hilda, whose golden-blonde hair, pale blue eyes and petite frame ensured men's eyes followed her wherever she went. Hilda would learn soon enough. No doubt the entire hall buzzed with the news. 'I've agreed to be Brand Bjornson's concubine. I suspect the Norseman thinks it is an honour. And, yes, I do know how people will react and what they will call me but I did it for them. I hope to soften his heart towards my people.'

Saying the words out loud helped.

A tiny tingle went through her. It might be different with Brand Bjornson. When their hands had accidentally brushed as he regarded the ledger, all her senses became aware of him. Something that had never happened to her before. She banished the thought as wishful thinking and false hope. She'd endured Egbert's touch and the bruises he had given her. She could cope with this Norseman. She was a survivor.

Hilda stared at her with shocked eyes and gaping mouth.

'Thank you, cousin, for your silence.'

'You're serious! That's your scheme?'

'Would I joke about such a thing?' Edith folded her hands in her lap. 'I have to remain here in order for my plans to work. Leaving would have meant that I had lost everything.'

Hilda's mouth dropped open, making her resemble a fish. 'I'd rather kill myself. Brand Bjornson is a monster. His very name causes grown men to quake in their boots. And he sports an ugly red scar about his neck. They say that even his own mother tried to kill him but failed. The man sups with the devil.'

'Unfortunately I didn't have that choice,' Edith said with a steady voice. Hilda was always overly dramatic, even as a young girl. 'If I die, who will speak for the people who till this land or work in the kitchens? And I dare say Brand Bjornson sups with whoever sits down at his table.'

'Stop trying to turn it into a joke, Edith. Why did you agree to it? How could you?' Hilda shook her head. 'Sometimes I fail to understand you, cousin. You should have drawn a knife, bared your breast and plunged it in. That is what any true Northumbrian lady would have done.'

Edith bit back the words asking why Hilda had agreed to be Egbert's mistress, then? Even now, she refused to stoop that low. There were some things which were better left unsaid. She accepted that Hilda had had her reasons and overall had behaved better than some of Egbert's other women.

'Why, Edith?'

'There were others to think of,' she said finally when Hilda's horrified gaze became too great to bear. 'I refuse to abandon everyone for the sake of my honour. In this way, perhaps I can tame the Norseman and prevent him from destroying all that I hold dear. Mayhap in time he will come to trust me and will install me as the steward.'

'As you say, it is your choice, my cousin.' Hilda stood up and made a brief curtsy. 'I wish you well.

I mean that. I hope you know what you have un-dertaken. These men…they are not quite human. You are gently bred. You haven't had to suffer—'

'I believe I understand the rudiments of the po-sition I now occupy.'

Hilda flushed. 'No offence meant, cousin. I want to be certain that you know what you are doing. When I was in the south—'

'Thank you, Hilda.' Edith inclined her head. The last thing she wanted to hear was a horror story about how Hilda had experienced the hab-its of the Norsemen. If she did, her courage might give out. Right now, not thinking about what the night might bring was the only way she'd survive. 'We have a feast to prepare. Busy hands mean neither of us will have time to think or consider.'

'A feast? How can you think about eating at a time like this?'

'The Norsemen will expect to be fed,' Edith re-torted, touching the keys to remind herself that she still had control. He hadn't taken that away from her! 'We must show them true Northum-brian hospitality. Thus far they have not started looting, pillaging or worse—something to be cel-ebrated, surely?'

Hilda rolled her eyes. 'You can be such an innocent, Edith.'

'I prefer a realist,' Edith said between gritted teeth. She wasn't going to lose her temper. 'I prefer this hall with four walls and a roof. I prefer to have a place to lay my head.'

'And that's it, the end as far as you are concerned?' Hilda snapped her fingers under Edith's nose. 'You are giving up without a fight? You should have allowed me to speak to them. I would have fought them with my bare hands before I allowed them to take this hall. I never took you for a coward.'

'I can hardly fight.' Edith's jaw ached and she tried to force her muscles to relax. 'Egbert took every able-bodied man with him and not one has returned. How many widows did he leave in his quest for glory?'

'And you believe you will be able to tame this Norseman warrior of yours?' Hilda looked her up and down. 'Do you have the womanly skills, cousin? You would be happier amongst the vellum and ink or out riding and looking at how the crops are doing. What do you know of the art of love? What will happen when this Norseman discovers you prefer learning to the arts of love?'

'You forget yourself, cousin.' Edith slammed her fists together. 'You're a guest here and asked for my protection, protection which I have sought to give. Always. Your behaviour here was your own affair and I've never questioned it.'

Hilda flushed scarlet and dropped her gaze. 'Forgive me, Edith, for speaking plainly, but you must not hold on to false hope that you will be able to hold on to this place for the long term. Did you have another choice? Something that might save us both?'

Edith clenched her fists. She didn't want to think about the night or what would happen when Brand discovered all of her inadequacies. She had to hope that he had another purpose in mind when he made her his concubine. Or that if Hilda had been there, she might have been the one he chose. 'I will face that when I have to. These Norsemen may have different expectations.'

'I hope for all of our sakes that they do.' Hilda put her hand on Edith's sleeve. 'I really do, cousin. I just hope this one is worth it. That's all. For once I don't envy you.'

'Thank you. It will be.' Edith bowed her head and concentrated on the keys. It had to be. The alternative wasn't worth contemplating.

'Where do you expect me to be during this pro-posed feast?' Hilda put a hand to her head. 'You know how those Norsemen unnerve me. My mind goes all to pieces, but I want to play my part. Give me a job and I will do it, something out of the way. Just for a few days, until I know what they are on about and whether I need to find somewhere else to live.'

'You may stay in the kitchen if the Norsemen upset you that much.' Edith thought quickly. She agreed with Hilda that having her in the main hall would not do at all. Edith wanted to be able to concentrate on her role rather than wondering what Hilda might do next. 'The cook can always do with another scullery maid. I doubt they will give you any bother there, so long as you don't mind getting your hands dirty. I will have a word with him.'

Hilda's cheeks reddened. 'Thank you, cousin. I do appreciate your kindness. The kitchen it shall be. Should you need any advice…about…you know…I am happy to give it.'

'It is kind of you to offer and I will remember it, should it come to it.' Edith silently vowed that Hilda would be the last person she'd ask to tutor her in the arts of love. The humiliation would be far too great.

Hilda hurried off, her narrow hips swaying and her skirts swishing to give a glimpse of her ankles. Even the way she moved emphasised her sensuality and highlighted Edith's own awkwardness.

Edith raised her fist. 'I will do it. I will succeed. Or die in the attempt.'

Chapter Three

'What are you contemplating, Lady Edith? You appear lost in your thoughts.'

Brand's rich voice caused Edith to jump. He stood far too close to where she rested in the alcove. Where had he come from? And how much had he overheard? For a large man, he moved silently. She bit her lip. She'd have to remember that. Egbert had always announced his presence with heavy walking and a litany of complaints.

'I was resting.' Edith forced her hands to stay calmly in her lap, rather than gesturing wildly. Hilda's story about Brand's mother trying to kill him had to be a wild fantasy. No one surely could be that wicked. 'The day has been traumatic for me. My entire life has been altered and it isn't even midday. It has given me something to contemplate.'

'You regret your decision now that you have had time to consider your position? You wish to leave for the nunnery, but worry about summoning the courage to inform me?'

The sun made it impossible for her to see his eyes. All she knew was that he wanted her to give up and admit defeat. That wasn't going to happen. Retreating would be a defeat, not only for her but for everyone she cared about. Despite what Hilda thought, she could be a concubine even to a man like Brand Bjornson.

'Not in the slightest.' Edith tilted her chin upwards and met his penetrating blue gaze full on. 'Were you searching for me? Has something happened?'

His dark blond hair fell in disarray about his shoulders and he'd shed his axe and overtunic, but that only emphasised the way his shirt clung to his chest. She was more aware than ever of the power in his shoulders. He was most definitely not a man to cross lightly. 'Nothing unexpected.'

The strange warm tingling feeling invaded her body. This was the man she would have to play the concubine with, if she could. Her heart sank. Hilda was right. What had she been thinking of? The enormity of the task crashed into her. She should have taken the easy route out and saved her own skin. What if she didn't please him? What would happen to everyone then?

'It is good to know.'

He tilted his head to one side. 'Did you think something would be wrong?'

'Why should there be?' She hurriedly smoothed her skirts and her hand touched the circlet of keys that she always wore. The tiny action gave her courage. She was doing it for her home. The keys were a comfort. She had them and it meant certain things were safe and hidden.

'You are very quick with your answer.' He regarded her with speculative eyes.

'How long have you been standing there?' she asked with a faint breathless catch in her voice, swallowed hard and tried again. This time her voice sounded firmer. 'Is there something you require?'

'Long enough.'

Edith rubbed the back of her neck. He'd overheard her conversation with Hilda, but she had to hope it was only the tail end. 'It's been a tiring day and your men will need to be fed. I have to make sure the servants understand the new situation. I wish to keep the incidents to a minimum.'

'It is kind of you to be concerned, but my concubine doesn't give the orders to any member of the household. She exists only to please me.'

Edith pursed her lips together—a subtle way of saying she lacked power. 'I'd considered ordering a feast was pleasing to the *master.*'

She hated how the word stuck in her throat and how the sound of it brought home the precariousness of her position. She was little better than a shackled slave.

He raised his eyebrow. 'It is good that you so readily acknowledge who I am. I had wondered if you would have to learn a hard lesson.'

'I've never been a concubine before.'

A ghost of a smile flickered in the corner of his mouth. 'I'd never have guessed, my lady.'

'Spare the laughter and jest. I fail to find the joke amusing.'

'Perish the thought.' He inclined his head, but the twinkle in his eye deepened, turning his irises to the colour of the sky after weeks of grey cloud. A blue so vivid it hurt to look at it. 'Maybe a little, but I enjoy teasing my women. But I remain serious about our bargain. I want you, Edith of Breckon, in my bed.'

Edith concentrated on a spot just above his

shoulder, rather than gazing into his eyes. His woman. One of many? She could well imagine the sort of women they were. She had experienced Egbert's parade and found positions and marriages for them after Egbert discarded them, so they wouldn't suffer humiliation.

'You should know that I am not very good at being a decorative object.' She allowed her mouth to turn upwards. 'I've never seen the point of flirtatious teasing.'

'You'll have to learn.'

'I'm far too practical. If I see a thing that needs doing, I do it. I like to keep my hands busy and my mind occupied.'

'But not with spinning. My men uncovered a number of broken whorls from the hall. Do they have a purpose?'

'Spinning is not my best skill,' Edith conceded with a shrug. Explaining about Hilda's drama of this morning was beyond her. 'I do try, but my mind wanders and the tread tangles. I prefer writing and reading.'

'Unlike the woman who just left for the kitchen.' His eyes flashed with barely concealed contempt. 'I do not believe she makes a good scullery maid. Her dress is far too fine and her accent refined.'

Edith's breath stopped in her lungs. He'd seen Hilda and her embroidered gown and guessed. Who wouldn't? There was just something about the way Hilda moved. She attracted men like honeycomb attract the flies.

'She was my late husband's mistress,' she admitted, dipping her head as her stomach clenched. Had she inadvertently delivered her cousin to another man's bed? She felt sick. 'Your men unnerved her. She had a traumatic time two summers ago and saw things no one, especially not a gently bred lady, should see. I thought it was for the best if she went to the kitchen and helped out there until I found something better for her.'

'And you allow this former mistress a place here? Give her charity? Is that how you take your revenge?' Something akin to disgust flared in his eyes, but was quickly masked.

'Where else could she go? She is my distant kinswoman. I have a duty towards her.' Edith pinched the bridge of her nose. The last thing she wanted to explain was how guilty and powerless she'd felt when Egbert made Hilda his mistress as if some of it was her fault. She'd promised Hilda that she'd be safe. But Egbert had seduced Hilda, promising her the moon. Before he'd left, she'd started to experience Hilda's tantrums at being ignored and Egbert's bad temper.

'Not many women would be as generous as you.'

'Hilda had little choice when my husband's eye lighted upon her.' Edith shrugged and hoped that he wouldn't guess the pain she'd suffered because of it. The marriage had been one of duty. She had no right to expect anything, but she'd hoped that a sort of friendship might emerge. It never did. And she wasn't cold or unfeeling as Egbert had claimed. She did feel things deeply. 'I'd planned to send her away once things quieted down, marry her off to a farmer, but it will not be my choice now.'

'Whose choice will be it?'

She made a careful curtsy and her keys jangled. The tiny sound comforted her. She might be a concubine, but she had privileges. 'Why, yours as you are the new lord.'

His entire body stilled. 'Are you always that involved with your household? Ordering their lives?'

'Someone has to care for their welfare, but Hilda is my kinswoman and merits extra-special care. We share a grandmother. She lacks a dowry and everyone knows about her former position. It limits her marriage prospects.'

'And what does she do here when she is not being a scullery maid? What does she prefer to do?'

Edith bit her lip, thinking quickly. Confessing about Hilda's hatred and fear of the Norsemen would be a bad idea. She had to find a way to protect Hilda. She'd given her word that Hilda would not have to go into the hall today. In a few days' time, she might feel differently and Edith could bring her back into the main household. 'She works in the kitchens now. She prefers it that way.'

'So then, this is the way you take your revenge?' His face became colder than the moors on a winter's day.

She squared her shoulders. Brand Bjornson did not need a further explanation. He'd already humiliated her enough for one day. 'Hilda asked for the position. It suits her needs.'

'No doubt she did.' His mouth became a cynical white line. 'Make sure she appears at the feast. In her best gown.'

'Is that an order?'

His long fingers clenched at his side as if they

were searching for the axe he'd carried earlier so he could bury it in her head. 'If you will not do it any other way, then, yes, consider it an order. Seeing two Northumbrian women enjoying themselves will do much to allay the fears of the people who farm this place.'

'Very well, I will inform her.' Edith put a hand to her head. With each passing breath she knew her impulsive decision to accept his offer was more of a disaster waiting to happen than an inspiration. She touched her keys and drew strength. He wouldn't stay. She would regain her position. 'No more kitchens for my cousin.'

'In future, leave the ordering of the household to me. No more giving disagreeable tasks to people you dislike.' He held out his hand. 'I will have your keys as well. You will have no need of them. The food shall be kept under my control.'

Edith struggled to gulp a breath of air. Those keys had hung from her waist ever since her mother had died. Without them, she'd be naked and the entire household would cease to function. 'I'm not used to having idle hands. I am good at the practical things. I know where everything is, what needs to be done and in which order.'

'Such as?'

'Seeing to the accounts. I like being efficient and do it every evening. You need not worry. I'm no thief.' She bit her lip. She had to admit it before they went any further. Seeing Hilda just now and the way she moved brought it home to her. She was no concubine, made for a man's pleasure. She was the sort of woman that a man married because he had to and she had sufficient dowry. 'You appear to have the wrong idea about me. I've no experience at being a…a concubine, but I can run a household.'

'I run my own household.' His tone allowed for no dissent. 'The keys, Lady Edith. Or do I tear them from your waist?'

He would. The barbarian! Hilda's story held more than a ring of truth. She could imagine him going berserk on the battlefield and slaughtering indiscriminately. Silently she undid them and placed them in his hand. Suddenly her entire being was lighter, but her waist felt naked and exposed. If anything, the bareness symbolised her new status as a slave. Edith schooled her features. She refused to burst into tears. She should have expected the request earlier.

He weighed the keys carefully and placed them in a pouch that he wore.

'A large house is different from a warrior's camp,' Edith argued. 'It takes a lifetime to master.'

'I have a lifetime.'

'I only wanted to help in case...'

His lip curled. 'In case I was only fit for the pigsty?'

'I never said that.' Silently she prayed he'd see reason. Surely he couldn't be that blind. He had to know that she could never play love games and that she alone should have control of the keys. Men did not control the keys.

If anything, his face became harder and more unyielding. It was easy to see why the rumours about his ferocity swirled about Northumbria.

'I know what needs to be done and rest assured I will discover which door each of them unlocks. You will find I learn quickly.'

A shiver crept down her spine. He would discover precisely where she'd hidden everything. Instead of listening to Hilda, she should have been dismantling the key ring and retaining those keys she needed. Hindsight was a luxury she couldn't afford.

'And what do you suggest I do? Take up pig-keeping?' She gave an arched laugh.

A distinctive heat came into his eyes. Bedchamber eyes. 'It is always good to learn a new skill. You will see flirting will come to you in time. I've no intention of forcing you to keep pigs.'

Edith's throat went dry. She swallowed hastily, trying to ignore the warm tide flowing through her. No man had the right to look that good. 'A new skill! What sort of skill? And who will teach me? You!'

'Having second thoughts, my lady? You can beg for the convent if you wish.' He put his hands behind his head. 'I might be open to begging.'

'You know nothing of me.' She crossed her arms. 'I gave my word and will endeavour to keep it. I have always done so, regardless of what other people have done.'

'Then what is the problem?' He ran a finger down her cheek, sending a delicious shiver throughout her being. She attempted to banish the feeling, but it grew. Edith concentrated on a spot above his shoulder, rather than falling into his gaze again.

'I merely wanted to warn you of my failings. Personally I have always found it most profitable to employ people where they were best suited.'

He made an impatient noise in the back of his throat. The rest of her speech died on her lips.

'I assume you know how to play tafl, sing and make amusing conversation?' he asked in a voice laced with heavy irony. 'That you are not devoid of culture in the North Riding?'

'Yes, of course,' Edith said, tapping her slipper on the ground. How dare the Norseman infer that she was some sort of barely cultured barbarian, instead of him! 'Those are the things people do in polite society.'

He leant forwards until their foreheads touched. 'You should have no problem in your new role. Keep in mind that you need to please me and we will get along well. I'm far from ungenerous to those who please me.'

'But…'

His breath caressed her cheek. 'You fear we won't suit. That I will have no idea of your tender sensibilities as I have spent my entire life soldiering and sleeping on the ground rather than on a soft bed. You fear the barbarian.'

Edith shook her head quickly, too quickly. Her body tingled with awareness of him and his proximity to her. She tried to think straight, but all she could think about was the blueness of his eyes, the broadness of his shoulders and the strength in his arms. 'I hadn't really considered where you have spent the night. I have no idea of your needs.'

'Shall I demonstrate? My needs are simple.' He put his hands on her shoulders, preventing her from moving, even if she wanted to. Edith found her feet had turned to stone, but his touch was oddly gentle rather than rough. A warmth radiated outwards from his fingers, infusing her body.

Edith lifted her chin and met his sardonic gaze. He intended on teaching her a lesson. She shuddered slightly, remembering the lessons that Egbert had taught her and how her body had borne bruises for weeks afterwards. Swallowing hard, she screwed up her eyes and hoped.

'Don't be frightened of me,' he murmured. 'It won't hurt. I never hurt my women.'

His mouth descended, brushing hers. Far more gentle than she had considered possible, but firm enough to be there and not her imaginings. Questing and seeking, rather than hard and demanding.

Her eyes flew open and she saw all traces of mockery or sardonic dark humour had vanished.

Her body arched towards him and collided with his hard muscular frame. Her hand reached up and her lips parted slightly. She tasted his lips and the warmth grew within her. She moaned slightly in the back of her throat.

He lifted his head. The kiss was over. He let her go, stepped away and eyed her with a cynical expression.

'I have found the correct person for the position, despite your protestations.'

Edith knew her breathing was coming a little too quickly and her lips felt far too full. Shame washed over her. She'd done it again, responded inappropriately.

'What was that supposed to prove?' she asked, forcing her eyebrow to arch. She hated that her voice sounded breathless.

His lips turned upwards. 'That you will prove to be an adequate concubine…in time.'

'I have no idea what you are talking about.' She clenched the folds of her skirt with her hand.

'You don't? Think on it. No doubt the answer will come to you, Lady Edith.'

Brand forced his body to remain still and unmoving as he sought to master his emotions. He never chased after a woman. They came to him. Lady Edith might stride away as though he represented the devil incarnate, but there had been something in her kiss. She'd be back, demanding more. He tasted his lips to see if the taste of her mouth lingered or merely the memory of honey-sweet lips.

Women were to be enjoyed for the moment, rather than taken into one's heart and cherished. He'd seen what happened when you fell in love and bore the scars for daring to love a woman who was destined for his half-brother. Brand absently fingered his neck. He'd learnt his lesson early—never to rely on a woman, particularly one who declares her love in troubled times.

'You think you'll win, Lady Edith, but I know your type. You might have a pretty face, but you possess the same steel selfishness that my father's wife had,' he said softly, touching the pouch where the keys now resided. She hadn't wanted to give those up! He would find what each opened and what she sought to keep hidden. Above all she'd learn that he was not to be treated like a fool. 'You will learn who the master is now. And I will find out exactly what you think is not mine! I will unlock all your secrets.'

'Ah, there you are, Brand,' Hrearek said, striding towards him, his craggy features split with a wide grin. 'You told me to find you when we discovered something hidden. We've found a locked storehouse.'

'You admit I was right.'

'The gods love you, Brand.' Hrearek slapped his hand against his trousers. 'The woman didn't lie. This is a hugely profitable and well-run estate, even if they have tried to hide it well. You are truly fortunate. How do you do it? Time and again?'

'The harder I work, the more fortunate I have been. It is the only secret.'

Hrearek frowned. 'If that is the way you wish to play it, then so be it. I am sure there is more to your success. You must have been born under a lucky star.'

'It only seems that way now. No one would have said that ten years ago.'

'I hadn't thought of it like that.'

'You should. Now, where is this locked storeroom? Hopefully you have obeyed orders and not forced the door.'

'How will we get it open?'

'I have the means. Lady Edith has been most accommodating.' Brand pulled out the circlet of keys. He didn't doubt that Lady Edith knew of the stash. Whether or not she was responsible for the estate's profitability remained to be seen. Keeping it hidden from the casual raider was one thing, but keeping it hidden so that it could be used for another rebellion was quite another. 'It belongs to me. Show me.'

'With pleasure.'

Brand regarded the large quantity of sheep's wool that Hrearek and his men had found carefully secreted in what looked like a disused hut. The barns and other storage areas had a few bits in them, but this hut possessed a great quantity of wool.

'You were right, Brand!' Hrearek exclaimed. 'Some day you must teach me to read. That witch never mentioned this stash of wool. I listened hard enough and remembered. I don't trust these Northumbrians. They'd steal and lie quick as you like. You are far too soft. There will be another rebellion unless they know we are the masters with iron fists.'

Brand fingered the wool, good wool which could easily be sold in Jorvik. 'She expected us to leave after a quick inspection. We were supposed to take her offering and go. She had it completely planned.'

'She doesn't know you!' Hrearek laughed. 'You have a cunning mind.'

Brand frowned. This haul had been far too easy to find. There was something more here. Had to be. From a distant place in his mind, he recalled his mother explaining how, as a girl in Ireland, her mother had always made sure that any raiders would find some items easily and the family would not lose everything.

Had Lady Edith played the same trick? What was the true reason that she put staying here above her honour? She wasn't a natural concubine, despite the passion in her kiss. She possessed a calculating mind. He looked forward to playing tafl with her, pitting his wits against hers and unwrapping her many layers. It added to rather than detracted from her appeal. He wondered what she'd be like in bed and why her late husband had deserted it.

'I want the wool cleared out of here.' Brand pushed the thought away. Bedding a woman always ended the mystery. It was as simple as that. He should look no further. 'Find somewhere else to store it.'

'Why?' Hrearek widened his eyes. 'It is safe and

there is naught else here. It is absolutely pouring down outside. The wool will get wet.'

'The wool will be safe enough.' Brand tapped a finger against his mouth. 'The Lady Edith has hidden something else here and I mean to find it.'

At his word, his men hauled the wool out of the hut and onto the muddy ground. The final bundle of wool revealed a trapdoor with a lock. Brand fitted several keys before finding the correct one. When he lifted the door the gut-wrenching stench of salt and fish filtered out—salt cod. A most surprising choice.

Financially, salt cod would do Lady Edith no good. It was difficult to transport and easy to acquire. He should know. He'd made a small fortune by transporting the stuff in the last few years. What else was there in that room?

'Thor's hammer. What does she want this stuff for?' Hrearek put his hand over his mouth and started for the open air. 'It makes me vomit. Let's go.'

'To keep intruders away.' Brand smiled. Lady Edith was not as clever as she thought. 'We go nowhere but forwards. We find everything. When I am finished, this hall will hold no secrets and this salt cod conceals something big.'

Hrearek stopped. 'You amaze me, Brand. Even after all these years, your capacity to think ahead never ceases to astonish. Do you remember when we were stuck in Constantinople and you—'

'Allow me. We need to see what lies behind this salt cod.' Brand bent down and started to empty the hidden room. He had no time for reminiscences about what had happened. His past was behind him. He'd been lucky rather than clever. Others had died and he'd learnt once again that you could not trust a beautiful woman.

Behind the salt cod stood a short passageway that lead out to the woods. 'You see, there is more behind.'

Hrearek wiped his hand across his face. 'We could have been murdered in our beds.'

'If they had advanced through the salt cod and the wool…' Brand said drily.

A faint noise sounded outside the hut. Hrearek immediately reached for his sword. Brand shook his head and went out of the hut.

'Who goes there? Show yourself!'

'Me, Godwin,' came a small voice from the trees.

Brand crouched down and held out his hand. 'What are you doing there?'

'There are bad men coming. The lady said. I wanted to make sure that they didn't come through here.' Godwin gestured towards the hut. 'The lady told me not to worry, that she'd taken care of it, but I don't want anything bad to happen to her.'

'There is no need to hide. All the bad men are gone. You are safe now. You are under my protection.'

'And you are?'

'Brand Bjornson.'

A young boy of no more than seven years came out, dusty and dishevelled. He held out his hand. 'I will accept your protection.'

Brand took it gravely and shook it. The expression in the boy's eyes reminded him of his youth. 'And what do you do, Godwin?'

'I serve the lady.'

'Lady Edith?' Brand crouched down so his eyes were level with Godwin.

'That's right. My da said I had to as he went with Lord Egbert. Only Lady Edith told me that she didn't need any help.' He scuffed his foot in the dirt. 'Except she can't watch for the bad men like I can.'

'I can imagine.' Brand rubbed his temple. Whichever bad men Godwin feared, Lady Edith had feared them as well. The passageway was blocked deliberately.

'There you are, Godwin!' Lady Edith called out, hurrying forwards. 'Your mother is looking for you.'

'I fear I detained him, Lady Edith.' Brand put a hand on Godwin's shoulder. Lady Edith knew. She had more spies than one boy. 'He has been enlightening me.'

She put her hand to her neck. Several tendrils of black had escaped from her headdress and framed her face. 'He is just a boy.'

'I know what he is. What is his role here?'

'He is the son of one of my husband's retainers.' Lady Edith nodded to Godwin. 'Your mother has been searching everywhere for you.'

Brand put his hand on Godwin's shoulders. 'He was here, watching for the bad men. I've explained that no bad men are here and he is under my protection.'

Edith faked a smile as her stomach knotted. How much had Brand guessed? She had to hope that he hadn't discovered the blocked tunnel. She'd blocked it so that Egbert could not sneak back and catch them unawares after he'd left for the rebellion.

'Godwin, come with me, your mother is worried. She wants you to look after your baby sister. You are the man in the family now.'

Godwin screwed up his face. 'I want to stay here with the warriors.'

Edith glanced at Brand. He had made a conquest.

'You should do what Lady Edith requests, Godwin. A good warrior always looks after his women.'

Godwin scampered off, leaving her alone with Brand. Edith regarded the piles of wool and salt cod, rather than looking at his broad frame silently looming before her.

Her prayers had gone unanswered. Even when John the tallow maker's son had told her about the find, she'd hoped that he had not uncovered the salt cod or the passageway.

'You discovered my hiding place,' she said when the silence grew too great.

'The salt cod had spoilt. The wool remains good.'

Edith pressed her fingers together and tried not to scream as the rain started to fall heavier, soaking her to the skin. He enjoyed prolonging the torture. He knew about the passage. He had to. But she couldn't blurt out about it in case by some miracle it had gone unnoticed. 'And you are an expert in salt cod?'

'My father was a trader and I learnt at his knee.'

'I see.' Edith wiped the rain from her eyes and the end of her nose. 'I obviously made a mistake. It won't be the first time.'

'It is good to know you can admit to mistakes.'

'I've no trouble taking responsibility for my mistakes.' She raised her chin defiantly. 'Ruined salt cod is not good. I paid good money for it and now it has no purpose except to go on the rubbish heap.'

His face grew thunderous. 'You didn't come to find Godwin. You came because you knew the wool and salt cod were discovered. What else is there, Lady Edith? What should I be looking for? What was worth spoiling a year's supply of salt cod for?'

'You're wrong.' Edith forced her shoulders back. She had excellent reasons for keeping quiet about the salt cod and the wool. 'Godwin's mother asked me to find him as she worries. I happened to search here.'

'A happy coincidence, then.'

'Yes. That's right. Is there anything else?' She

waited with bated breath for him to ask about the passageway.

'I wish you to look your best for the feast. You should be attending to that rather than searching for a lost child.' Brand's lips turned upward. 'Your cousin might be able to help you with your hair if you are not used to such things. Now if you will excuse me, I have an estate to explore. On my own.'

Edith clenched her fists as her confidence plummeted. He enjoyed baiting her and he hated her wimple! She would keep her secrets. Her people were counting on her. Somehow the thought lacked comfort.

Chapter Four

The sound of Hilda's outraged shrieks combined with the pandemonium of cauldrons crashing and heavy objects falling filled Edith's ears even before she reached the kitchens. Edith gritted her teeth. Hilda never liked to make things easy.

'Hilda,' she called out as she entered the kitchen. 'I need you. Immediately, if not sooner.'

At the sound of her voice, the tableau froze. The cook gesturing towards a black cauldron, and Hilda's sulky expression while a variety of ladles and spoons lay on the floor as the kitchen boys cowered, told Edith everything she needed to know. Brand was right. The kitchen was no place for Hilda.

'Hilda, it is time you leave the cook and his staff to do what they do best.'

Hilda stuck her nose in the air and marched out

of the kitchen. 'Me being a scullery maid was not one of your better ideas, cousin. That cook actually expected me to wash the cauldrons! Do you know how long it takes me every night to keep my hands soft? I was born a lady, not a thrall.'

'Then you will be relieved to know that you are to be in the main hall tonight. Lord Bjornson has requested your presence at the feast.'

The colour fled from Hilda's face. 'You told him about me? You promised, Edith! What else have you done?'

'After your little performance back there, I don't wonder King Halfdan in Eoferwic doesn't know about you!' Edith crossed her arms. Hilda could not have it all her own way. 'Try taking some responsibility, Hilda. Brand Bjornson saw us talking earlier. You should know that I do endeavour to keep my promises.'

Hilda had the grace to flush. 'You should change the cook. He has not the least idea about proper respect.'

'Fulke has been with us since before my father died, first as a kitchen boy and now the head cook.' Edith took a calming breath. Screaming at Hilda wouldn't serve any purpose. Hilda had never liked hard work. 'In the kitchen, he is king.

It has always been that way. What precisely did he do, besides ask you to clean the pots?'

Hilda picked at her sleeve. 'If you must know, I became angry at that blasted cook for saying you were a Norseman's whore. He had no right.'

Edith winced. She could well imagine the insults which were bandied about, but they were only words. Words only had the power to hurt if she let them. She'd learned that lesson long ago with Egbert. Inside she knew her reasons and some day everyone who mocked her would be grateful. 'I believe that is what a concubine is.'

'But it isn't right. It hurts to be called such things.'

Edith drew in her breath. 'All I have is your word, Hilda. Fulke has not dared say it to my face.'

Hilda blushed and Edith breathed easier. Hilda had spun another tall tale to get someone into trouble.

'Did you know they are slaughtering two of the cattle? You refused Egbert cattle when he left. And Fulke wants the spice cupboard unlocked because Lord Bjornson asked if we had any cinnamon bark. Who uses such a thing?'

Edith fumbled for her keys, only to grasp thin

air. She looked up at the ceiling and blinked back tears. 'Fulke will have to ask Lord Bjornson for the key.'

'He has taken your keys!'

'The hall and all its contents belong to him.'

'I can't believe you, Edith. You are so calm about the whole thing. All your spirit is gone. I thought you were a Northumbrian through and through, yet you surrendered your keys. Your mother's keys!'

'Who can I fight, Hilda?' Edith held out her hands. Somehow she had to make Hilda understand that it was dangerous to be belligerent. She was playing this game for the long term. No one would be helped if she broke down now. The gold, silver and jewellery were well hidden. You had to know where in the lord's bedchamber to look. Brand Bjornson would never find it. 'We are in this mess because Egbert decided to fight, rather than accepting my father's pledge of fealty. The Norsemen would have left us alone if we paid that tithe. Yes, it would have been hard, but we could have done it.'

'But don't you care?'

'I don't like it any more than you do. I don't like the increased demand of tithes, but the Norsemen won. The rebellion is no more. I have a duty to look after the living. Petty vengeance solves nothing.'

Hilda looked thoughtful. 'I dislike working in the kitchens, Edith. It makes me want to pour poison in their soup. And I hope they choke on the beef.'

Edith shuddered slightly at the thought of her cousin poisoning someone. Hilda was far too impetuous.

'Then it is best that you don't have to work in the kitchens any more.' She gave a wry smile. 'Orders. We all have to obey them, some time, even me. You're to help me do something with my hair. Lord Bjornson dislikes my headdress.'

'I am to dress you now? Like a common servant?'

'You are to be my companion and help me. I can use your eyes and ears,' Edith said, thinking quickly. 'It is quite important. It is why you must dress in your finest clothes.'

'Served up for some Norseman's delectation so I can spy?' Hilda went pale. 'It is all right for you, but I wanted something more from my life.'

Edith bit back the words asking Hilda about

why, then, she had agreed to be Egbert's mistress? 'Hilda, for once, help.'

'Very well, but I won't wear my best gown. I want to be overlooked.' Hilda's entire body shook and her eyes were wild. 'You promised, Edith. I came here to be safe from the Norsemen. Keep me safe.'

'You never will be overlooked, Hilda.' Edith put her hand on Hilda's shoulders. 'Hush now. I'll do my best to keep you safe, I promise, but neither of us is in charge of our destiny right now. Some day we both will be. You have to believe that. The Norsemen never stay long. Here we have the chance to regain the land.'

'You don't really believe that, do you, Edith?'

Edith looked over Hilda's shoulder to the blank wall where she could see the shadows move. The memory of Brand's kiss surged through her. 'I have to believe it. I need hope. If I give that up, the world will truly be black. The only thing which keeps me going is my duty towards my people.'

Her cousin leant her head against Edith. 'I'm sorry, Edith. You are so good to me and I am such a beast. Egbert and I—'

'We don't need to talk about him, Hilda. Ever.'

Edith put her fingers across Hilda's mouth. 'He is dead and bears a large part of the blame.'

Hilda's eyes filled with tears. 'So you knew. You never said anything despite...'

'Egbert was my husband. How would I not know?' Edith rolled her eyes. 'It is in the past.'

'What is this Brand Bjornson actually like? I've heard terrible stories. I'm worried about you. You seem strong, but can you withstand his sort of lovemaking? It could all go so wrong.' Hilda brushed away her tears. Where crying turned Edith blotchy, Hilda managed to weep prettily. 'You are so brave to take on this role. I do want to help you. We could try dressing your hair differently. Something to add colour to your face. And you could try not talking back. A man likes to believe he is right.'

'Far too late for that, Hilda.' Edith gave a little laugh. She might be about to become a concubine, but she refused to be subservient. 'He knows what I look like and I've never been able to keep silent.'

Hilda grabbed Edith's arms. 'If he is not good to you, Edith, I will scratch his eyes out. But I'm serious. I want to help. Our lives depend on your success.'

'I believe you would too.' Edith laughed. Her entire being relaxed. She was far from alone. Hilda would help in her own way. She had to hope that included being civil to the Norsemen.

The smell of roasting oxen filled the hall, making Brand aware of how long it had been since his last meal or since he'd last had beef. He knew it was extravagant, but it was one more promise fulfilled—his first meal in his hall. He had to hope that it tasted as good as it smelt.

He glanced over to where Lady Edith sat. She had changed out of her shapeless gown into a dark blue one which highlighted her grey eyes, but her expression remained mutinous and she kept glancing over to where her cousin sat. He'd placed the cousin between Hrearek and another of the warriors. She appeared full of gaiety and charm. It was pure spite that had made Lady Edith banish her.

Brand took a sip of his mead. He would bed Lady Edith, but not yet. The fun with her was in the chase. He wanted to unwrap her layers naturally, rather than forcing the pace. He had a year to seduce her. He wanted to prolong this feeling of interest.

'Is the food up to the standard you require, my

lady?' Brand asked, breaking the silence which had wrapped about them. 'You appear preoccupied and have barely tasted your meat. I had the cook use some of the spices I brought. They are imported from Byzantium. Are you waiting for me to feed you?'

She ducked her head. 'Hardly that.'

'Then what is it?' He gave in to temptation and put his hand on her shoulder, making sure his breath caressed her ear. 'I'm hardly likely to make love with you in front of my men. I prefer privacy for those sorts of endeavours and I always make sure the lady is willing.'

Her cheeks flushed scarlet and she took a long draught of mead. 'It is good to know. My husband…'

'Your late husband holds no sway over the proceedings or the estate. He has vanished as if he never was.'

'Have you explored the entire estate?' Edith choked out. She had to change the direction of the conversation before it became out of hand. Brand's voice had conjured all sorts of images and possibilities in her head. Could she go back to the girl she once was? She had been so full of optimism then. 'You can hardly blame me for attempting to keep something back. Most Norsemen want to take rather than settle. We who remain behind need to live.'

He regarded her with sharp eyes before relaxing against the back of the chair. His fur-lined cloak brushed her thigh, sending a small pulse of warmth through her. Edith schooled her features. She was behaving worse than a virgin on her wedding night. She knew what the basic procedure was, though she'd never quite understood what was enjoyable about it. Egbert had always been rough, taking his pleasure before falling asleep with a drunken snore.

For some reason when Brand was near, her body reacted in unexpected ways. Hurriedly she gulped her mead down.

'Everything is fine.' His mouth quirked upwards as if he knew how he affected her and why she'd chosen this topic. He motioned for her goblet to be refilled. 'The estate as you said is more profitable than I was first led to believe. You are right about how Norsemen used to behave. We saw no reason to settle here. This time we have come to settle. The land is ours now.'

'Is that what you call it—settling?'

'You have another word?'

'Conquering and annihilating.'

'We must agree to differ. I've no wish to spoil my food with a fight.'

Edith placed the goblet back on the table with a clunk. 'I warned you that my skills as a conversationalist were not great. I've trouble keeping my opinions to myself.'

'You should never be afraid of expressing a sincerely held belief. I judge men on their merits, rather than on their past beliefs.'

'It is good to know.' Edith concentrated, but all her thoughts revolved around the breadth of his shoulders and the shadowy hollow of his throat. 'What are you curious about?'

'Shall we discuss why you chose to hide such a quantity of wool in an out-of-the-way place?'

'I feared raiders.'

'It wasn't just to keep it away from the Norsemen. You had another purpose. Who else knows about the passageway, Lady Edith?'

Edith tapped her finger against the ceramic goblet. He knew or rather had guessed. She'd underestimated him. 'We had to take precautions with the wool. It was done under my orders. I take full responsibility if you are seeking to blame someone.'

'For what?'

Edith took a sip of her mead. The back of her neck prickled. 'Must we play games? I gave orders for the salt cod to be put there. I can't abide the smell, if you must know.'

'It is your responsibility, rather than your husband's.'

'Yes.' Edith lifted her chin and looked directly in to his piercing eyes. 'I gave the order. Egbert enjoyed eating it, but it turns my stomach. I thought it best to keep it safe for his return. I was being prudent.'

He lifted an eyebrow. 'Is that what you call it?'

'What else should I call it?' Edith took a cautious sip of the mead, just one rather than gulping it down again. Allowing the mead to go to her head would only result in a headache tomorrow and she needed all her wits about her.

Her stomach knotted and she once again felt that she was playing a high-stakes game where she wasn't entirely certain of the rules. All she knew was that one misstep and everything would come tumbling down. She pushed the goblet away.

'A passageway to the woods.' He toyed with his knife. 'Who are you trying to keep out? Your late husband? Did he know about it?'

'It no longer matters. The cod has served its purpose.' Edith kept her head up and her gaze focused somewhere over Brand Bjornson's shoulder.

There was no need to explain that she'd blocked the entrance to the passage to prevent Egbert from sneaking back in. The last thing she wanted was for this Norseman to know the true state of her former marriage and the threats he had made. Egbert was dead and buried, along with his men. She never had to think about him hurting her again. And Brand Bjornson would soon discover what she was like in bed. Suddenly she wanted the feast to continue for ever. Here she knew she could hold her own. In the dark, she'd be lost.

'It matters to me.'

'Very well.' Edith put her hands in her lap and clenched them tightly. 'My late husband did know of the passageway. My father showed him all the hall's secrets before he died. My father trusted him. It was not until later that Egbert changed. I believe one of the Romans built the passageway before they departed these shores.'

His eyes danced. 'Not a fairy or the wee folk?'

'This estate originally belonged to a Roman or so my grandmother used to say. My father used to say that one of them had hidden huge quantities of silver about the land, but he never found it. He reckoned that it was one of his mother's stories.'

'Why would Egbert return that way?'

'I had little expectation of him winning. I was in Eoferwic when it was first overrun. I saw the hordes of Norsemen with their gleaming axes and swords. I know what happened when the Northumbrians attempted to retake Eoferwic. Every building burnt to the ground. Even the great church was scorched. When I last saw the city, the ash still smouldered.'

His cool blue eyes assessed her. Then his face relaxed into a smile. 'I have it finally! You thought your husband would return with his tail between his legs and didn't intend to be taken unawares. You should have said something, rather than speaking in riddles.'

Edith shifted uncomfortably. 'I like to plan for all eventualities.'

'Your cousin is enjoying herself.' He nodded towards where Hilda sat in between two Norsemen, effectively changing the subject.

Edith clenched her hands tighter, torn between the desire to move the conversation away from her previous behaviour and her fear of Hilda's volatility. If she looked closely, she could see signs of forced gaiety. Hilda's laugh was far too shrill and her gestures extravagant.

'My cousin enjoys feasting far more than I do. Shall I call her up here so that you may converse with her?'

Edith started to rise, but Brand's hand went around her forearm, pinning her to the chair. He gave a quick shake of his head and the heavy gold torc about his neck gleamed in the torchlight.

'I would hardly wish to disturb her pleasure.'

Edith glanced quickly at Hilda. Hilda's hand inched towards a knife. 'I'm sure she wouldn't mind. I had best go and fetch her.'

'Leave her.' Brand's mouth turned down and his tone allowed for no dissent. 'She knows who holds the power here and is far from stupid.'

'She is intelligent,' Edith agreed. 'But impulsive. Acts and then regrets her actions when they fail to work out as planned.'

'You were wrong about her wishing to hide in the kitchens. Relax and stop using her as a shield.' His fingers turned more gently, lightly stroking the inside of her wrist. Little butterflies flew up her arm.

'All is peaceful now.' Edith focused on Hilda, rather than on Brand's fingers. Hilda's hand relaxed and she laughed up in the Norseman's face, fluttering her lashes. Edith released her breath.

'Did you think it wouldn't be?'

'Hilda has no love for the Norsemen. They burnt her house and murdered her husband,' Edith explained, gently pulling away from Brand. Instantly he released her.

'But she knows who holds the power now and accepts it.' Brand Bjornson took a long draught of his mead.

'I hope so. I also hope your men realise that they shouldn't behave like conquerors and decide my cousin is one of the spoils.'

'Seeking to tell me what my men should be doing now? You Northumbrians will need to respect us, rather than treating us like overgrown oafs who have no culture or manners. I will have no woman forced under my roof.'

'An observation.' Edith reached for her goblet and delicately took a sip. The liquid burnt a pathway down her throat. Drinking the mead helped to keep her thinking from what the night might bring or the potential for disaster from any number of areas. That there had been no serious incident was more from good fortune than anything. 'Respect has to be earned.'

'I will keep it under consideration.' His hand stroked her cheek, turning her head towards him. 'Where do you bathe?'

'Bathe?' Edith blinked. 'There is the lake for bathing if one wishes. The priest believes that bathing leads to sinful behaviour.'

'Luckily I am not constrained by such things.'

Edith put her hand on her stomach. Sin. The priest would no doubt consider her behaviour un-redeemable. Her immortal soul would be damned for ever, but she had made her decision. 'And neither am I any longer.'

His smile grew. 'I'm pleased you understand.'

A shrill scream rent the air. Edith watched in horror as Hilda was pulled into one of the Norseman's laps. The man roared with laughter. She screamed again and pushed at his chest, but the Norseman roared with more laughter. Edith slammed her fist down on the table. The resounding crash made everyone stop and stare.

'This is how your men behave?' Edith said, pointing at the pair. 'My cousin should be treated with respect.'

Brand shrugged. 'Hrearek always treats his women well. It is the manner of his wooing she objects to.'

'Hilda is not his woman!'

'Yet.'

Edith retained a narrow lead on her temper. How arrogant of Brand to assume that Hilda was an apple ripe for the picking. 'Until such a time that she readily agrees, she shouldn't be man-handled.'

'You are making too much of it. It is a bit of play-acting and fun on both their parts.' Brand leant closer. 'Hrearek knows my wishes and will not cross lines. I remain the leader of the felag. All my men obey my orders. Your cousin is safe. Nothing will happen to her if she does not wish it.'

Hilda gave Edith an agonised glance and Edith knew she had mere heartbeats to avoid disaster. Thankfully she had dealt with this situation many times before with Egbert and his men.

Edith stood up and smoothed her skirt. She made sure that her voice could be heard in every part of the hall. 'If you have finished playing your game, Hilda, I wish to retire and leave the men to their feast.'

The entire hall fell silent. Hilda flushed scarlet. The Norseman made another lunge for Hilda. Hilda pulled back her hand and struck the Norseman, a loud ringing slap. The silence deepened.

Hilda's arm froze in mid-air. The colour drained from her face, recognition of what she'd done dawning far too late. The air hissed with the sound of drawn swords.

'He pinched my bottom! Next time I will plunge a dagger in his heart.'

'Hilda, it is time we left the men to their stories and drink. We retire now.' Edith pressed her hands together and offered up a silent prayer that she could get Hilda out of here without any blood being spilt. 'You know what feasts can be like. Leave the men to enjoy the mead. It is a particularly fine vintage, one that my father laid down.'

The Norseman who held Hilda started to protest in his native language, but Brand lifted his finger. At Brand's gesture, the Norseman released her. Hilda twitched her skirt out of his hand.

'The women wish to retire. Allow them.' Brand's voice boomed. 'Remember your manners. The women are under my protection. You disobey me on this and you will feel the full weight of the felag on your shoulders.'

The man muttered something, but then he let Hilda go.

'Thank you,' Edith whispered. Relief washed through her. He understood what had nearly happened and what she'd tried to do. Somehow it made things easier. But she hated being indebted to him.

He put his hand on her sleeve. 'We are not through, you and I, but I release you for now. Your cousin is volatile. Hrearek is not a man to cross, particularly in this mood.'

'I didn't expect it to be finished.' Edith hated how her stomach trembled, but she had to speak up for Hilda. She wanted to know what sort of man Brand was. 'I know what I agreed to. I don't recall my cousin being offered the same.'

His eyes danced slightly. 'I only have one woman at a time. It makes for an easier life.'

Edith's face immediately went hot. Like it or not, she was shackled to this man for the time being. When he discarded her, she had no idea of what would happen to her, but she had to take each day as it came. 'That is not what I meant. She should be allowed to retire to a convent if she likes, rather than becoming some Norseman's plaything simply because he has had far too much ale or mead.'

A muscle jumped in his cheek and his scar stood up more sharply from just above the gold torc. 'You are asking for her? Why? What concern is

it of yours? She was your husband's concubine.
You must have hated her for it.'

Edith kept her head up. What sort of women
was the Norseman used to? Of course she was
concerned! 'She is my kinswoman. She deserves
some respect. I have no wish for her to be passed
from man to man like some plaything. I know her
story. My marriage to Egbert is none of your concern, but I know what sort of man he was.'

'I shall take your views into consideration.' He
waved his hand. 'Since you begged so prettily.'

'It is most kind of you.' Edith held out her hand
to Hilda, who scampered over to her. Hilda's cold
fingers clasped hers.

'Where are we going?' Hilda whispered.

'Away from here,' Edith answered in an undertone. 'Next time remember where we are. You
know what nearly happened. I can't promise to
keep you safe if you behave like that.'

Hilda blanched. 'I'll…I'll try.'

'We walk out of here, slowly. Do not make eye
contact with anyone.'

'I understand.'

Edith started to walk towards the door. All the
Norsemen's eyes were on her and Hilda.

'Hold!' Brand's voice boomed out before she had taken ten paces.

Sweat trickled down her back. What had she done wrong this time? 'You require something, my lord?'

'You may retire to a convent, Lady Hilda, if you wish,' Brand said with a lazy wave of his hand. 'Lady Edith fears that you might not wish to be here or might find being with my men distasteful.'

Edith stared at him, astonished. He was giving Hilda the option, something Egbert had never done. A tiny flicker of hope burnt within her. Perhaps this Norseman was not the barbarian she'd first considered him to be.

Hilda shifted from foot to foot, ducking her head and not quite meeting Edith's eye.

'Hilda, do you understand what you are being offered?' Edith asked in an undertone. 'A new start. A place away from these men. Tell them all in a loud voice what you want. Don't be shy. You are under my protection.'

'I wish to stay here.' Hilda suddenly straightened her back and shoulders. Her blonde hair gleamed in the torch light. 'I refuse to abandon Lady Edith to men such as you. She is a gently reared lady despite what you seem to think. She has chosen to stay and so shall I. But I demand the right to choose my own man, if I desire. I believe the women from the north are allowed that privilege.'

'Spoken like a woman from the north!' someone called out.

The hall erupted with laughter.

Edith blinked in surprise. She never knew that Hilda felt that way. She had always considered that Hilda only stayed because she had no choice or because she enjoyed the power she had from being Egbert's mistress. And she knew precisely how much Hilda feared the Norsemen.

'I'm honoured, Hilda, truly I am,' she muttered. 'Are you certain you know what you are doing?'

'You are doing this for everyone. I heard the talk in the kitchen of how it came about,' Hilda said in a low tone. 'I couldn't leave you with these men. Your bravery has given me courage. I was so wrong and selfish earlier to doubt you. Forgive my temper, cousin. Allow me to make sure that you are the best concubine. You are the only hope we have of civilising this brute. I see that now.'

Edith gave Hilda's hand a squeeze. Somehow it did make a huge difference to know that Hilda was willing to stay. A pang of guilt washed through her. Perhaps she'd done Hilda a disservice in thinking her selfish. Right now she had an ally and she was awfully short of people who'd help her.

'We shall have to look after each other, then.' She wrinkled her nose. 'Besides, I don't think either of us would enjoy a nunnery.'

Hilda gave a small shiver. 'No. I'm no nun given to praying all day. Can you imagine?'

'It is settled, then,' Brand said. 'Both of you women are staying of your own free will. And you, Lady Hilda, shall choose the man who shares your bed. You are right—in Norway, our women are allowed to choose. In Jorvik, they are also allowed to choose.'

Edith dropped a curtsy in Brand's direction. She had misjudged him. Once he had recognised the danger, he took steps. 'We shall retire now. I bid you adieu,' she said loudly.

'And you go to keep *my* bed warm.' He, too, lifted his voice, she noted. 'I will join you in due course.'

Edith swallowed hard. He'd said the words she'd feared all throughout the feast, the true reason why everything had tasted of ash. Unlike Hilda, she'd already made her choice. 'I have my own bed. It is where my husband…'

Her voice trailed away under his hard gaze.

'Not when you are my concubine. Or did you forget that little morsel? You sleep where and when I want you to.'

His gaze was clearly fixed on her lips, and against her will, Edith found herself remembering the kiss they'd shared earlier. Her mouth tingled as if he had just kissed her. She rubbed her hand against it, banishing the thought. He wouldn't do such a thing in front of his men.

'Where would you like me?' She forced her trembling legs to curtsy.

A wide smile split his face as coarse laughter resounded from the entire hall.

'My bedchamber will suffice…for now.' He paused and his hot gaze travelled all over her. Edith frantically wished that she hadn't drunk all that mead. It was making her head spin. She wanted to sit down again and have the room stop spinning, but that wasn't an option.

'Is that an order?' She tilted her chin upwards.

'Yes.' The word hissed from his lips. 'I trust you to obey it.'

'Very well, I shall use the lord's bedchamber

instead of my own.' Edith hated how the blood pounded in her ears and the way the room slowly spun around. Somehow she had to do this—find a way to please Brand. It was the only way to ensure no one would get hurt.

'Wait.'

'Have I done something wrong?'

He reached her in two steps and pulled her against his hard body. Her body collided with his muscle. Unlike Egbert, there was no soft layer of fat. He was a warrior through and through. Edith swallowed hard—what had she been thinking about in provoking him?

'You need this.' His mouth swooped down, capturing hers.

He tasted of honey-sweet mead and something indefinably male and him. The kiss seared and branded her as his.

He put her from him amid loud catcalls and cheers. Edith knew her face burnt. She wiped her hand across her aching mouth. 'What was that for? Uncalled for and unasked for!'

She was furious with him and with her body for wanting more. She crossed her arms over her suddenly aching breasts.

His finger traced a burning line down her cheek.

'A taste of what is to come, Lady Edith, and you will find the experience enjoyable. I can guarantee you that.'

Edith picked up her skirts and ran as hearty male laughter rang out behind her and Hilda. More than anything that kiss demonstrated how little control over her body she actually had.

Chapter Five

'Thank you, Edith,' Hilda said as she brushed Edith's hair, turning it as smooth as the raven's wing. 'You were marvellous back there. Truly formidable. You saved my life. That Norseman would have…'

'I couldn't have you slaughtered before my eyes.' Edith gave a hiccupping laugh. Ever since they had left the hall, Hilda had stuck close to her side, insisting on helping her to undress, even going and getting some scent to dab on her wrists. Edith allowed it, but she couldn't help thinking that a true lady would have had more control. She silently tried to remember what her mother had said on the subject when she told her that she'd have to endure her husband's touch, but she'd have children to hold at the end.

Edith bit her lip. She wasn't going to think about

children or how Egbert's well-chosen punch to her stomach, followed by a swift kick when she refused to allow him to beat one of the serving girls for spilling his drink ended her dream of being a mother. She'd miscarried a beautiful boy. Ever after she could not bear his touch. Thankfully he had never tried to get in her bed again.

Now, his last mistress regarded her with an intent expression.

'Do you have something to say, Hilda?' she said, expecting another tirade about the Norsemen and their brutish ways.

'I was very foolish, I know that now. I thought… I thought it might be the same as with Egbert, but it wasn't.'

'These Norsemen are of a different breed.' Edith took the brush from Hilda's hand and gave her hair a few last vigorous strokes.

'You can say that again. The scar on Brand Bjornson's neck! It goes right round. I'm sure it is true what they say about his mother.' Hilda shuddered. 'He appears too wild, but he can control his men.'

'Warriors have all sorts of scars. By all accounts Brand Bjornson has been fighting for ever.' Edith put the brush down. 'But it did give me pause. I do know the rumours of how well he performed in battle. They say he is the main reason why the rebellion failed.'

Hilda nodded and began to pace the room, moving as if she was completely unsettled again. Edith's heart sank. The last thing she wanted to be bothered with was Hilda's problems. She had enough of her own. Brand's latest kiss seemed imprinted on her brain.

Her body wanted to believe it would be different with him, indeed she'd never experienced that tingling soaring sensation even in the heady days before her marriage when Egbert had made her feel like she was the most precious object in the world. Her head kept telling her that all men were the same. And she had no idea how Brand would behave if she failed to please him. She flinched, remembering how Egbert had taken his revenge for her shortcomings—first with snide remarks and then increasingly with his fists.

'Tell me something I don't know, Hilda. Give me some courage.'

'You should know that I never shared his bed, not in the sense everyone thinks.' The words rushed from Hilda as she knelt in front of Edith.

'He couldn't… Something had happened and he couldn't. He blamed you.'

Edith froze. Never? Egbert had been incapable? 'But I thought…'

'He couldn't.' Hilda glanced over her shoulder. 'He drank far too much ale and mead. He fell into bed, fumbled my body and snored his head off. I wanted you to know after what you did for me today, saving my life and all. He lied to me when I first arrived. He had said that he was the one who had given me shelter and spoken up for me. And if I didn't do as he said, he'd give me over to the Norsemen. You did what you said, just as you spoke up for me back there. I feel so guilty.'

'You are my cousin, my kinswoman. Of course I will look after you.'

'Egbert made it clear that if I didn't play along, I would have no place to lay my head. He'd throw me to the wolves. He slapped me when I didn't agree at first and called me a fool. I was scared, Edith, scared and wrong.'

'That sounds like my late husband,' Edith commented wryly, her mind reeling.

'You can't know what it was like when the Norsemen came. How I lost my world. I couldn't lose what little I had gained.' She hung her head.

'I was jealous of you and all that you had. Egbert's actions and words tipped the balance. I took what I could to survive. Only now I see I had it all wrong.'

'It is all in the past now.' Edith put her hand to her stomach to try to quell the butterflies which had suddenly begun to circle. Egbert had been incapable. Even with Hilda.

Tears shimmered in Hilda's eyes. 'Do you truly mean that?'

Edith's shoulders grew a bit lighter. Perhaps it hadn't been just she who had failed at the marriage bed. Egbert might have had a part in it, but what mattered was tonight and how she performed with Brand Bjornson, a man whom all her instincts told her was very different.

She put her hand under Hilda's elbow and raised the girl to standing. One good thing had come from this evening—she was speaking to her cousin. 'You'd best go. We already had one close call this evening.'

Hilda's lips curved upwards. 'I know what you mean. I doubt Brand Bjornson would be pleased to have onlookers. My heart quite soared when he kissed you like that. He is attracted to you. I know these things. You can try being pleasant to him, rather than wiping your hand across your mouth as if it stained you.'

'It was deliberately done to make his mark on me. He doesn't want me to forget my status. I'm not his wife. I'm his concubine. I serve at his pleasure.' Edith rubbed the back of her thumb against her aching lips.

Hilda fluffed out Edith's hair so it flowed over her shoulders. 'There, you look fit to eat. I do wish Egbert had not broken your mother's mirror so you could see how pretty you look.'

The mirror incident had happened during their final fight when Edith had refused to turn over her mother's jewels. Edith held no great store by her looks, but she'd loved her mother's mirror. Many of her earliest memories revolved around her mother having her chestnut hair brushed and watching herself in the mirror. On special occasions Edith had been allowed to peek into it. Her own features never matched the delicacy of her mother's. And her black hair was so dull compared to vibrant red.

'My late husband deserved all the ill fortune he received after breaking the mirror,' Edith said as steadily as she could.

Hilda gave a little giggle. 'I suppose you are

right. I had never thought about it in that fashion. He should never have done that.'

'I know I'm right.' Edith covered Hilda's hand. She had to know the worst. Had her desire for a peaceful life made Hilda's a misery? 'He never...'

'He never beat me after that one slap. He treated me much as one would treat a beloved dog.' Hilda finished for her. 'He saved his violence for you if servants' gossip is to be believed. He was jealous that you could run the estate so well. He used to rant about it, over and over.'

Tears pricked at Edith's eyes. She was grateful for the knowledge, but it still didn't make the situation any easier. The one thing she could do well, Brand had no interest in her doing.

'We will get our lives back.' Edith grasped Hilda's hand. 'I have to believe that.'

'You treat Brand Bjornson well.' Hilda slipped her fingers from Edith's and Edith knew that she didn't really believe the words, any more than Edith believed them. 'A well-satisfied man makes life easier for everyone in the household, as my mother used to say.'

'The saying is new to me.'

'That doesn't make it any less true. You can do it, Edith. Please him rather than confronting and challenging him. I've faith in you. We're all counting on you.' Hilda hurried away.

'That is what I'm afraid of,' Edith whispered after Hilda had gone.

A faint pink-grey light seeped into the room. Edith lay on her bed, hardly daring to move a muscle. The noise of the feast had died seemingly hours ago and still Brand had not come to bed.

She hugged her knees to her chest. At first she had feared he would arrive and be disappointed and then she had wondered why he had not come. But she lacked the courage to go looking for him.

In the early days of her marriage, she'd gone looking for Egbert and had ended with a hard slap to her face for her pains. Lying in this bed brought all the horrible memories back about every time she'd displeased Egbert. Hilda's confession helped slightly, but she knew she'd contributed to it. Egbert's touch had never excited her, never made her feel anything but repulsion, whereas Brand's insulting kiss had sent her senses aflame.

What could she expect from a Norseman with Brand Bjornson's reputation?

For some reason, he had found a better place to sleep. This entire exercise had been designed as a humiliation. That ended now! Edith slammed her fist down on the bed.

She wasn't going to stay here, waiting for someone who might never appear.

Edith knew once the hall started to stir that everyone would know and no one would look her directly in the eye. She'd experienced this before with Egbert and had always vowed that she was never going through such a thing again. Ever.

'I obeyed your order. Now I'm doing what I want.'

She pulled her gown on, but didn't bother with any head covering, leaving the bed unmade to show that she had been there and left the room without a backward glance.

The entire hall was silent. Various different Norsemen lay sprawled asleep where they had passed out. Edith delicately picked her way around them. They smelt the same as Egbert's men after a feast—ale-soaked.

Outside, the sky was tinged pale pink. Edith breathed in the morning-scented air. Always this time was her favourite part of the day, when she could think and plan without interruption. For a heartbeat she allowed herself to believe that all this was as it had ever been. Here was home.

She went into the stables and discovered that the stalls were now full of the Norsemen's horses. Rather than being silent as they had been since Egbert left, they were full of stamping and soft breath. The huge barn smelt right again. Edith went over to Meera, her horse, and rubbed the mare's nose.

'I wonder what you make of all these creatures invading your stable, Meera?'

The mare whinnied and butted her head against Edith's hand, searching for a treat.

'I haven't brought you anything.' Edith glanced about her. 'You can have some hay.'

She went over and gathered some. She saw with a frown that whoever had been in charge of feeding the horses yesterday had made a mess of the hay, scattering it everywhere. The mare gave her a look of disgust when she put the hay in her manger.

'It is no good hoping for an apple. There won't be any of those until the autumn.' Edith scratched Meera behind the ears as the horse bent her head and gobbled the hay. Strictly speaking, she supposed Meera did not belong to her any more, but the horse was more than an animal which she rode, she was a friend and friendship wasn't dictated by arbitrary ownership.

Her hand stilled in mid-stroke. She had to hope Brand had different views than Egbert about women riding as well. Her fingers grasped Meera's forelock. She would ride, no matter what he said.

'But I will try for a carrot,' she said as Meera lifted her head. 'Surely Brand can't begrudge me one carrot or parsnip. Or one ride either.'

After talking softly to the horse for a little while longer, Edith left the stable. Even without trying, her mind had made a list of things that needed to be done in the stable and yard. Little things if left unattended would result in much larger things happening. She tried to forget it, telling herself that it wasn't any of her concern now that the fencing was loose or the straw not evenly distributed. And goodness knew how those horses were shod and how much iron would be needed. She had to physically stop herself from going and checking the iron supply.

She pressed her fingers to the bridge of her nose. It wasn't any of her concern. Her sole responsibility was pleasing Brand in bed and she hadn't been given a chance to do that. The thought made the whole morning seem gloomy. She kicked a pebble and sent it skittering across the yard.

A slight movement by the stable alerted her to the fact that she wasn't alone and this was no longer strictly her home. Her body tensed. She wasn't supposed to be here. Brand had said specifically that she should wait for him in his bedchamber.

Quickly she thought of her excuse if it happened to be one of the warriors, something that tripped easily off her tongue rather than the real reason. Silently she prayed that she wouldn't have to use it.

She watched as the figure grew bigger. Brand. His hair gleamed as if he had been swimming. His shirt clung to his chest, revealing the hard planes and muscles. He might be large, but there was not an ounce of fat on him.

Her heart beat faster. What gave him the right to look so good in the early morning? She knew she must look a fright, but she also knew that she didn't have time to withdraw into the shelter of shadows. She brushed her skirt, trying to remove some of the wisps of hay which clung to her gown.

He stopped. His gaze slowly travelled down her form. Edith forced her shoulders back and silently wished she'd taken the time to put on her headdress. Rather than being the perfection of beauty that Hilda had declared her to be last night, she suspected she looked like she had been dragged through a hedge backwards.

'You're awake and dressed, Lady Edith,' Brand called out. 'Ready for another busy day? Or did you have another purpose?'

'I had trouble sleeping.' Edith pressed her hands together so that she would not be tempted to pick any more hay from her gown. Why did he make it sound like she was up to no good? 'I did obey your orders. I did go to the lord's bedchamber.'

He lifted his eyebrow. 'You *can* obey orders. Good. I wondered if you could only give them.'

Edith clenched her fists. He hadn't even bothered to check if she had! He'd simply assumed. Next time, she'd not make the same mistake. From now on, he came to her room, rather than her spending time staring up at the blackened beams in his. 'Is there some reason you failed to join me?'

Instantly she wished that she could unsay the words.

He tilted his head to one side. 'You looked like a scared rabbit in the hall. I like women willing and eager when I indulge in bed sport. There is no pleasure in intimidating the woman. Both should derive pleasure. Some in the felag do not understand, so I wanted to make sure my stamp was on you.'

Edith ducked her head. The low purr of his voice rolled over her. She had done it wrong again. Her fear of intimacy had shone too much.

She swallowed hard. The old Edith would have apologised but he didn't deserve one. The old Edith was the one who'd allowed Egbert to make fun of her. The knowledge of his deception helped calm her nerves. No man was going to do that to her again. 'And I prefer a different sort of wooing, but we can't always have what we want.'

He came over to her and put his finger under her chin, raised her face so she had to look him in the eyes. They were deep pools of blue. A woman could drown in those eyes.

'There was no need to hurry. I'm interested in more than just bedding my women.'

Edith put her hand on her stomach and tried to quell the sudden butterflies. What sort of wooing did this mountain of a man have in mind? 'What sort of wooing do Norsemen do?'

'I like to know a woman's mind before I know

her body. Long gone are the days when I needed the comfort of a warm body in the night.'

Edith crossed her arms as swift anger went through her. She'd spent a sleepless night and he had never had any intention of bedding her! It had been a cynical ploy to teach her some lesson.

'What was last night about? Why put me through the torment? What precisely did you hope to achieve?'

He cupped her cheek with his hand. The simple touch sent a warm pulse radiating out through her. She kept her body rigid, but an insidious warmth filled her, winding its way around her belly. She wanted to lean into his touch.

'Miss me that much?' he whispered and his breath caressed her ear. 'Is that what you are cross about? I will have to remember for the next time—you dislike being kept waiting. Tonight we will unlock the passion.'

She bid the weakness in her limbs to be gone. He was attempting to unsettle her again, like he had last night. Or worse, he expected her to fall into his arms like a ripe plum. It was all a mind game with him, an intellectual exercise much like playing tafl. He thought she was starving for affection.

'It wasn't a question of missing precisely,' she said meeting his gaze directly. 'More a question of unexpected thanksgiving for deliverance from something I feared. You had no right to put me through it.'

'I'd every right. You serve at my pleasure. When it pleases me to come to you and not before. Would you deny me that right? You were the one who agreed to the arrangement.'

She shrugged. She'd no choice but to agree. He seemed content to forge that little fact. 'So you say, but treating another person like that is not how I do things.'

His eyes flashed. 'And you believe you are superior to me? That I should treat you different than other women?'

'You need to learn about Northumbrian manners if you wish to rule here successfully.' Edith tapped her foot. She wasn't going to think about other women.

He drew his eyebrows together. 'You think me ill mannered.'

'Yes.' Edith glared back at him. She no longer cared if he did anything to her. He was the one in the wrong.

'You wound my pride.'

'I suspect your pride isn't even in the slightest dented. You have more than enough pride for the both of us.'

'And you have none.' He arched his brow. 'A veritable saint. Well bred and always correct.'

Edith rolled her eyes. It was such a typical feint, trying to change the subject. Her father had been that way whenever he lost an argument.

'I am proud, proud of things that matter, such as how I have run this estate and how I've looked after the people on it.' She held out her hands. 'Why should I deny that? Is it wrong to be proud of one's accomplishments? The sort of pride I despise is the sort which seeks advantage over another.'

'You have a tart tongue.'

'I've never seen it necessary to sweeten it with honey and have no wish to start now.'

'You prefer honesty.'

Edith straightened her shoulders. 'Yes, I do.'

'This is all about you sacrificing yourself for the good of others, serving yourself up as the innocent lamb.'

Edith swallowed hard. It amazed her that Brand knew of something of Christian imagery. There again, he had been in England for ten years. 'I don't recall you making a demand that it had to be one thing or another.'

Her body stiffened and she waited for the blow. Instead, he threw back his head and laughed.

'That will teach me, little one. Make a foolish statement and you will get the better of me. I won't make the same mistake twice.'

'I'm not little. I'm tall.' Edith moved the conversation away from the potentially difficult problem of why she'd done it. It appeared that Brand never had any real intention of making her his concubine in truth. Somehow that fact hurt.

'Maybe for a Northumbrian, but in Norway our women match us.' His countenance took on a faraway look. 'Strong women are needed to breed a race of warriors as my father used to say.'

'A woman's strength depends on things other than her height.'

'We are in agreement. Norsewomen are forged differently.'

Edith's heart panged slightly. There was a woman back there who'd claimed his heart. It shouldn't make a difference, but somehow it did. There was no good hoping for more. She was his concubine, not his love. 'I was the same height as my late husband,' she said quietly. 'I'm not used to being little.'

He put his hands on her shoulders. 'You are smaller than me.'

Edith moistened her suddenly dry lips. 'I know.'

'That makes you little.'

'Or you big.'

'It's all in your point of view.'

'I hadn't thought of that.' Edith knew her breath was coming far too quickly. Her heartbeat raced and her entire body was aware of him and how close he was standing. She could see the droplet of water which had gathered at the base of his throat.

He dipped his head. This time, his lips nibbled at her mouth, teasing and provoking. Edith arched towards him and his arms came about her, holding her there. Her mouth opened and she tasted his clean taste.

He lifted his head and she moved away immediately.

'What was that for?' she asked, a little too breathlessly for her liking.

'No particular reason.'

'I think you wanted to end the argument.'

Brand looked down at her upturned face. He fought against the instinct to crush her to him again and truly explore the depths of her interior. He wanted to savour the pursuit. He'd forgotten what it was like to spar with a woman. Too often these days women seemed to fall at his feet. Most had an eye on his position or his money.

He shook his head at his folly. It was the exhaustion, rather than feeling for this woman. Had to be. He'd spent the night searching for hidden cavities in the hall, knowing she was safely tucked up in his chamber where she could do no damage.

'And you prefer the final word.'

She tilted her nose up, but her cheeks coloured prettily. 'There is nothing wrong with that.'

'But I've found the perfect way of silencing you.' He gave a hearty laugh.

'The household is beginning to stir.'

His hand traced a line down her shoulder. 'I will allow you to escape this time, Edith, but we are far from finished. In fact, we have not yet begun.'

He watched her backside with appreciation as she turned, her skirt swinging. The exhaustion melted from his body. She would make a good bed-partner when the time came.

She hadn't gone thirty paces when she gave a stifled scream.

He crossed the yard in a few short strides.

'What is wrong, Edith?'

With a trembling arm, she pointed. 'There in the mist, a man is hanging. What goes on at these feasts of yours?'

'How do you know it is one of my men?'

'I don't.' She wrapped her arms about her waist. 'The one thing I had hoped to avoid was bloodshed.'

'You have no idea what it is.' Brand put a hand on her back. 'Shall we go and investigate?'

'Together?' she squeaked.

'Unless you'd rather I do it on my own.'

Her white teeth nibbled her bottom lip. 'It is kind of you to offer, but I want to know as well. It startled me, that is all.'

They walked in silence towards the figure. Halfway there, Brand's shoulders relaxed. Not a body but a childish trick, a set of clothes, stuffed with straw. But a challenge to his authority as lord. The perpetrator had to be found and punished before other incidents happened. He'd witnessed other men's authority ruined when they overlooked such petty tricks.

Edith saw it an instant after he did. She let out a shuddering breath and the colour drained from her face. 'What is that?'

'A straw man.'

'We won't have to bury anyone at the cross-roads, thank God.' She shivered. 'It is always awful when that happens.'

A deep-seated anger filled Brand. The petty trick had unnerved Edith. He wondered briefly who she had buried at the crossroads. 'I assume you know nothing of this.'

'Why should I?' Her eyes flashed fire and she became more like the woman he had encountered before. She glanced down at her skirt and tried to brush off the straw. 'I was in the stables earlier. Someone had spilt hay everywhere. I went to see how my mare fared.' Her hand faltered. 'You must believe me.'

'Did anyone see you?'

'No one else is awake.' She balled her hands into fists. 'I would never do a cheap trick like that! Ever! It is cruel beyond imagining.'

To his surprise, Brand believed her declaration. Her face had been far too shocked and white when she first spotted the figure hanging in the tree. She was not that good at mumming or play-acting. 'I believe you.'

Her tirade stopped. She opened and closed her mouth several times. 'You do? Why?'

Whoever had done this failed to consult Lady Edith. Interesting. 'Is there some reason why I should think you are telling less than the whole truth?' he countered.

Slowly she shook her head. 'When I was young, I discovered my aunt hanging like that. Her mind had become unhinged after she lost her baby to a fever. Even to this day, there are times I wake with dreams. There have been others over the years. I have had to arrange for the burials. The priest will have nothing to do with it. And my husband also refused.'

'I'm sorry.' He put his hand on her shoulder and felt her quiver. 'Should it happen for real, I will deal with it. They should be treated with dignity.'

'What are you going to do?'

'Cut it down. Discover who did it and why. An air of suspicion hanging over the estate serves no good purpose.'

'How are you going to do that?' She put her hand on his arm. 'I deserve to know. If you punish everyone, you will only breed resentment.'

'You deserve nothing, but know it is my estate and I will handle it my way.' He shook off her arm.

He crossed over to the straw dummy, withdrew

his knife and, with a single stroke of the blade, the figure tumbled to the ground. Brand saw, to his disgust, that whoever had done this had somehow managed to acquire a Norseman's helm.

He picked it up and examined the markings. With a start he realised who it belonged to. The audacity of it nearly took his breath away.

'Whose helm is it?'

He balanced it on his hand. 'Hrearek will be embarrassed when I return his helm to him.'

Her eyes widened. 'Is Hrearek the Norseman who attempted to molest Hilda last night? That was very brave of them. My people are not that brave.'

'Foolhardy, you mean.' Brand shook his head. 'He must have been drunker than I thought. I shall have fun when I present it to him.'

Her brow knitted. 'After what happened, why would any Northumbrian dare?'

'We have a different interpretation of events.' Brand tapped his finger against the helm. 'Hrearek did nothing to be ashamed of. However, some Northumbrian might have objected. After all, your cousin was the late earl's mistress.'

Her mouth became a stubborn white line. 'I tell you that none of my people did this.'

'Your people?'

Her cheeks reddened. 'Northumbrians then. The conquered.'

'You are saying that a ghost did this?'

'Or a Norseman,' she retorted. 'Seeking to cause mischief. Maybe someone holds a grudge against you.'

'Why? What could one of my men hope to gain from this? If any has a grudge, he is welcome to speak up. He may even challenge me for the leadership of the felag.'

Her teeth worried her bottom lip. A smug expression came into her eyes. 'If I had an answer to that, I'd tell you, but I could ask the same question—why would any of the people who live here risk displeasing their new master? They live in fear of you and any punishment you might dish out.'

'When I require your counsel, then I will ask for it.' Brand started to march away. He wanted to hit something hard. This was the first test of his authority here and he was not going to fail. Despite her story and shocked expression the most likely culprit stood before him. The hay on her gown proclaimed it. But he doubted she could have accomplished it on her own. He should have joined her in bed and taken his pleasure, rather than leaving her free to do mischief.

'Wait, please wait.' The plea in her voice echoed about the desert yard.

He retained a lead on his temper. 'Why?'

'You have made up your mind before you know all the facts. You need to call everyone together and ask. Then and only then will you know the full truth.'

'Why on earth should I do that?'

'You said that you are to be the lord over everyone in this place. Northumbrian and Norseman.' Her chin tilted upwards slightly. 'You don't want to be divisive and sow the seeds of discontent.'

Brand froze. He could remember his mother complaining about his impatience. 'And you are certain that it is not one of your people.'

'I'd stake my life on it.'

'Once I demonstrate to you that the guilty party is one of yours, then I expect you to show me where everything hidden is buried.'

'I believe you've found everything.'

'Insulting my intelligence will get you nowhere.'

She fingered her neck. 'How do you know I will have buried things?'

'Because it is what I would have done.' Before

she could protest, he shook his head, silencing her. 'You needn't worry. I'll find everything. It'll go quicker if I've your cooperation.'

Her eyes warred with his and she was the first to look away. 'Very well, if it turns out to be one of my people, I will show you all of the hiding places I know about. I refuse to have any suffer on my account. But what will you give me if it proves to be a Norseman?'

'The right to remain here, unmolested for as long as you desire it.'

'As your adviser?' She tilted her head to one side.

'If you wish to be.'

She held out her hand. 'I accept your offer with pleasure. I know my people. Shall we gather everyone and question them all at once?'

'Do you have a better plan?'

She bowed her head and screwed up her eyes. 'We should do it your way.'

Brand smiled slightly. She'd fallen into his trap. He would expose her for what she was. Today was turning out better than he'd planned.

Chapter Six

Edith waited in the yard, her head held high, but her stomach roiled. It was one thing to agree to Brand's terms with fake bravado and quite another to wait for it to happen.

She had to be right about no one from her household being involved in the practical joke. Her entire future depended on her following her gut instinct. If she could prove to Brand that she was correct, she would not have to be his concubine. She would become his adviser instead and the sword which had dangled over her head would lift. If not, she would lose everything.

She watched silently, keeping her hands at her sides and her head erect as everyone filed in—Northumbrian and Norseman—until the yard was full of sleepy and yawning people. Everyone had been roused, from the Norsemen warriors to the lowliest pig keeper.

Brand stood in front of everyone, dressed in his battle gear, his double axe resting against his calf as he balanced the helm from the straw man in his right hand.

'What is this all about, Brand Bjornson?' Hrearek asked. 'Why have you woken us? I thought we'd have one day to sleep in, particularly after a feast like the one you gave us.'

The other Norsemen warriors echoed the grumbling. Brand's face became sterner. He cleared his throat and the grumbling instantly ceased. The men stood straighter, but there was no disguising the malevolent glance she'd been given by the Norseman who'd caused the trouble last evening.

Edith reached for her circlet of keys for comfort before remembering. If she was wrong, the mood of distrust and discontent created would be far worse than she'd ever imagined. She crossed her fingers and hoped. Her instinct had to be right. The person who had done this was not from Northumbria. It was a set-up designed to sow distrust.

'There is something which needs to be sorted,' Brand said in a tone of voice that allowed for no dissent. He nodded towards the most vocal of the

Norseman. 'You appear to be missing your helm, Hrearek.'

Hrearek shuffled his shoulders importantly, thrusting out his chest. 'It isn't where I left it. I've had no time to search for it. Whoever took it will regret it when I'm through with them. I promise you that. On my honour as a Norseman.'

'Funny, that. I found it straight away.' Brand tossed him the helm, hitting him square in the chest. 'Next time, look after it better, Hrearek. It can be a matter of life or death. We have been together for too long for me to risk losing you because of your inattention.'

Hrearek scowled as he jammed the helm on. Edith clenched her jaw and concentrated on looking straight ahead, rather than returning the Norseman's arrogantly malevolent gaze.

Of all the people to have had their helm stolen, it would have to be him, the man who had wanted to bed Hilda.

She'd made an enemy last night, but she knew she'd do the same again to protect Hilda or any woman belonging to this house. Edith gulped a mouthful of air as her heart contracted. Silently she prayed that the straw man wasn't Hilda taking some sort of childish revenge. She could remember an incident with some nuts which went wrong last Christmas. Egbert had laughed, but the kitchen boy suffered a beating before the truth came out.

'Next time, Hrearek, I expect you properly dressed before you come on parade,' Brand thundered.

Hrearek stood straighter. 'Yes, sir.'

'The incident is now closed.'

Hrearek moved to stand behind his jaarl. The remainder of Brand's men followed his lead—a definite show of strength by the Norsemen and a statement that they all stood together with their leader.

Edith's heart sank. Had her instincts been wrong? Swiftly she silenced the little voice which urged her to withdraw before she was utterly humiliated, before Hilda was exposed. Nothing was proved. Just because Hilda had made a straw family last Christmas, it didn't mean she had done so this time. She just wished she'd remembered that particular jape before she had opened her mouth, pledging hidden treasure against the freedom to live how she wanted. She glanced about her and saw that Hilda was missing.

Edith balanced on the tips of her toes, debating

if she should ask Brand for permission to fetch her cousin when Hilda entered the yard, wrapped in several shawls and yawning her head off. Edith waved.

Hilda ran up to her. 'What is going on, Edith? Why have we been dragged from our beds? What new tortures have the Norsemen devised? Is this your fault?'

Edith put her fingers to her lips. Right now, whatever happened, she had to keep Hilda calm. A hysterical Hilda was not worth thinking about. 'All will be explained, but a straw man has been found.'

'A straw man. How wonderful!' Hilda clapped her hands. 'Was it poking fun at the Norseman? How clever.'

'What do you know about it?'

'Ask me no questions, dearest cousin.' Hilda waved a dismissive hand. 'I'm simply pleased that others want to fight back. It was a warning to all the Norsemen that they may control the land, but ultimately we will prevail.'

'Petty tricks are not fighting back,' Edith retorted sharply. 'They can come back to haunt you. Or, worse still, hurt innocents who might be caught up. Have a care, Hilda.'

'You treat me like a child, cousin. As if I would do something so foolish!'

'Only when you act like one.' Edith put her finger to her mouth. 'Brand Bjornson is in a fearsome temper over this little incident.'

'You haven't done anything foolish, have you?' Hilda's eyes grew wide and she clutched the shawl tighter. 'You were wrong to try. This whole adventure has been a mistake from start to finish. You should have been keeping him sweet.'

'I hope not,' Edith whispered back and her stomach knotted worse than ever. She had cast her dice and now she had to hope for the best. 'I told him that it could not be someone from my household. We made a bargain.'

'What did you promise him, cousin?'

'Shall we begin, Lady Edith?' Brand's voice cut through her panic.

'Yes, of course.' Her voice sounded far calmer than she considered possible. 'Like you, I wish to get to the bottom of this. I dislike mysteries.'

'Lady Edith and I discovered a straw man hanging from a tree,' Brand thundered. Somehow his shoulders broadened and he seemed to grow in height and ferocity. 'Who put him there? Who seeks to mock me and my men? Confess this instant! We are not criminals who deserve to be hanged but the rightful lords and masters of this place. We acquired this land with the might of our swords and we will keep this land!'

He lifted his sword and planted it in the ground.

The entire yard fell silent, far more silent than she thought a crowd could be. Edith bit her bottom lip. She didn't blame them. With Brand looking like that, was it any wonder?

Somewhere in the crowd a baby let out a thin wail, swiftly followed by a mother's hushing. But still no one spoke.

'No one?' Brand raised his eyebrow after the silence seemed to last for a lifetime. 'You are saying that the straw man just appeared. Conjured out of thin air?'

There was a mumbling and shuffling of feet.

'It might be one of the rebels returned!' someone shouted.

Brand put his hand to his ear. 'I have trouble hearing you. Someone is responsible for this. In the end, I will discover who has done this. I am a peaceful man, but it does not do to rouse my anger. If any of you harbours this person or any of the rebels, it will go ill for you.'

Again there was silence, but Edith could see the resentment growing in the Northumbrian faces.

'If none will speak, all will be punished.'

'What are you going to do, punish everyone including the children?' Edith asked in an undertone. 'The innocent and the guilty alike? None has returned. I am willing to swear an oath on this. It will not be one of the men who left here with Egbert who did this. The person who did this is standing in this yard.'

'What do you suggest, Lady Edith?' His voice was carved from chipped ice. 'I will find the guilty party. Trust me on this. The longer it takes, the worse it will be…for everyone. Are you sure you didn't see anything?'

'And you remain convinced that it was a Northumbrian?' Edith resolutely kept her gaze from Hilda. The longer it went on, the less sure she was that Hilda had anything to do with it. Hilda would never put others in jeopardy like that. She had a kind heart.

Brand made a sweeping gesture. 'As you can see, my men had nothing to do with it. They would have answered swiftly and truthfully. It is part of the felag's code. If a man cannot trust others in the felag, it cannot hold. If someone had been misguided enough to do this, he would have confessed. It is part of our code.'

'You trust your men.'

'With my life.'

'I feel the same about my people.' Edith crossed her arms. 'They're not warriors, but they do know what warriors can do. They fear you!'

'What do you suggest? This calling together of everyone has not given the result you declared it would.'

'If you must punish someone, punish me,' Edith said in a steady voice as she made a sudden decision. She had to take the punishment, rather than have innocents suffer. It couldn't be worse than what she'd suffered with Egbert.

'You?' He lifted an eyebrow.

'If someone must take the blame for this practical joke, punishing me will send a message.' Edith clasped her hands together and raised them in supplication. 'It is far better than burning a storehouse or torching a barn. They've lost so much, why should they lose more?'

She made sure that her voice could be heard in the furthest corner of the yard. At her words, people shook their heads.

'She should be flogged,' Hrearek called out. 'For

daring to defy you. There is no need to look further for who the culprit is. Your concubine should suffer a hundred lashes for her defiance!'

The other Norsemen beat their swords against their shields. Edith's legs became jelly. A hundred lashes. There was no way she could survive that!

'You think that little of me?' Brand asked, ignoring the growing chorus. 'You think I intend to burn some storehouse? Or deprive people of food? Is that why you want this to happen?'

Edith forced her shoulders to straighten. 'I want this ordeal to end. You are intent on punishing a Northumbrian. Punish me and be done with it.'

'This ordeal, as you call it, was your idea. I thought you wanted to find the true culprit. Who do you suspect?'

She wrapped her arms about her middle. She couldn't accuse Hilda without proof and Hilda would faint before the first lash hit her flesh. 'I've no idea. I wish I knew.'

'You must have an idea.' Brand's fierce face turned towards her. 'Are you going to confess, Lady Edith? Is that the true reason why you had straw on your gown?'

Edith put her hand on her throat as the day suddenly became more like a bad dream.

'I simply don't want to see any innocent suffer,' she whispered between parched lips. 'I told you the truth about visiting my horse. I will take the punishment because I have to.'

'I…I know!' a young voice piped up. 'I know who did this and it wasn't a lady. You must not punish Lady Edith. It is not right.'

A ripple of astonishment went through the crowd as the words sunk in.

'Who speaks?' Brand thundered, shading his eyes. 'I wish to see him and hear his evidence.'

'I do, sir. I wish to speak.'

Edith's heart pounded. Godwin. It couldn't have been him. He wouldn't have had the strength to lift the straw man up and she doubted if he would have stolen a helm.

Godwin's mother rushed forwards and raised her arms in supplication. 'Forgive my son. He knows not what he says. He is just a boy. Spare him. I will take the punishment for him. Just spare my son. I beg you! He is young.'

'I know what I say, Mother. And I do know who did this,' Godwin replied in a strong voice, shrugging off his mother's hand so that he darted forwards again. He put his hands on his hips. 'You should listen to me, earl of the Norseman, if you want justice done, rather than simply punishing the lady.'

Edith bit her lip. There was no way Godwin could know anything. It was a gallant but misguided attempt to protect her. 'Brand,' she said in an undertone, 'he is just a boy. He is the only male relation his mother has. He won't have done anything. He is a good boy.'

'Come forwards, Godwin, so that all might see and hear your testimony. You have nothing to fear.' Brand beckoned imperiously with his hand. He gave Edith a pointed glance. 'You will see that Norsemen justice is fair to those who tell the truth.'

Godwin stepped forwards. He stood bareheaded in front of Brand. He raised his chin and his gaze never wavered. Edith knew his father, Athelstan, would have been proud to see the sort of man his son had begun to become. 'I trust you to be fair, sir.'

'How do you know, Godwin?' Edith ignored Brand's glower. He had to understand how misguidedly brave Godwin was being. 'You should have been at home, asleep.'

'He was, my lady.' His mother stood up, her face white and her eyes fearful. 'I swear it. With all those Norsemen about, I couldn't risk something happening. I bolted the door and sat up all night just in case. My son was asleep in the loft.'

Edith turned to Brand and held out her hands, willing him to understand finally the impossibility of Godwin's claim. 'You see.'

'I wanted to watch the warriors, Lady.' Godwin bowed low. 'I beg your and my mother's pardon. I climbed down from the loft on the outside.' Godwin stuck his chest out and hooked his thumbs in his trousers. With each word, his voice grew in strength. 'I'm an excellent climber. I saw you and the Lady Hilda depart and heard the bard's songs about the deeds of Brand Bjornson. Then I was afraid of going back and waking my mother, so I decided to sleep in the stables. I curled up amongst the straw.'

'That much is true, my lady,' one of the stable hands called. 'I discovered him curled up like a dormouse in the hay loft.'

Brand crouched down, so his face was on a level with Godwin's. This lad had seen something. He could feel it in his bones. In an odd way, Godwin reminded him of another boy back in Norway. Brand had a clear memory of hiding beneath a table so that he could see his father feast. Godwin had seen something. Edith might protest but he knew it was the truth. 'What did you see, young man? Which of the Northumbrians did this?'

'It wasn't a Northumbrian, sir. He was unknown to me.'

Brand stood straight up. His stomach twisted. He hated the thought. One of his men? The lad had to be mistaken. None of his men would dare. 'Not a Northumbrian? Explain. Do you mean a Norseman did this?'

Godwin gave an almost imperceptible nod. 'I think so, sir. Aye, I'm sure so.'

'You are going to allow this lad to accuse us?' Hrearek shouted. 'You should punish the Lady Edith.'

The other members of the felag rattled their swords and axes against their shields. Brand frowned. Hrearek's words were far too quick and undisciplined.

Brand held up his hand and instantly the Norsemen fell silent. 'I wish to hear the boy speak.'

'Who did you see, Godwin?' Edith put her arm about Godwin's shoulders. 'Don't be afraid. Tell the truth and shame the devil.'

'I saw…I saw him.' Godwin raised his hand and pointed toward Hrearek. 'He did this and now he seeks to punish you, Lady, and that is very wrong.'

The big Norseman turned crimson and began to bluster. 'Me? Why would I do that? I've been searching for my helm. It was why I was late. I've never been in the stables. Me? I don't even like horses.'

'Do you have any proof, Godwin?' Brand asked. The significance of it slammed home. Hrearek. Over the past few weeks since he'd been honoured by Halfdan, Hrearek had become more and more insolent, bordering on insubordinate, but not quite. Would Hrearek truly attempt to undermine his leadership in this way? Things like this happened in poorly run felags. He prided himself on running a good felag, just as Sven had done before him.

Brand clenched his jaw. He desperately needed proof. Hrearek and he had been together for far too long for him just to accept this boy's word. But he knew deep within his gut that Godwin was telling the truth. He had seen Hrearek. It explained about the helm.

'It is a big thing to accuse a warrior.'

The boy swallowed hard and tears filled his eyes. Brand was taken back to a time when he was a little younger than Godwin. He had faced his father and told him the truth about how his wife was bullying Brand's mother and setting her up. No one had taken his part. He'd been beaten for lying, but later, after his mother died, the truth had emerged.

'I know that, sir, but I couldn't allow Lady Edith to get hurt.'

'He accuses Hrearek? A mere boy? That is a brave boy!' some of his men called.

'Are you going to stand for this? One of the felag! Where's the proof?' others retorted.

Brand's shoulders tightened as the noise behind him grew. The worst of all possible outcomes. Hrearek enjoyed great popularity with a certain section of the men. And the last thing Brand wanted to do was to split the felag and force his men to choose sides.

He would have to find a way to get Hrearek to reveal his hand. If, in truth, Hrearek intended on challenging for the leadership, he needed something solid which would enable him to act at a place of his choosing. The sagas were littered with men who had waited too long and lost everything.

A faint glimmer of tears showed in Godwin's eyes. 'He didn't speak…'

'I see. No proof.' Brand nodded. 'Could you have made a mistake? No doubt the stable was very dark.'

'There was a full moon last night,' Godwin said. 'I could see. And I know who I saw. He walks with a slight limp and smells of hair oil.'

'Godwin,' Edith said, kneeling down. 'You can't just accuse one of the Norsemen. You couldn't be sure, not in the darkness. Brand Bjornson needs something he can hold or see with his own eyes. Did he make a mark or do something?'

Godwin tilted his head to one side. Silently Brand urged him to remember something of significance. Godwin's face brightened.

'I do have this brooch. I found it on the floor after he went.' Godwin dug his hand into his pocket.

'May I see it?' Brand held out his hand.

The boy dropped it into his palm. Brand silently blessed the boy. He didn't need to ask whose this brooch was. He had seen it enough times pinned to different cloaks, over the past ten years. He could even remember when Hrearek purchased it. He grasped it tightly, the clasp biting into his palm as surely as the betrayal bit into his soul. He wanted to shout in rage. He should have seen the difficulty weeks ago, but he had chosen to ignore the pointed remarks and the needling.

'You say you have never been in the stables, Hrearek?'

'He said never, my lord!' one of Hrearek's close friends called out. 'It is good enough for me. A member of a felag would never lie to his leader.'

'Unless he intended on challenging for the leadership,' Brand said quietly. 'Do any of you wish to challenge?'

Brand waited for Hrearek to make a noise, but his sokman was silent, looking anywhere but at him. His stomach twisted. Hrearek's hesitation sealed his fate. It had to be done, but it didn't mean that he had to enjoy it.

'What did you say the perpetrator should have happen to him, Hrearek? Refresh my memory!'

'Flogged with a hundred lashes,' Godwin supplied.

'I said that she should be flogged. Aye!' Hrearek's eyes blazed defiantly.

'Can you explain why Godwin discovered your brooch in the stables?' Brand thrust the brooch under Hrearek's nose.

'I...I...'

'You thought you'd teach me a lesson, maybe?

You believed that you should be the one who had the honours, is that right? You rather than me should have become the leader of the felag after Sven's death and should have been made an earl?' Brand felt righteous anger surge through him. Hrearek had a few things to learn if he was going to challenge for the leadership.

Hrearek's tongue flicked out. 'I don't know what to say. You are an able leader, Brand. I would never challenge you. You know that. We go back to Constantinople.'

A sense of disgust and disappointment filled Brand. No, he would never challenge directly. Instead he would seek to undermine his leadership with little jokes and pranks and then step in when some other man had challenged him. The treachery of it all made him sick to his stomach.

'But I do!' Brand tossed the brooch at Hrearek's feet. 'What is the punishment for a man who breaks his solemn oath?'

'Death!' All of his men uttered as one, rapping their swords against their shields.

'Perhaps, Hrearek, I misheard you. Why were you in the stables? Or are you going to deny that brooch is yours?'

Hrearek fell to his knees. His face showed craven cowardice and fear. 'Please, by Thor's hammer, I didn't mean any harm. It was done in drink. A silly joke. I thought you'd find it amusing. I was about to say something when the lad spoke up. You must believe me.'

He gave a hollow laugh. No one else joined in.

'A joke, Brand. Don't tell me you have lost your sense of humour!' Hrearek made a gesture of supplication. 'Surely you haven't lost your famous sense of humour? I know you have played jokes before. We both have. No one was hurt. Come on, man. Lighten up.'

Brand struggled to control his temper. He wanted to rip Hrearek's head from his shoulders. Who did he think he was, behaving in such a fashion? But he couldn't run the man through. He had to think of this as a game of tafl. One false move and he could lose everything.

'No, you meant for me to distrust the Northumbrians. You meant for me to punish an innocent. You proclaimed the Lady Edith's guilt and demanded a punishment of public flogging.' Brand slammed his fists together and regained control of his temper. 'All because you were not able to bed a woman last night. You have dishonoured the felag. That much is clear. I have no use for a warrior who cannot keep his vows and seeks to take petty revenge.'

Hrearek went white and the men who had stood closer to him when he'd swaggered into the yard fell away as if he were diseased. Brand did not look at Edith. He owed her a debt. If she had not been so insistent, he would have punished the wrong person and would have allowed Hrearek's malign influence to grow and spread.

'In light of our past, Hrearek, I will be merciful this time. I will allow Lady Edith to decide your punishment as you were so quick to implicate her.'

Hrearek raised himself to standing. A faint light gleamed in his eye. 'Merciful?'

'Do you wish to challenge for the leadership?'

Hrearek's tongue flicked over his lips. He glanced to his right and left and saw how alone he was. 'No. I have no wish to fight you, Brand Bjornson. Ever. You have saved my life too many times. It won't happen again. Spare my life, I beg you, in view of our long past together.'

Brand bowed towards Edith. He gave a half-smile. Lady Edith fancied that she knew how to run an estate. That assertion deserved to be tested. Did she possess the nerve required to deal with men such as Hrearek? 'What say you, Lady? Shall I put this man to death as my custom demands?'

He waited and hoped that he had the measure of the woman.

Slowly she shook her head. 'Death should be for something far less trivial. You say he is an able warrior?'

'One of Halfdan's best. He has fought long and hard. His timely warning prevented the rebels from gaining the upper hand when they broke the truce.'

She nodded as if she understood his predicament. Silently he willed her to make the right choice.

'Then he should be sent back to Halfdan with your compliments. Halfdan must judge.'

Hrearek fell to his knees. 'May the gods bless you, Lady.'

Brand regarded Edith with faint astonishment. He'd expected her to ask for the man to be flogged and bear the same punishment that Hrearek had planned for her. Getting rid of Hrearek solved a number of problems.

'Bind him. Take him to Jorvik and Halfdan. He can be his problem and not mine. I will keep this part of North Riding peaceful. The Lady Edith has spoken and I concur with her request. Hrearek is far too valuable of a warrior.'

The men obeyed his order instantly and Hrearek was led off. Brand chose two of the men whom he considered were not overly friendly with Hrearek to provide escort duty. They obeyed instantly.

Some of the tension in Brand's shoulders eased as the yard emptied of people. Hrearek had not terminally damaged his leadership, but he was not going to allow anything or anyone else to interfere. He'd take over Hrearek's job of training the men himself until he could decide on the best man for the position.

He glanced over to where Edith stood, her dark red lips softly parted. A light breeze moulded her gown to her curves. No one was going to distract him. Lady Edith was a headache which would have to wait. Without acknowledging her, he walked into the hall to begin the tedious process of finding where the accounts had been altered.

Edith patiently waited until everyone had departed from the yard. She clenched her fists. If Brand thought he could ignore her and their agreement, he had another think coming. The culprit had been unmasked. True, it wasn't strictly entirely her doing, but he should honour his part of their agreement.

Perhaps now he could see why she needed to be a steward. If she had nothing to do, she would go mad.

Without giving herself time to consider, she strode into to the hall. Her feet came to a sudden stop. Brand sat at the high table, looking at the accounts with an intent expression on his face.

Edith cleared her throat. He glanced up.

'Have you come to gloat?' he asked, turning the page.

'To thank you for listening to Godwin. The true culprit has been unmasked, but you have lost your right-hand man. I can't believe your men would have had him killed for such a thing.'

'I know what happened. I was there.' He frowned slightly as his finger travelled down the page. 'You were not entirely honest here about the salt cod, were you? You really did not trust your husband. You mention it was disposed of.'

'You can read?' Edith's mouth dropped open. Astonishment gave way to quick anger. He had made a fool of her. He knew how to read. Here she thought she was being clever and he had used the accounts to help him find the hidden stores.

'Like you I learnt my letters a long time ago.' His eyes twinkled and he did not appear in the least repentant. 'It saves time when people are less than honest.'

Edith sat down on a bench, trying to collect her thoughts. Brand Bjornson could read. He'd played her for a fool as she stood reciting the stores. She'd been arrogant and condescending yesterday in assuming that he was an ill-educated barbarian. Edith shook her head. In retrospect she probably deserved it.

'You should've told me. It would have saved trouble.'

'And spoil your fun? Hardly. You seemed to enjoy showing off.'

'How well do you read?'

'Better than most scribes and I can write as well.' He gestured towards the book. 'I've no need of a steward, Lady Edith. I've no plans to leave this place. I'm through with wandering and fighting other men's battles. Time to beat my sword into a plough.'

'Battles will always need to be fought. Your king will demand it.'

'Halfdan will have to find other men. I intend to hold this piece of land for him.'

She pressed her hands together. 'We had an agreement. You and I.'

'If you had succeeded, you would have your reward.'

'Would have?' Edith crossed her arms and attempted to control the fury which coursed through her veins. First he misled her about being able to read and now he dared say she remained his concubine despite everything.

'I wagered your freedom against gold if you unmasked the culprit.' He tapped his fingers together. 'I will not ask you for the gold as the culprit has been found.'

'How very generous of you,' Edith said through clenched teeth.

'I thought it was. We have reached an impasse, you and I. No one won in my view.'

'But I did…or rather I helped.' Edith tapped out the points on fingers. 'It was only through my intervention that Godwin spoke up.'

'It was Godwin who provided the clue and, knowing the boy, I suspect he would have come to me in due course.' He raised his brow. 'Are you going to argue with that?'

Edith raised her chin, rather than reeling from the blow. Despite everything, she was to remain his concubine. It was only a matter of time before he discovered how truly unfeminine she was and what then?

'You mean I am to remain in our present arrangement,' she said slowly, unable to frame the word—*concubine*. 'To sleep in your bed and all it entails.'

'The idea does not excite you?'

Edith ran her tongue over her parched lips. Excite her? She was terrified of proving less than adequate! But she wanted to taste his mouth again. What did that make her? 'Not in the slightest.'

She waited for him to call her a liar. He turned the page of the book. 'A pity that.'

'Do you truly think?' She pressed her hands together. 'I think you only wanted to make a point. I was never supposed to agree and now you are stuck with an arrangement that you do not desire.'

'You are seeking to put words in my mouth?'

'Merely to clarify yesterday's events. It is why you offered to woo me.'

Something flared in his eyes. 'It might not have happened how you planned it, but Hrearek was discovered before he could truly undermine me.' He closed the book with a slam. 'That is worth something. You need to be rewarded.'

'I don't have to be your concubine?' Edith bit her lip. A wild surge of happiness went through her, swiftly followed by a curious depression. She wanted to feel his arms about her and his mouth against hers, particularly after how he'd kissed her early this morning.

'You may retire to your own bed at night.' His eyes twinkled. 'Since I assume you do not wish to go to a convent, consider yourself my adviser… for now. It should make things easier for you.'

Her heart skipped a beat. He wasn't sending her to a convent. She was going to remain here as she had wanted. A faint prickling came at the back of her neck. He had not mentioned anything about sharing his bed in the future, but she'd worry about that later. 'Do you mean that?'

His eyes became the colour of the lake in summer. 'I do not make the offer lightly.'

'I understand.'

'When I have need of you, I expect you to come to me. Day or night.'

Edith gave a little laugh. 'You can hardly have need of an adviser at night.'

He shrugged. 'Those are my conditions.'

The back of her neck prickled. He was up to something. But her heart argued that it didn't matter. It was a small price to pay for the entire issue of her being his concubine to vanish as if it had never been. He never need find out what a failure she was at bed sport.

'Very well, I accept your conditions.' Edith held out her hand. 'I shall sleep in my own chamber rather than waiting on your pleasure.'

He wrapped his warm fingers about hers. The small thrill that always seemed to go through at the slight brush of his hand ricocheted through her again. Edith knew her cheeks burnt and that he was aware of the effect he had on her.

'I…I will inform Hilda of the new arrangement.' Her voice appeared to have gone all breathless. She screwed up her nose and tried again. 'Immediately.'

His smile deepened and he slowly removed his hand, making it seem like a lingering caress. She snatched her hand back and covered her fingers, but all it seemed to do was to make her more aware of his touch.

'Why?' The single word rippled over her nerves.

'She will need to vacate my bed.'

'That would be good idea. I dislike the idea of you sharing your bed with anyone else.' He inclined his head. 'Pleasant dreams, Edith.'

She took a cautious step backwards. 'It isn't time for bed yet. I want to allow Hilda time to make other arrangements.'

'Really? I gathered you had a disturbed night last night. You should rest as you do not know what tonight will bring.'

'I doubt it will bring anything but peace.'

'One can hope.' He paused and a shadow of a dimple showed in the corner of his mouth. 'Peace is what one requires when one rests.'

Edith hurried from the hall and pretended not to hear the sound of hearty male laughter. She knew she should be relieved that everything had worked out how she hoped, but it seemed like she had just made a bargain with Lucifer himself.

Chapter Seven

Brand took a cautious sip from his mead and watched Edith as she took her place for the evening meal. Rather than sitting next to him, she stopped a few places away and sat down with a great flourish of her gown, dark blue shot with silver. And her head was bare. She carried herself like a queen.

He smiled inwardly. The next part of his scheme was about to go into operation. He wanted to probe Edith's mind and get to know her before he bedded her. He had little doubt that it would end in a bedding and not a wedding. He had chosen the sort of woman he'd marry years ago—biddable, excelling at homemaking and a woman who accepted his word was law. Edith was more akin to one of the Valkyries than the women he'd left behind Norway.

The memory of her passionate response to this morning's kiss haunted his brain.

Edith might feel that she was no longer his concubine, but he knew differently. This title or that didn't matter; it was the actual job which was important.

She'd made a tactical error in accepting his terms, but he saw no point informing her of it. She would surrender to him…eventually. He looked forward to her next move. Playing this sort of tafl made him feel alive.

Brand motioned to one of the servants, but made sure his voice would carry. He pointedly looked where Edith sat laughing with one of his men. She had no business laughing with Starkad. Starkad had more women chasing after him than there were stars in the heavens.

'Inform Lady Edith, she is to sit next to me, rather than making merry with one of my men.'

Edith reddened and moved quickly to sit beside him. She wore a dress which brought out the blue in her eyes. 'I had assumed you'd wish to dine with your men. I find them to be quite amusing.'

'You are to be my adviser, it is only natural you should sit here.' He nodded, ignoring the implication that he wasn't amusing. He could be as witty as the next man when called on. 'In case I need advising. What is the point of having an adviser who is elsewhere?'

'I will attempt to remember that in the future.' She sat down with a natural grace. 'I only wish to please.'

Brand frowned, feeling that she had won the point without even trying.

Throughout the meal she ate very little and answered his questions in an overly sweet manner. Brand made his questions more and more outrageous to see if he could provoke a response, but her tone remained one of distant politeness.

'You mentioned you play tafl? I've lost a most formidable opponent with Hrearek's departure,' he asked finally in desperation as the meal drew to a close and she started to rise.

She sank back in her seat. 'None of your men…'

'My men offer little challenge. You, on the other hand, have potential.'

Her body became instantly on alert. However, her eyes concentrated on the table, rather than meeting his.

'My father taught me.' Her voice was studiedly toneless.

'But you haven't played in a long time. Your husband failed to live up to expectations,' he said, making a quick guess. 'He lost to you.'

'Unfortunately my husband felt it was a game for men, but I used to be very good.'

'You liked winning.'

'There is very little fun in playing a game to lose.'

'I agree entirely.'

Her gaze raised and he could see the hidden shadows of vulnerability in her eyes.

'Why do you ask?'

'I would like to play with you and test your skill.' He resisted the temptation to cover her hand with his. She wouldn't thank him for it. Not yet. She had her wild expression in her eyes. 'I like to make sure my advisers understand the rudiments of strategy.'

'When?' She tilted her head to one side.

'Here and now.' He gestured towards where one of his men sat tuning a lute. 'A little music for the background, Starkad. "Ragnar's saga".'

'That is the one where Aella was made into a blood eagle,' Edith said with a faint shudder as she named the man who had done more than most to bring about the Norsemen invasion ten years ago.

'Did you know him?'

'My father did not think much of him.'

'Then we shall have the Lindisfarne one with Haakon the Bold. It might be ancient, but I still enjoy it.'

'You would have it sung here!' Edith seemed genuinely shocked.

'To the victor, the spoils.' Brand raised his glass to his lips. 'The man who led the raid was an ancestor of mine through my father's line. They say I take after him.'

'And you are proud of that?'

'He was a great warrior.' He quickly moved to set up the pieces. 'If you are ready to begin?'

'You will need to explain the rules as I've only played according to my father's.' Her long lashes swept down, covering her eyes. 'I would hardly wish to make a mistake, given the ferocity of your ancestor.'

The back of his neck prickled. Sometimes she was far too transparent. Edith wanted to win—not this game of tafl, but this game between them. She was fighting her instincts, and only allowing her personality in short bursts. He should have seen it earlier.

'Modesty does not become you, Edith. You are trying too hard.'

Her mouth gaped opened and her hand froze in the act of moving her piece. 'What do you mean? I haven't even begun to play.'

Brand leant towards her so that his breath caressed her shell-like ear. 'Relax. You're trying too hard to be pleasant. You really want to tell me to go to the ice cold of Hades, particularly as I brought up Lindisfarne. You were hoping to depart before I trapped you into this game and now you are afraid that you are going to enjoy this.'

'Hell is hot.' She folded her hands in her lap and adopted a falsely pious expression. Only the gleam in her eye gave her away.

'Not where I come from.' He motioned for more mead. 'Now admit I'm right about the game.'

She laughed, the first genuine laugh he'd heard from her. 'Yes, you are right. I do enjoy pitting my wits against you.'

Edith regarded the tafl board. Another move and she'd win. Her fingers trembled on the carved ivory piece. Did she dare? She hated that she had enjoyed herself far more tonight than she had in years. It was as if that horrible time with Egbert had never been and she could be herself.

Hilda had sent her several warning glances. Edith had tried to pay attention to her words of wisdom from just before supper, but it was proving impossible. All the joy she'd once experienced playing with her father came crowding back. She wanted to play to win, rather than allowing Brand to win as Hilda had advised.

'You might be right. A man might like to think he is superior, Hilda,' Edith muttered under her breath as the saga reached a screeching finale. 'But it doesn't have to mean that I cave in—but I can do something.'

'Did you say something?' Brand enquired, leaning forwards.

'I believe it is my game and the match,' she said, giving in to an impulse and making a move that was reckless. If he was good, Brand could still win.

'Not so fast.' Brand's hand stilled hers. 'You've not won yet. I have one more move.'

'You think that will save you?'

'Yes.' He moved his piece. 'My match, my lady. It does not do to become overconfident.'

She looked at him open-mouthed. He had done it. Egbert had always failed that test. 'You've won.'

His eyes turned serious. 'Edith, promise me that you will never again be tempted to just allow me to win again.'

Her hand flew to her mouth and a hot flush crept up her cheeks. 'Can I claim the music put me off?'

'Your eyes gave you away. I saw your cousin's nod.' His hand covered hers. 'I prefer my opponents honest. It makes the victory sweeter.'

'Enjoy the feeling while it lasts.' Edith withdrew her hand and started to set up the pieces. 'I demand a rematch! This time without a saga as background noise.'

'That is easily done.' Brand moved his first counter. 'Shall we set everyone a challenge as well? Something to keep them occupied.'

'What sort of challenge?'

'I will give a bag of silver to the man who produces a song which is pleasing to your ear.'

'Do warriors play music?'

'You should have faith, my lady. We Norsemen can carry a tune as well as any other man. I don't want you claiming the music is bad just to get out of playing me at tafl.'

* * *

Edith marked the fourth tafl win down on her diary in as many days. It was not a bad tally and she was beginning to gain ground on Brand. She looked forward to their nightly matches. After Brand had issued his challenge about the music, the hall reverberated to the sound of lyres and flutes as the warriors attempted to outdo each other.

'Lady Edith, I had hoped to find you here.' Margaret, Owen the Plough's wife, lumbered in. Years ago, Margaret had served as Edith's nurse, leaving only when she married the farmer after his young wife died in childbirth. She had never approved of Egbert and had stayed away.

Edith put down her book and held out her hands. Margaret enfolded her in her warm embrace.

'Margaret, to what do I owe this pleasure?' Edith asked after they had finished their greeting.

'Father Wilfrid has been to see us.' The elderly woman's brow creased. 'The new lord has ordered the corn be planted now, rather than waiting until Lady Day. Owen is afraid we will have no crop if it is not properly blessed. Father Wilfrid agrees with him. What am I to do, my lady? If my husband angers our new lord, he could lose everything, but he dares not displease the priest.'

Edith rolled her eyes. Father Wilfrid was stirring up trouble—nothing overt, just a few words in appropriate people's ears and suddenly people started questioning the decisions. She had battled him before. She did not envy Brand. 'Where is Owen?'

'He is here.' Margaret clapped her hands together before running off to drag her elderly husband in front of Edith. The farmer stood there, silently twisting his cap.

'Margaret tells me you are in trouble, Owen the Plough.' She held out her hand. 'If I can help, I will.'

'I knew you would do something, my lady.' Margaret's face became a wreath of smiles. 'Didn't I say my lady would help us, Owen? She will make the barbarian see sense.'

Edith cleared her throat as a distinct prickle went down her back. 'How do you know Brand Bjornson is a barbarian?'

'He is a pagan Norseman, what else can he be?'

'He reads and writes Latin,' Edith said quietly. 'Which is more than Father Wilfrid can do.'

'The more is the shame, then. He should know

what is right and proper. Everyone knows that the corn must be blessed before it goes in the ground. It is in the good book. Father Wilfrid says so,' Owen the Plough proclaimed. Tears filled his eyes. 'Please, Lady Edith. Help us. Soften his heart.'

Her shoulders felt like a heavy weight had been placed on them. If Owen the Plough believed this, how many others would believe it as well? And the last thing anyone needed was more trouble, particularly around planting time.

'Have you told Lord Bjornson how you feel?'

The colour drained from Margret's face. 'We could never…'

'I understand.' Edith pressed her hands together. She had to do it. Somehow she had to make Brand understand what was at stake if he persisted in demanding the concession.

'Here I find you! I've been searching every-where for you. No one knew where you were,' Edith said when she finally discovered Brand in the exercise yard.

The sight of him in his shirt sleeves with his tunic plastered to his chest took Edith's breath away.

'Where else would I be?' Brand tilted his head to one side. 'I've no wish for my skills to get rusty. It is where I am every morning. Not to be here would be wrong. The men need to be put through their paces.'

'I understand you have ordered the corn planted immediately.' She took a deep breath and continued, aware that she had stared a little too long at his chest, rather than saying anything coherent or deeply meaningful. 'Without having a blessing of the seed on Lady Day. It simply isn't done. It will be a catastrophe otherwise.'

He tossed a wooden pole to one of his men and strode over to where she stood.

'You have a problem? The year is getting on. If the corn isn't planted soon, we will have nothing to eat come autumn. Why wait when the soil is ready?'

Edith resolutely kept her gaze from where his tunic clung to his muscular arms. But every particle of her being was aware of him and the fact that he stood close enough to touch. It made her thinking all woolly. Her entire speech vanished from her mind. She stole another glance at his arms before continuing.

'One of the farmers came to me with tears in his

eyes.' Edith hated that her voice seemed breath-lessly at odds with her words. She swallowed and tried again. 'He is very upset about being asked why he has failed to plant and being told that if he does not plant, you will take the corn away from him.'

His jaw became set. 'No one has complained to me.'

'They fear you.'

He raised his eyebrow. 'What are you saying, Lady Edith? Why have you interrupted my sword practice for superstitious nonsense?'

Edith struggled to take a deep breath. Superstitious? 'The blessing means a lot to the farmers. It has always been on Lady Day when the rents are paid.'

'Times change.'

'Have you ever actually planted corn?'

'My father farmed.' His eyes became hard-ened points of blue ice. 'I grew up on a farm. We planted corn when the ground was able to be worked, whether or not Freya's priest had given her blessing. The soil can be worked. I pointed this fact out to the priest when he came bleating the other day.'

Edith tapped her foot on the ground. Hot anger

flowed through her. He wasn't even going to listen to her or consult her, despite telling her that she was to be his adviser. And he'd insulted Father Wilfrid. She could imagine the priest's jowls quivering at being informed that he behaved like a pagan priestess. 'When did you speak with Father Wilfrid?'

'Do we have to discuss this now?'

'It is getting near Lady Day. It is necessary to ask for Our Lady's blessing. Then we plant it after the first full moon,' she said, making sure that each word was clear. 'It is very simple and effective. It is how matters are arranged here in the North Riding.'

'I would have considered how warm the soil was to be more important.'

'It is not what the priest says.'

He rolled his eyes. 'Am I expected to listen to that black crow? He has already given me a lecture about how my soul is in peril unless I dismiss all pagans from my retinue and make an act of contrition for acquiring good Christian land. He suggested a donation to his church.'

Edith winced. She found Father Wilfrid overly officious as well. And he had gone beyond the bounds of looking after his flock. 'I didn't know about this.'

'It was not your problem.' If anything, his jaw had become more set.

'Did you assure him that you could look after your soul?'

His mouth dropped open. 'How did you know?'

She burst out laughing. She could see Father Wilfrid's jowls shaking with rage. She almost wished she'd been there. To see the priest meet someone who was not going to bend over backwards. 'Because it is the sort of thing I would say.'

'You are not overly enamoured of him.'

She waved an airy hand, suddenly realising that she was on shaky ground. She might not care for the priest, but his office was important. He did do good work in this parish and the last thing she wanted was for it to be undermined. 'He takes his responsibilities very seriously and has certain set ideas.'

'I told him that I was less concerned about how a man prays than the strength of his sword arm. It is none of his business how I pray or if I bathe.'

'He dared speak to you about that?'

Brand crossed his arms and his brows drew together in a stubborn line. 'He wished me to be a good example. My habit of bathing in the mornings has apparently been noticed and commented on.'

Edith rolled her eyes. She could well believe it. The priest, like the others before him, believed bathing was sinful and allowed demons in. It was better to wash, than to immerse. As a little girl Edith had asked why Jesus was baptised in the River Jordan if what the priest had said was true? Both her parents had hushed her, but ever since all priests had treated her warily as if she was a cross to be borne, rather than someone to be embraced. Father Wilfrid had much preferred Egbert's company.

'It doesn't change the rightness of the argument about the corn. The farmers look forward to his blessing on Lady Day. They regard it as necessary.'

'And my answer remains the same. The corn needs to be planted now. I refuse to have such a man bless anything.'

'But…but…'

'Consider it an order unless you wish to challenge for the right to be earl. I'm surprised you felt the need to intercede on this matter. How were you hoping to convince me?' His gaze raked her up and down. Insulting, lingering on her curves.

She crossed her arms and tried to ignore the sudden heaviness in her breasts. How dare he imply she'd attempt to seduce him to get her own way. As if that would work!

'You are making a mistake! A serious mistake!'

'I think not.' He gestured towards the practice area. 'Now, unless you wish to join me in testing my sword arm, I will return to my task with my men.'

He turned his back on her and picked up his wooden sword, calling to his men to start the bout again, effectively dismissing her and her arguments.

'Won't you even listen?' she whispered, balling her fists. 'I'm trying to help you. To keep you from making mistakes and harming these people.'

The set of his shoulders spoke volumes.

Brand scowled and picked up his opponent's sword. Six men he'd faced since Edith stomped off in a huff and each time they had been painfully easy to disarm.

'Shall we try again, Starkad? This time, attack

like you mean it. You make things too easy. I expected more from a warrior of your experience.'

'You have been knocking lumps out of us all morning,' the grizzled veteran said. 'Hrearek never worked us this hard, even when we knew we were going into battle. What is the purpose if we are not going to fight?'

'Hrearek has no part in this. We need to be ready in case of trouble.'

'I'm aware of that. You and I have fought shoulder to shoulder for too many years. You should know my worth.'

Brand narrowed his gaze. 'I will not have either of our skills getting rusty, just because we are looking after the land now.'

'But does it need this fierceness?' Sigmund stuck his sword down in the ground. 'I swear, Brand Bjornson, you should just bed the woman. It would save everyone a great deal of bother. Get on with it. What are you waiting for?'

'You trespass, Sigmund.'

'You are worse than a bear who has been woken from his winter's nap. Snapping here and there and demanding these endless hours in the exercise yard.'

'Only because we need it. Remnants of the

rebels remain. They might try to return here.' Brand shook his head. Was his lust for Edith that obvious? 'I refuse to have my relations with Lady Edith used as a cover for sloth and indolence.'

'We have been through too much, you and I.' Sigmund clapped Brand on his shoulder, rather than backing down. 'I was with you in Norway before Byzantium. I saw you kill your first man.'

Not his first man. That had happened when he escaped from his father's farm. It had been a case of kill or be killed, but Brand had been physically ill in a ditch afterwards. The second had happened on the battlefield and he'd managed to retain the contents of his stomach. 'What of it?'

'You need to bed that woman. It is a pleasanter way to pass the time, rather than seeking to knock our heads off.'

'When I require advice, I will ask for it.' Brand bent down, picked up the wooden sword and tossed it to Sigmund, hitting him squarely in the chest. 'In the meantime, shall we have at it?'

Edith sat in the hall, trying to spin but inwardly fuming. Brand had dismissed her without listening to her arguments. What was worse was the horrible look he gave her.

'You worry too much, Edith,' Hilda declared, neatly finishing one distaff of wool as she grabbed more wool with her other hand. Edith watched the process with envy. Hilda seemed to excel at all womanly tasks, whereas Edith had managed to break her thread three times this morning and lost her spindle whorl once, only finding it when one of Brand's dogs snuffled it out from under a bench.

'On the contrary, corn is hugely important to this estate.' Edith leant forwards, eager to explain her reasoning, everything she should have said to Brand but which she had thought of far too late. 'What do you think you will be eating next winter if the corn isn't planted at the right time with due consideration given to the local saints? And you don't want the farmers muttering against you. That is when trouble happens. My father used to say that all the time. And he might not have always agreed with the old priest, but he never mocked him.'

'Does the planting of the corn matter that much? A day here or there?' Hilda snapped her fingers. 'You should allow the men to do their job and get on with yours. Do you think they will dare complain, knowing Brand Bjornson's reputation?

Brand and his warriors are more than a match for any farmer who fails to comply and they know it. And that priest should never have made those remarks. He enjoys making people feel small. He'll be the one stirring up trouble, rather than our new earl.'

'He was doing his job as he saw it. But I agree with you. He'll be causing trouble for the sheer pleasure. He was one of Egbert's creatures. But Owen the Plough had tears in his eyes.'

Hilda adopted a pious expression. 'Brand Bjornson is doing his duty, in the manner he wishes. When are you going to learn that it does you no good to argue with men, be they priests or earls? The other night, I kept sending you messages with my eyes and still you played tafl like you wanted to win. And then you pointed out the mistakes he'd made.'

'I play to the best of my ability. To do anything else is to dishonour Brand.'

'Your problem, Edith, is that you hate losing. Learn to lose gracefully. And if you win, make it seem like an accident, rather than grinding his pride into the dust. Men like to feel superior.'

'It is one lesson I hope I *never* learn.' Edith gave her spindle a vicious twirl. 'And I know what the people who farm this land are like and what can happen. The priest has a certain standing and it is better to work with him than against him.'

'You really do care deeply about this land. I hadn't appreciated it,' Hilda commented. 'You take your responsibilities seriously.'

'Always.' A small sigh escaped from Edith's lips as the thread broke once more. That was part of the trouble—knowing what the probable outcome was. They might not complain out loud, but the resentment would build. She'd seen it happen with Egbert and in the end he'd had to reluctantly admit that she did know what she was doing.

Worse still, she didn't know what her job was. She had spent so long running the estate that being here, spinning and gossiping with Hilda, felt alien. She seemed to be all fingers and thumbs, rather than completing her spinning quickly and efficiently. Perhaps she ought to investigate going to a convent, but somehow something always came up.

'There are some things I know about and one is the correct time to plant corn on this estate. And we have always used a priest to invoke the blessing. Tradition.'

'Traditions are made to be broken, I say.'

'And when did this new attitude towards our conquerors come about?'

Edith narrowed her gaze. Hilda wore a new shawl, one which brought out the blue-green in her eyes. A little twist of jealousy curled around her insides. She wasn't going to ask who had given it to her. It was not her business if Brand had found another woman to warm his bed.

It bothered her that she looked forward to their nightly tafl game. He made her think.

Hilda flushed slightly and tightened her shawl. 'All I know is that it is not in your interests to quarrel with the new lord. Didn't you learn anything from your experience with Egbert? A man likes to be flattered, not have his pride ground to dust under your heel. You insisted on trying to win at tafl and now you berate him for making hard choices.'

'Why are you being so sympathetic to the Norsemen all of a sudden? Do not attempt to change the subject, Hilda. I know you too well.'

Hilda gave her distaff a twirl. 'Some of them are quite mannerly. Starkad has the sweetest singing voice. He sounds like a robin in spring. He was the one who sang the saga of Lindisfarne the other night but he prefers other more romantic songs.

He sang me the one he is working on for Brand Bjornson's challenge. It brought tears to my eyes.'

'And how do you know this?'

Hilda made a little moue. 'We met and he sang me a song. Pure poetry. I have no hesitation in admitting that some of the Norsemen might be different. He smiles more than Egbert ever did. And you are right about the scars. On some men, they give a face dignity.'

'Lady Edith, Lord Bjornson requires your presence in the stables.' One of the servants rushed in before Edith could question Hilda further. 'Immediately. You are to give no excuses.'

Edith's heart leapt and then immediately the doubts crowded in. Why now after their quarrel? Had he uncovered another of her hiding places? Or provoked more unrest with the priest? 'I'll go to him. Since he asks so politely.'

'You should go slowly, cousin.' Hilda put her hand on her shoulder. 'You don't want him to think you were too eager.'

'Hilda!'

'I was only saying,' Hilda protested. 'I've seen how he watches you like you were some sweetmeat ripe for eating. Whatever you two quarrelled about, and I refuse to believe that it was about corn, you should get it sorted out. If the jaarl is in a good temper, the entire household benefits.'

'And who says Brand is in a bad temper because of me?'

Hilda made a little tsking noise in the back of her throat. 'You are blind, sweet cousin, blind.'

Edith rolled her eyes and left before she was tempted to say harsh truths to Hilda. Snapping at Hilda wasn't going to solve her immediate problem. When she got outside, she picked up her skirt and ran towards the yard, trying to keep her imagination from seeing the worst.

Chapter Eight

To Edith's surprise, Brand stood in the middle of the stable yard. He wore fresh clothes, far richer and more ostentatious than the ones he'd worn earlier to exercise in. The red cape trimmed with fur and gold arm rings screamed that he was a nobleman. Water sparkled off his hair like diamonds.

Edith smiled. He had obviously bathed in the lake again. Her heart gave an odd little thump.

He stood with one hand on her mare's bridle and the other holding a much larger stallion. She pinched the bridge of her nose and ruthlessly suppressed the sudden leaping of her heart. Simply because Meera was saddled, it did not mean that she was about to be invited for a ride. There were so many possibilities, far more sensible reasons why he had Meera ready.

'Is there some problem? Hilda and I are hard at work with the spinning. It needs to be done.' She clenched her hands. She was not going to apologise for earlier either. She'd been right to confront him about Owen the Plough's fears. 'Are you leaving for parts unknown immediately? And you intend on using my mare as a packhorse? I will have you know that she is high spirited and needs care when handling.'

'Not in the slightest. Your mare sounds like her mistress.'

'What is wrong, then?' Edith rubbed her hands up and down her arms. She wished now that she had grabbed a shawl. She wasn't going to think about his linking her to Meera's high spiritedness.

'I want to put your knowledge to work, rather than have you do something you dislike such as spinning. Since you appear to know so much about the planting of corn, I require your assistance this afternoon.' His eyes turned harder than flint. 'We can visit the farmers together and you can explain to them why it is in their best interests to obey my orders.'

A spark of hope shot through her. He wanted to go for a ride with her. True, she'd have to explain why various farmers and tenants should obey

Brand, but it was nothing when set against the sheer joy of being on a horse again. 'You mean now?'

'I would have hardly ordered your mare to be saddled if I meant tomorrow morning. Show me the estate.' A faint smile tugged at his mouth. 'That is…if you do ride.'

'Much to my late husband's disgust.' Edith gave a small laugh, but it was impossible to know Brand's feelings about this. 'He felt no true lady should ride like a man. My dear mother would have agreed with him. She used to despair at my ways, but my father encouraged me. A good leader knows everything that happens in his territory, he used to say, and some day I would have to look after this land as if it were my first-born child.'

'But you do ride.'

'How else would I be able to visit all the parts of the estate in a single day?' Edith glanced down at her gown. Thankfully she was wearing one of her old ones, rather than one of her best ones. 'I designed my gown to be modest when I ride. It was my concession to my mother's sensibilities, but practicality meant I had to ride, particularly when my late husband was away.'

Even that had been fought over every single time and she had never really dared to, except when he was away. When she had found out about his death, a wondrous peace had settled over her. She was never going to have to give up riding again. There was something about feeling the wind in her hair and the reins between her hands as she gave Meera her head and they galloped over the moors. She'd had Meera saddled and they rode long and hard that day.

Brand's eyes turned sceptical. 'Show me you can ride. Here and now.'

'You don't believe me.'

'Northumbrian women rarely ride. All the ones I've seen in Jorvik take a cart.'

She forced her lips to smile. 'Norsemen rarely read Latin. Even fewer write it with a fair hand.'

He inclined his head. 'There is riding and then there is riding like the wind. I need you to be able to keep up with me if you wish to assist me. There again if you need to ride in a cart, you should say and stop pretending.'

Edith balled her fists. She looked forward to seeing his face and that of the other Norsemen when they saw she could ride. She might have failed to win the final tafl match last night, but she knew she could do this. 'I adore riding and I never back down from a challenge. It is no problem to demonstrate my prowess.'

'Do you need help getting on the horse?'

'I can do it on my own.' She refused to think about his arms about her waist.

She took Meera over to the mounting block and mounted the horse. With a slight click of her tongue, she rode the horse about the yard.

When she finished the circuit, she stared defiantly at Brand from where she perched. His look of amused scepticism had changed to one of astonishment. 'Well, do I ride well enough or do you need more convincing?'

'You tell the truth.'

Edith stared at Meera's ears, rather than looking at Brand. The words stung far more than they should. He still did not trust her. 'Why would I lie about something like that?'

'Shall we ride out and put your skills to a true test?'

With one bound, he mounted his horse and rode out of the yard, not bothering to wait for an answer. Man and beast moved as one. Edith's breath caught in her throat. She could understand why the bards sung of half-men and half-horse after seeing how Brand looked on his stallion.

She gave her head a little shake as some of Brand's men began to place bets on when she'd catch up with him. Edith counted to twenty to ensure he had a proper start.

'You will have to do better than that,' one of them called.

Edith dug her heels in and urged Meera forwards. The horse moved swiftly and Edith soon arrived where Brand waited.

'Where to first?' she asked, keeping her voice deceptively casual but her heart rejoiced at the astonished look on his face. 'Meera and I are more than able to keep the pace with your horse. I believe a few of your men will have lost their bet.'

'Serves them right. One never bets against a lady without being involved in the race, of course.' He inclined his head and his lips curved up in a secret smile. 'Then one plays to win.'

'Where to now?' Edith asked, pushing away the thought that they were playing a very different sort of game, much like when they had played tafl. But she'd won in the end. She tightened her hands about the reins. She would win at whatever game Brand played now.

'I want to see the outlying farms.'

'Any particular reason?'

Brand glanced at the woman riding at his side. Horse and woman were moving as one. He hadn't truly believed her when she said that she could ride, but now he had to admit that she could. She rode better than a number of his men.

He'd allowed her a few days' space, but he remained determined to unlock her secrets, not where she'd hidden her treasure, but why she sought to hide her beauty. His dreams had been full of her and the way her mouth had moved under his. She needed to become his in truth and to realise that he had never given up his claim of having her as his concubine. He wanted to possess her.

'My reasons are my own, but I do want to see if what you say is true. If this Owen the Plough needs his corn blessed by the bleating crow.'

'What is wrong with needing a little divine intervention?' She looked at him defiantly. 'You must understand that Owen the Plough is a highly religious man. He takes what the priest says and holds it in his heart.

'I want to see what the farms are like and hear you talk about them directly.'

She nodded. 'You don't trust my assessment.'

'I want to see what you are made of.'

'And you thought to test my riding ability.'

'It surprised me. Very few women ride.'

'I'm not most women.'

He laughed. 'I'm beginning to discover that. You have hidden qualities.'

Her eyes narrowed. He was laughing at her. 'Shall we race to Owen the Plough's farm?'

'If you like…'

'Yes, I do. And if I demonstrate to you that I can ride, will you listen?'

'I'm never one to refuse a challenge.'

She dug her heels in and her mare started off at a gallop before he had a chance to change his mind.

'You see all is resolved, quickly and satisfactorily. The priest will bless the corn on Lady Day after it is in the ground,' Edith said as they left Owen the Plough's farm. The interview had gone far better than she had anticipated. Owen the Plough kept bowing and saying how honoured he was. And Brand had listened.

'You won the race to the farm,' Brand said, very definitely changing the subject.

'Meera is a fast horse.'

'We should have wagered to make it more interesting.'

'Is it necessary to wager when you are racing? I simply enjoyed allowing Meera her head.' Her body felt as if a thousand butterflies were fluttering through it.

'There has to be some reason for racing.' A shadow of a smile showed on his face. 'But I will give you a chance. Shall we see who will be the first to make it to the river?'

'And what are we racing for? It had better be something that is worth my while.' Her heart gave a little lurch. She was flirting. Effortlessly. And it was pleasant, rather than a chore. She ran her tongue over her dry lips. 'Something special?'

'Something simple.' He leant forwards and patted his horse's neck. 'A kiss.'

'A kiss?' Her limbs became liquid. He wanted to kiss her. He hadn't attempted to kiss her since that first time.

'A kiss freely given, if I win.' His smile turned positively wolfish. 'If you win, you may choose the forfeit.'

'You're going to lose,' Edith said firmly, banishing all thought of how his lips tasted. He was seeking to unsettle and distract her. Meera was faster than his warhorse.

'You are certain of that.'

'I wouldn't race if I wasn't.' She had to win for the sake of her pride. 'You want an honest opponent.'

'I will give you a head start.' His face appeared entirely innocent. 'But you need to specify a forfeit before we begin.'

'Very well, I will claim the right for the priest to bless the corn,' Edith said quickly before she gave in to the impulse to ask for a kiss as well.

He tilted his head to one side, assessing her. 'You always think of others before yourself.'

'Someone has to consider them,' she argued back. He was so certain and sure that he'd win, even to offering her a head start. 'And I have no need of pointless gestures. I mean to win this race. Why not race for something that truly matters?'

'And a kiss has no significance?'

Her heart skittered. 'None whatsoever.'

She hoped she sounded far more confident than she felt. Kissing him again would bring up all the feelings she tried to keep buried. Last night had been the first time that she'd been able to sleep, rather than lying and looking up at the ceiling while her mind went over each time she encountered him. She tried to tell herself that it had to do with the running of the household, but increasingly she found her thoughts turning to his hands, or the set of his shoulders.

'Choose something else. Something just for you. A new dress or a hairnet?'

She tightened her grip on the reins. It was hard to remember the last time anyone asked her to choose a present. After they were married, Egbert had never bothered and her mother had drummed into her head that it was rude to ask. She hesitated and then she knew what she wanted. Hilda would no doubt tell her that she had it wrong and that she should ask for something that would enhance her, but Edith knew precisely what she wanted.

'I would like a book of *Beowulf*. My copy was lost years ago.' There was no need to tell him that Egbert had sold it to pay a gambling debt of his. She had drowned her sorrows in the estate, rather than letting him see how angry it made her. 'I used to love the language of it. My heart positively soared when I first heard it recited on a midwinter's evening. I must have been about four.'

'*Beowulf* it shall be, if you win.' He inclined his head. The feather in his hat bobbed up and down, highlighting the planes of his face. 'It is always best to race for something that really matters.'

'Shall we begin?' Her limbs seemed wobbly. He thought a kiss from her would matter? Impossible!

'Count to three. First one to the old oak tree by the water. And we shall see which is the more important—a book or a kiss.'

At the sound of 'go', Edith dug in her heels and Meera took off at a gallop. She concentrated, hunching down over Meera's neck. The race was less about winning, and more about proving to Brand that he was supremely arrogant. But a few hundred yards from the end, Brand passed her.

He laughed as she drew up. 'You lost. A kiss obviously means more.'

Her hands ached from clenching the reins so tightly, but her heart leapt. She wanted to be kissed. 'Yes, I did. I tried very hard to win. *Beowulf* will have to wait.'

'Overconfidence does you few favours.' He leapt down from his horse and looped the reins about a branch. 'Time for you to pay the forfeit.'

'Here?' She glanced over her shoulder. They were entirely alone in the peaceful glade beside the river, but it was also out in the open. Anyone could see them. Her mouth dried. 'You want me to kiss you right now?'

His eyes twinkled. 'I believe in collecting such debts immediately before the woman in question changes her mind.'

Before she could object, he took Meera's reins and looped them around the same branch. His strong hands went about her waist and lifted her down onto the spring grass. All around them, the white wood anemones and yellow primroses carpeted the ground. The woods had gone from the barrenness of winter to a riot of spring in a few short days.

Her body brushed against his muscles and thrummed with awareness of him and the fact that they were alone. She was amazed at how alive she felt. It was as if she, too, had suddenly emerged into the warmth and light of spring after spending years in a cold hard winter. She took a step backwards and strove to maintain her dignity and calm, twitching the folds on her gown into place.

'I can get down myself.'

His face became ultra-serious save for the deepening of blue in his eyes. 'I will strive to remember that.'

She had the distinct impression that he was

struggling against laughter. Edith made a show of straightening the folds a second time, trying not to think, but one thought kept hammering at her brain—she always failed at such games. Her ability to seriously flirt was non-existent.

'Why have we stopped?' she asked when the silence became too great. 'Was there some particular reason why you chose this glade, pretty as it is?'

'I want my reward.' His voice flowed over her like silky fur, warming her in the fresh spring air. 'I claim it as my right. I want it here and now, not in the distant future. Wagers are always best when collected on at once.'

'A kiss?' She strove for a natural tone, but her blood started to sing.

'One single kiss from you. Here and now.'

'That is the work of a moment.'

She rose up on her tiptoes and pressed her lips to his cheek. His masculine scent filled her nostrils and she knew all she had to do was to turn slightly and her mouth would meet his. It would become the sort of kiss which had haunted her dreams for the past six nights.

She stepped back, and refused to give in to the impulse. Hilda's admonishment rang in her ears, making her recall her mother's long-ago advice—a true lady endures the physical, rather enjoying it. It was wrong of her to want more. She needed to go slower and be submissive rather than always trying to win. It went so against her nature.

'A proper kiss.' His breath caressed her ear. 'I believe I've been patient, little one. It is time for your education to properly begin.'

She glanced up at him. Her heart thudded against her chest. A sudden trembling came into her limbs. Excitement rather than nerves. He was going to kiss her. Properly. He wanted to kiss her, despite Hilda's dire predictions that men never wanted women who argued. 'Patient? Education? I'm in no need of instruction.'

'Yes.' He gathered her closer to him. Her body instantly curved into the lean planes. 'You are in desperate need of instruction. This is the proper way to kiss. Learn and remember for the next time we wager.'

He lowered his mouth to hers. To begin with, his lips were light like the wings of a butterfly, but rapidly hardened as her lips began to move of their own volition under his.

His tongue stroked her bottom lip, demanding entrance. She opened her mouth and allowed him to feast, allowing her tongue to tangle with his. He tasted of spring air and the newness of life— all honey and clean, unlike anything she had ever tasted before, but ultimately leaving her craving more. A wave of sensation crested within her, breaking and building to another one. She was aware of how his mouth covered hers, how his tongue felt deep within her mouth and how his body moved against hers.

A small moan emerged from her throat as her body arched closer, demanding the solidness and strength of him. Her body seemed to acquire a will and instinct of its own.

'And now you know how to kiss,' he murmured against her lips. 'Shall we see if you learnt the lesson properly?'

'You want me to kiss you like that?'

'Until you have done so, the forfeit remains unpaid and we would have unfinished business. Do you wish to finish this in front of everyone?'

'That would be wrong, particularly when I'm only a novice at your type of kissing.' She looped her hands about his neck and stood on her tiptoes and brought his mouth down to hers again. He stood unmoving for a moment, forcing her to run her mouth over his as he had done to her, trying to coax a response. When she thought it was hopeless, his mouth yielded, inviting her in. She darted her tongue between his lips, running it over his teeth. This time, the kiss had no chasteness about it, but was dark and carnal, demanding more of the same. A heady sense of power swept through her. She had started this kiss. She was in control and in charge. It was up to her how long it lasted.

His arms instantly tightened and pulled her closer against him, moulding her curves tightly to his hard planes, allowing her to feel his arousal pressing into her.

His mouth left hers and pressed small kisses along the line of her jaw to her ear, sending licks of fire throughout her body. Tiny little gasps emerged from her throat. Her hands gripped his hair.

'Hush, hush,' he murmured, his accent becoming more pronounced. 'Relax and enjoy, little bird of mine. We have all the time we need.'

'Bird?' She looked up at him and was lost in the blue-green pools that were his eyes. 'You make me sound like some delicate creature. I am quite tough, I swear to you.'

'Stop beating your wings against the cage. You'll fly soon enough.' He drew a finger down the side of her face and gave a half-smile. 'You understand how to kiss properly now when you have lost a race, yes? You are a quick learner.'

She nodded and knew she could tease a little. She leant back against the circle of his arms. 'If that is all there is…I have given the kiss. The wager is finished. Perhaps we should consider returning to the hall. There is bound to be someone who requires your attention.'

'Such a kiss deserves the appropriate response.'

'Do I need more than one lesson?'

'You need many lessons.' His teeth caught her earlobe and tugged. The sensation was far more exciting than anything she'd experienced before. She had thought that somehow she could never experience pleasure from a man's touch, but Brand had amply demonstrated how wrong she was.

His hands tangled in her hair, releasing it from the headdress and sending it spilling out over her shoulders. He wrapped some of her hair about his hand and brought it to his lips.

Burgeoning warmth swept through her, blotting everything else out. She wanted more from him than a kiss. She needed more. She wanted to feel his skin slide against hers. Her body arched towards him, seeking his heat. Her breasts ached with sudden heaviness. Out here with no one around, she felt reborn. Something stirred and awakened in her, making her feel beautiful and desirable for this man.

'What is it you want?' he rasped in her ear. 'Tell me now.'

'You,' she answered, giving in to impulse and raising her hands to his face. Her fingers brushed his throat. It no longer gave her pause, but seemed an integral part of him. She pressed her lips to his scar and felt the solid thrum of his heart. 'Please.'

'You shall have me.' He placed a kiss in the corner of her mouth. 'Since you ask so politely.'

He stepped away from her, took off his cloak and laid it on the spring grass before removing his tunic and shirt. His skin gleamed in the spring sunshine. She could see a network of white scars across his front and shoulders, a map of the hard life he'd led before coming into hers. He was a warrior in truth, barely tame despite his learning. She started as she saw the heavy gold cross.

She put out her finger and touched it. 'Where did you get this?'

'A gift from the emperor for saving his life.'

'Are you…?' Her voice trailed away.

'I have always found it best not to ask how a

man prays or to which god, but how strong his sword arm is. The way I speak to my God is my business, certainly not some ignorant priest's who can't be bothered to learn Latin.'

'I should've guessed when you said you could read.'

'My mother was Irish and she used to tell me stories. My father believed in the old gods as did his wife. It was an easy choice.'

'Was it?' She couldn't see how it could be.

He laid his finger against her lips. 'There are more important things to discuss.'

He took off his trousers and she forgot how to breathe. His arousal sprung forth, declaring his desire for her.

She took a step forwards and ran her hand down the warm pliable skin, feeling the hard muscle contract under her touch. Her fingertips traced the network of scars and indentations. She brushed the golden hair on his chest and his nipples contracted to hardened points. Each touch was more seductive than the last and she wanted to feel his skin against hers. Edith resisted the urge to smile. Her mother most definitely would not approve! But her body demanded the contact with him. Something which felt so right could hardly be wrong.

His hands eased her back onto the cloak. The soft fur trim brushed the back of her neck, sending a delicious shiver down her spine.

She lifted her hand to his face. The soft bristles brushed her palm. 'And the next lesson is?'

He gave a throaty laugh. 'Allow me to see all of you. I've dreamt of you and the things we will do together. How good we will be.'

He'd dreamt of her! And from his expression, it was easy to guess that his dreams had resulted in the same frustrated excitement that hers had.

She reached her arms up and he pulled the gown off. Her undergarments swiftly followed. The spring breeze caressed her flesh, bringing an awareness of her nakedness.

Her hands went over her breasts and groin, suddenly uncertain of what he might think. All the doubts she had about her body crowded back in. Her breasts were too small and her hips too large. She waited for him to turn away in disgust.

He gently moved her hands to her sides. He gave a sharp intake of breath as his hot gaze roamed all over her, warming her far more than the sun ever could.

'You are so beautiful, Edith,' his low voice rasped. 'Far more so than I imagined. I wish I could show how you look lying against the redness of the cloak with your dark hair spilling out over your creamy flesh.'

Edith's cheeks burnt and she turned her face away. 'Should I believe your flattery?'

'You need to see my appreciation? Very well, it shall be done.'

He bent his head and caught one of her nipples, suckled, wrapping his tongue about it and turning it into a hardened point. He repeated the exercise with the other breast while his fingers toyed with the nipple he'd just suckled. Her body arched off the ground. A thousand lights burst inside her.

His mouth slowly travelled down the length of her, leaving a trail of fire behind. She knew she should be ashamed of her response, but it no longer mattered what was acceptable, all that mattered was what he did to her body and how he played it as the finest bards play a lute, coaxing and demanding a reaction.

Her body arched off the cloak when his mouth touched the apex of her thighs and his tongue found her inner core. Deep within the heat exploded and circled outwards.

'What was that for?' she asked after her senses stopped reeling and she found him propped up on one elbow watching her.

'Next time,' he growled, cupping her cheek with a surprisingly gentle hand. 'Don't belittle yourself. It doesn't become you. Now are you prepared to accept the compliment? You in the flesh are a thousand times better than you in a dream.'

'I'll think on it.' She gave a throaty laugh which he joined in. It felt good to be laughing, with her skin touching his. She'd never thought of a man joining with a woman as a time for humour and teasing, but with him it was. And that made it all the better.

She buried her hands in his long dark blond hair, pulling his face to her, making it a curtain about them. 'Is that an order?'

He nipped her chin. 'You may take it as such.'

He moved his hips and the tip of his erection pressed against her. Her body opened and welcomed him in. She wrapped her legs about him and pulled tighter. The length of him slipped in and filled her with pulsating warmth.

Always before when this moment of joining came, she had resisted and tried to lie as still as possible, thinking of other things. Now she welcomed it. Her hips began to move, urging him to delve deeper and harder. Wave after wave of sensation crashed over her. Each time, she seemed to be lifted up to greater heights. Finally a great shuddering engulfed her.

Brand watched Edith sleep, a tiny crease between her brows and her dark red lips faintly puckered as her long dark hair flowed over them both. He hadn't intended for this to happen when he suggested the ride. But he refused to be sorry. Already his body wanted to be with her again. This time in a warm bed, rather than on the cold ground. With plenty of time to truly explore all the facets of her. He hadn't lied when he said she was better than he'd dreamt. There was something about her, a bit like one of the mosaics he'd admired in Constantinople—the closer you were to it, the more intricate it became and the more you wanted to study it.

He smoothed a strand of dark hair away from her alabaster forehead. It amazed him that Edith was so confident in so many ways, but with lovemaking she was timid until she forgot herself and allowed her passion to take over. Her passionate response had been more than worth waiting for.

Brand stared up at the clouds skittering past. What did he want in his ordered life? Before Edith, he thought he knew his life's path, but now with her, he appeared to have taken a detour. Detours were fraught with problems. He'd learnt that lesson a long time ago. He knew what was important in his life and why he wanted it. His long-term future did not include this Saxon lady.

'Time to wake up, beauty,' he said more abruptly than he intended. 'We have tarried too long here as it is.'

Her eyes blinked. Her mouth trembled slightly. She stretched her arms over her head. His body reacted instantly. Desire, pure and simple. He'd be wrong to think more of it.

'I didn't mean to sleep,' she said, drawing her knees up to her chest.

'After that exercise, I'm far from surprised.' He ran a hand down her flank. He watched her nipples contract and knew she wanted more of him as well. 'Passion can tire you out.'

She sat up abruptly. Her black hair covered her like a veil, hiding her expression. 'It never has before. Normally my head spins with thoughts.'

'You've never been with me before.' He drew her back into his arms. He wanted to destroy all traces of the man she'd been married to, who had done this to her and imprisoned her spirit so she was afraid to show her passionate nature. When she forgot herself, the passion crackled from her fingertips. 'There is the difference.'

'I…I suppose so.'

'I know so.' He pressed his lips against her temple and attempted to control his temper. He wanted to run his sword through her husband for doing this to her. 'Was he that rough with you? How often did he beat you?'

She looked up at him. 'How…how did you know he beat me?'

He touched the silver scar on her shoulder. 'I assume this did not come by accident.'

'Egbert was a violent man.' She gave a sad smile. 'If you believe my cousin, it turns out that he saved his violence for me. He couldn't stand the fact that I was more intelligent than he. He used to mock my reading habits and my love of music.'

A jealous anger swept through Brand. 'Did he share your bed?'

'I always had to go to his.'

'The one I now sleep in.'

'Yes.' The word hissed from her lips. 'But it

stopped…after I lost our baby. It was then the real violence started.'

'I'm sorry. You don't have to speak of it.'

'I must.' Her throat worked up and down. 'I want you to understand why he said I was not a true woman. It was his fault. He beat me because I pointed out a tafl move he should have made.'

Brand wished he could kill Egbert slowly, piece by piece. Hitting a woman was bad enough, but to hit a pregnant woman was completely unconscionable. The worst thing was that he knew Egbert had died too quickly and without suffering. The only thing he'd wanted that day was to defend Sven against the treachery of the Northumbrians. He could not even say that it was his sword. He knew what Halfdan thought, but for his part, he could not be sure.

'It is good he is dead or otherwise I'd kill him.' He lifted her chin so she could look him in the eyes. 'A true warrior fights other warriors, not women or children. It is part of my creed. He also keeps his word and defends the others in his felag.'

She watched him for a long time, her throat working up and down. Finally she looked away.

'I could never forgive him. Ever, no matter what the priest said,' she whispered.

'You know my feelings about that man.'

She wrapped her arms about her waist and shuddered. 'It makes it easier to know that. It helps. Thank you.'

His heart contracted. He hated to think how she must have felt waiting for him that first night. He reached over and kissed her forehead.

'Shall we make new memories there or shall I come to you?'

Her eyes swam. 'I don't understand what you are saying.'

'The wooing is over, Edith.' He put his hand on her shoulder. 'You are now my concubine in truth. We will sleep together from now on…for as long as I have need of you.'

She scrambled out of his arms and dressed rapidly. Her head spun. She had been so stupid. She had never thought about the consequences. She had considered they had put all that nonsense behind them. Brand hadn't. She'd been very naive.

'Your concubine?' she squeaked when she had her clothes on. Brand, she noticed, made no move to cover his nakedness. He appeared to be totally at peace with it.

'After what we shared, you hardly think I want only one time? It is not in my nature to sneak around.'

'But…but…I thought… Did I please you?'

'It went beyond pleasure.'

She tried to form her thoughts into a coherent train rather than the chaotic jumble. The one thing that sang through loud and clear was that far from being a failure at this, she had succeeded. Brand wanted her as a man wants a woman. Egbert had been wrong. She was capable of being feminine and pleasing a man.

She had never dreamt that such sensation was possible. It had all been about finding the right man.

Her stomach churned. Neither was there some sudden offer of marriage. She had known that before she gave her body to Brand and it would be useless to pretend otherwise. She had become a fallen lady in truth.

'There'll be no need to sneak or hide,' she said slowly. 'I will share your bed. It is the person who counts, not the object.'

Chapter Nine

'There you are, Edith. I've been searching everywhere for you.' Hilda came up to Edith in their now shared bedchamber after she had washed her face and changed from her ride. 'You are seldom where I want you these days. You always seem to be busy with him.'

'I went out riding with Brand,' Edith answered and hoped her colour wasn't too high. She took one last look at the bed. Did she tell Hilda now or later that she would not be sharing it with her tonight? Her body ached in places that she had not dreamt possible and her lips remained pleasantly swollen. Even now, she fancied she could feel the rasp of his bristled chin against her flesh.

She wanted to hug the time they had shared to her bosom. It was like some time out of mind. She had never dreamt such things were possible. She

felt truly connected to Brand as if they had become one person. She knew it was a good thing,
no matter what anyone might say. And some day,
who knew if they remained compatible, he might
decide to make her his life's companion?

'Only riding?'

Edith turned to her trunk and lifted the lid. She
forced her hands to start rearranging the combs,
anything to stop them from covering her cheeks.
'Brand wanted to visit the outlying farms.'

Hilda stamped her foot. 'Brand took you riding.
I know. Everyone spoke about it. They wagered
on you coming off, but I told Starkad that you
ride better than most men. Never wager against
my cousin, I said. You were gone a long time. It
is nearly supper time.'

'Brand enjoyed it.' Edith chose her words with
care. 'So we stayed out later than he'd planned. I
think we will be repeating it soon.'

Edith moved the combs back to their original
place as Hilda started a long litany of why carts
were superior to horses and why she never rode,
how her day had gone and a variety of complaints.
Edith listened with half an ear while her mind
started to spin dreams. What if they married? It
was the best option. They were compatible and

she knew the estate. Their children could inherit. The thought took her breath away. Their children. She pushed the thought away. It was far too soon. She wasn't even sure how she felt about him except he made her feel alive. She had been dead inside for so long.

Hilda waved a hand in front of Edith's eyes. 'Have you listened to a word I've been saying? Or are you wool-gathering?'

'Of course,' Edith replied, frantically trying to recall Hilda's last remark. 'Brand is a different sort of man to my late husband. He sees me as a challenge rather than an affront.'

'I'm pleased.' Hilda put her hands on her head. 'I can't begin to tell you how much I feared that something had happened to you and that I'd have to cope with this on my own. Pay attention, Edith. This is important, far more important than what happened on your ride.'

'We are both experienced riders. You should have known that I'd return. The hall hasn't burnt down,' Edith explained, trying to work out Hilda's perplexed expression. What business of hers was it how long she took? It wasn't as if she'd disappeared for the entire day. They were only gone a few hours. 'We rode out to Owen the Plough's and the matter has been satisfactorily resolved. Besides, their women are not supposed to be quiet. He is used to women arguing.'

'Their women? You belong to him now?' Hilda regarded her closely. 'Truly? I had thought…that is…'

'Everyone has been talking about it. I refuse to be mealy-mouthed. I'm his concubine, Hilda. His woman.'

Edith marvelled that she could call herself his woman. But it seemed natural. And she hated lying. It would get easier. Soon everyone would know that they were sharing a bed. There again, they thought it had already happened on the first night. She had finally done what she declared she would.

Hilda linked her arm with Edith's. Her face became utterly grave. 'It could not happen at a better time. You are going to need to have him in a good mood. We all are. You remember we heard that everyone died in the rebellion? They didn't. Not all of them.'

Ice crept into Edith's spine, chilling her from deep within. Something was terribly wrong. She should have known that it was far too easy to be happy. She should never have gone on the ride or kissed Brand back. She should have been here to deal with the problem. 'What is wrong? What has happened? What have you done, Hilda? Why do you need me to cope?'

'Godwin's father has returned. Athelstan. He's back.' Hilda's hand gripped Edith's elbow. 'He's alive, Edith.'

Edith withdrew her arm from Hilda and walked over to a tapestry her mother had woven. She could recall clearly the many happy hours she'd spent, helping. Then when her mother fell ill, Edith had finished the last bit herself. When it was completed, Athelstan and her father had hung this tapestry to help keep her mother's room warm while she lay ill.

Athelstan had come back. If he'd returned, what about Egbert? What if he came back too?

Edith drew a deep breath and willed the sudden panic to be gone. Egbert was dead. She knew what had happened to him and how his body had been shown to everyone.

'I thought they all perished,' she said when she trusted her voice. 'It was what we heard. Halfdan ordered them all to be killed after they broke the truce and they were. Edward the baker's son only escaped because he crawled away in the brush.'

'Not all of them. Athelstan made it home. He came through the unblocked tunnel last night. Mary came to see me as she couldn't find you. He's been hurt. He is asking for you. Will you go? Will you tell him to leave us alone? We have suffered enough.'

Edith closed her eyes, remembering Brand's words from when Hrearek was unmasked. Anyone harbouring one of the rebels would be considered a traitor. Mary and Godwin were taking an awful risk, harbouring him, even for a night. Hilda was right, for everyone's sake, Athelstan had to go and make his way to the south. He was an able man. He'd survive.

There were some things which Brand would not forgive. She knew that after his decisive treatment of Hrearek, he was the sort of man who saw the world in black and white. Her father had been the same. Once he'd established a course, he wouldn't change. It was no good pleading with him for Athelstan.

She couldn't turn her back on a man who had served her family for so long simply because some king decreed it. His family and hers had always been intertwined. She could remember his father and grandfather and how her father set such a store about his advice. More than once he'd intervened when Egbert was in a murderous rage. He'd only gone with Egbert to look after the men when she'd insisted. At first he'd asked to stay as Mary had just had her baby.

She refused to allow such a man to be slaughtered in cold blood, simply because he had the misfortune to be on the losing side.

'Athelstan is a good man. He served my father well.' She concentrated on the tapestry and saw a few of her crooked stitches. Gives it character, Athelstan had laughed when she complained about it not being perfect. 'Will he live?'

'He was been injured in the shoulder and left leg, but Mary is convinced he will live now that he can be nursed properly. You know what she is like.' Hilda gave a crooked smile. 'And Godwin knows he will. He is pleased his father has returned and the bad man hasn't.'

'You will have to take me to him.' Edith reached for her shawl. A blinding pain shot through her head and she found it difficult to think straight. She stumbled back to the side of the bed.

The happy bubbly feeling from earlier vanished as if it had never been. She had a responsibility towards her people which transcended everything.

It gave her reasons for breathing. She wished she could see a way where it was going to end happily for Athelstan and his family and her. She doubted if Brand would ever be able to forgive her once he found out what she had done. She took a deep breath and squared her shoulders. No one ever said that being responsible was easy. She owed a debt to Athelstan.

'When do you want to go?'

'Now, without delay.' Edith covered her eyes and tried to think logically. 'The sooner Athelstan is made aware of the situation and danger he has placed everyone in, the better.'

'We won't be back for supper and it is the final of the singing competition. You are the judge. And Brand Bjornson has promised to sing as well after you have crowned the victor. Starkad said that he has the most marvellous voice.'

Edith sank back on the bench. Hilda was right. If she went too quickly, Athelstan's hiding place would be discovered. The best thing she could do tonight was not even to think about him. She had to put Athelstan in a little box and forget. Luckily she had experience with that sort of play-acting. It depressed her that until a few heartbeats ago she'd planned to share everything with Brand, but now there would be secrets between them. Edith bit her lip. 'You are right. And you are willing to help or shall I go on my own?'

'I know I am.' Hilda stood up and smoothed her skirts. 'I expect you to do the best thing for everyone, you always do. I remain ashamed of my part before the Norsemen arrived. You were trying to protect me all the time, even when I was consumed with jealousy and showing off. Other women would have turned me out. This time you will have my help. You are far from alone.'

'Wait, we will have to make a plan. It is best to gather provisions for Athelstan and make sure that we are not noticed. We will do this tomorrow while Brand puts his men through their paces. I take it he is safe right now.'

'Do you know what you are doing, Edith?' Hilda asked, looking at her suspiciously. 'Have you thought this through? You could put everyone in jeopardy if he stays. You should order him to go and save everyone else. There is no future for him here. The only thing that will happen is he'll bring misery down on everyone.'

'He has been a loyal servant. He returned. I owe

it to him and to his family to help. Should he be discovered, I will take full responsibility. No one else will be harmed.' She hugged her arms about her waist. A great hollow opened inside her. Brand would not understand. She knew that. She had to keep the news from him and hope that some solution came to her.

'And what if he is discovered? Do you think they will listen to you? What about Mary, Godwin and the little one? They are bound to be implicated. Have you thought of that? It is worse than I thought.'

'What would you have me do? Turn my back and pretend? Refuse to see him? He spilled his blood because of this place and my family. You may keep out if you think the risk is too great.'

'I never said that!' Hilda protested.

'Are you going to tell anyone?'

Hilda reddened. 'I know how to keep secrets. Mary did come to me when she failed to find you. She trusts me, even if you don't. Athelstan might not mean anything to me, but she helped to sew my latest dress. I've no wish for anything to happen to her.'

Edith smiled at her. It felt good to have a friend.

'We'll need food from the kitchen and medicine.

Tomorrow morning when the Norsemen are at practice would be ideal. I can slip away without any awkward questions being asked.'

'We both go.' At Edith's look, Hilda shrugged. 'I want to know if any more will arrive. And you need me. I can help with other things.'

Edith began to pace. She hated waiting, but it was the best way to keep him safe. If Athelstan was well enough, she could explain the situation and ask him to move on, with his family. She would raid the last of the silver and give him enough to live on. His skills would be in great demand down in Wessex. Her parents would approve. Brand would not have to know until much later...if ever.

The pain in her head eased slightly. 'How can you help, Hilda?'

'I can get the bread from the kitchen. The kitchen boy is sweet on me.' Hilda fluffed her hair a bit.

'The medicine is stored in a trunk.' Edith paused. It was enough that Hilda was willing to get the bread.

'I will get it. We're cousins. Kinswomen. No more nonsense about doing it alone.'

Edith reached out her hand and squeezed Hilda's. 'Thank you.'

'I believe you've a love bite on the base of your neck.'

Edith hurriedly drew her shawl tighter about her neck. How many other people had seen it and refrained from saying anything? 'None of your business.'

'You have lain with him.'

'What if I have?' Edith squared her shoulders. 'I did agree to be his concubine. There is nothing to be ashamed about. I have kept my vow.'

'It will make things easier. Starkad tells me that Brand has been in the fiercest of tempers, making them work at swordplay for no good purpose.' Hilda's eyes danced. 'And you don't, you know.'

'I don't what?'

'Have a love bite. I merely wanted to see your reaction. It told me all I wanted to know. I am happy for you, cousin. Truly I am. Your face has a certain glow about it. He is good for you. He is unmarried. There is every reason to think he might marry you.'

'Hilda! One thing at a time. I'm not sure I want to marry again.'

'But he would be a good choice and then people

will have to be silent about you, rather than call-ing you names.'

'Who?'

Hilda shrugged. 'Father Wilfrid has been speak-ing about the folly and weak will of women.'

'He enjoys causing problems.'

'It is far better to have Brand Bjornson in a good mood with Athelstan showing up. We are going to need all the help we can get.'

Edith bit her lip. He might be in a good mood now, but what was his reaction going to be when he learnt that she had gone against his direct or-ders?

'You appear distracted, Edith,' Brand com-mented, covering her hand with his as Starkad's song finished.

Edith jumped at the gentle touch and forced her mind back to the present, rather than the uncer-tain future. 'Merely making a memory.'

'A memory?' He raised her hand to his lips. The ease and naturalness of the gesture astonished Edith. It was as if they had sat at the high table together for a lifetime.

A great longing swept over her. She wanted this happiness to continue, but she had a responsibility towards Athelstan and any other former rebel who might appear. Surely it wasn't wrong to enjoy one night of happiness? There would be time enough to confess to Brand in the morning.

'I want to remember every aspect of today so I can recall it when I am old and grey,' she explained.

'As long as you are enjoying yourself. I don't envy you the task of choosing the winner.'

'If I must choose, I choose Starkad. Sometimes you just know in your heart one song is the winner.'

Brand made the announcement and the entire hall erupted in applause. Starkad turned a bright red and claimed the purse of silver.

She tilted her head to one side. 'I understand from Hilda that you can sing. Or was Starkad merely being kind?'

'I can.'

'Then why didn't you enter?'

'Because it wouldn't be fair.' He gestured to Starkad who rapidly brought a lyre. 'I can sing now you have made your choice.'

He began to sing and his rich baritone filled the hall. It was a song of longing and loyalty. Edith wondered that she had ever considered him a barbarian. There was so much more to him than simply someone who made war on others. When his voice faded, the entire hall was silent.

'Well?' he asked. 'Surely it was not so dreadful.'

'It was one of the most beautiful songs I have ever heard,' Edith confessed. 'I should like to hear songs of the north in this hall. More than that I should like to learn the song.'

'My mother taught me the song. She used to sing it to my father.'

'Your mother must have been special.'

He put his hand on her shoulder. 'You remind me of her. I made a mistake the first day. I thought you were like my father's wife, but you are not. You have an honesty about you.'

'I hope I do.'

Brand frowned as he listened to another litany of excuses about why various buildings were not being restored or were unsuitable for the purpose they were intended. His thoughts kept returning to Edith and yesterday afternoon.

She had been a bit subdued at supper, but later, he'd demonstrated the full use a bed could be put to and she had responded with a fevered passion. He'd been reluctant to leave her warmth this morning and had nearly called off practice. Several of the men made pointed comments when he arrived late, but he ignored them. To his astonishment, the last several days had shown improvement and the swordplay this morning had been short, particularly as his thoughts kept returning to Edith and the curve of her mouth.

He struggled to remember the last time a woman had dominated his mind in this fashion. He'd abandoned the practice and set his men to surveying the outlying buildings, a task which should have given him time with Edith but instead brought its own problems.

'Finally,' Starkad said with a great note of excitement in his voice, 'we discovered a bath house. There is no need to build one. It is already here!'

'A bath house? I thought their priest forbade such things. He certainly had been very vocal on the subject.'

'It looks like one. It has been used for storing grain, but I would have sworn I was back in Constantinople,' Starkad said. 'It can be easily made ready. The men are eager to start. It will save time.'

'That is one problem solved.' Brand smiled. He looked forward to initiating Edith into the delights of bathing. A few weeks or months of enjoying her was permissible, even if she'd seemed a bit distracted and distant yesterday evening. Later, the passion had overwhelmed them both, but in the hall, she had seemed on edge as if she waited for something to happen.

A few weeks to conquer and learn her secrets, then he'd return to the life he'd planned so many years ago. There was still time to send for Sigfrieda or some other woman who'd provide the sort of sons he'd dreamt of and who would be the sort of wife that Halfdan approved of. He couldn't risk Halfdan's ire, not after he'd been shown such favour. He wished he knew the precise reason why Halfdan had failed to order a marriage between Edith and himself.

'I thought you'd want to know.' Starkad stretched. 'By Loki's beard, it will be good to have a proper bath rather than freezing my arse in the lake.'

'Let me know when you are finished. I expect it to be ready by nightfall.'

'We all hope for that.' Starkad dug into his pouch. 'I nearly forgot. A rune arrived.'

'Why wasn't I informed? Immediately?'

Starkad shrugged. 'The messenger couldn't find you. He is seeing to his horse.'

'You should have given it to me at once. When he is ready, I wish to see the messenger and find out how things fare in Jorvik.'

'You insist on things being done in a proper order. Far be it for me to do otherwise.'

Brand rolled his eyes. 'The rune?'

He rapidly glanced at it. It told him nothing that he wasn't already aware of. Not all of the rebels were dead and some might try to return here. It was one of the reasons why he trained his men so hard. No one would take this land from him. He would fight to keep it. The rebels had given no quarter. They deserved none.

After speaking briefly with Halfdan's messenger and learning Halfdan remained as adamant as ever about punishing the rebels, Brand spied Edith walking in close consultation with her cousin. His senses went instantly on alert. If anything she looked more desirable now than she had when they'd parted this morning. He wondered that he had ever allowed her out of bed.

He frowned, trying to puzzle out if he should tell her about Halfdan's order about providing no shelter to any rebel warrior. There was no need. He had made his views clear on the first morning—he would tolerate no challenge to his rule and anyone who aided or assisted the former rebels for whatever reason would be punished.

'Edith, a moment of your time.'

Edith froze. How could he know? All she'd done was to collect the basket of food from the kitchen.

Hilda gave her a wild glance. She squeezed Hilda's hand. 'It will be well.'

'Will you tell him?'

'When he needs to know…' She handed the basket to Hilda. 'Take it to Mary now. Be quick about it.'

Hilda snatched the basket from her and hurried off.

'Is there some problem with your cousin?'

'She and I planned to see Godwin's mother. She wanted to make sure the cakes remained hot.' Edith was amazed at how steady her voice sounded. She wasn't lying. She simply wasn't telling him the whole truth. Early this morning, lying in his arms, she had decided to see Athelstan first before confessing the truth to Brand.

Until she had actually seen Athelstan, she only had Hilda's word. And there was always the possibility that he would wish to give himself up. She wanted a chance to speak with him and find out his story. She owed it to him for his long service to her family and to Godwin for saving her when he spoke out after that trap Hrearek had set. She wouldn't be the one to betray him.

Edith gave a faint shudder. The risk she was taking was dreadful but she owed it to Athelstan. She had to keep it a secret until she knew precisely what Athelstan wanted and why he was here.

'I'm pleased you reminded me about Godwin. I'd nearly forgotten the lad in light of other things.' Brand's eyes grew warm, reminding Edith why she had had little sleep the night before. 'I need to speak with his mother.'

'Why?' Edith schooled her features, trying to ignore the sharp prickle of fear. 'What has Godwin done now?'

'I want to have him train to be a warrior. He could have a great future in my service and, if he is good enough, I will send him to Halfdan in due course.'

Edith choked. Unexpected and generous. The offer was precisely what Godwin needed. He could go far. But it was completely at the wrong time. 'You want to speak with her now?'

'The sooner, the better. The boy needs direction. He reminds me of myself at that age. We can go together.'

Edith twisted her belt about her fingers. 'Now would not be a good time. Trust me.'

His brow creased. 'But you were going to see her.'

'There is…that is, someone is not well. It would upset Godwin's mother as she would be unable to give the sort of welcome her lord requires.' Edith released a breath. Not exactly a lie. Hilda had said that Athelstan was seriously injured. 'But I'll send word with Hilda that Mary should come and see you once she is free from her nursing duties.'

He nodded with a perplexed frown. 'And you are certain that everything is all right?'

'It will be. I know the honour you do Godwin.'

Edith hurried over to Hilda and rapidly explained. Hilda's eyes went wide, but she agreed to take the message to Mary. Edith's shoulders relaxed slightly. She'd bought a little time. Somehow, the solution would come to her—one which would enable Athelstan to live and allow her to retain this precious bit of happiness. Was it so wrong of her to put herself first for once? As Hilda had pointed out yesterday, it was important for everyone that Brand be contented and in a good temper.

'It is done.' She put her hand on Brand's arm.

Brand tucked her arm in his and started to lead her towards the old storage hut, intending to show her the bath house his men had unearthed. 'Your cousin seemed surprised at the request. Does she think that I wouldn't want someone as able as Godwin in my retinue? He is the sort of boy who will go far. And I intend to give him that chance.'

'Hilda thinks it is a kind thing.' Edith concentrated on keeping her voice steady. 'Godwin is a great favourite, but his mother may want him with her for a while longer. She's barely recovered from losing her husband.'

'His mother will do him no favours by keeping him as a little boy. He will quickly become a man, particularly now that his father is dead.'

A faint wistful note entered his voice. He had been the same sort of boy. The knowledge thudded through her. A kindred spirit. Edith knew she had to know more. Every time she'd asked before, he had expertly turned the conversation away from his childhood. Maybe she could find a clue this time to help Athelstan and Godwin.

'This concerns Godwin rather than my misbegotten past.'

Edith rolled her eyes. 'You came from somewhere. You didn't spring full grown from the earth, ready to slay Northumbrians. I want to know about it.'

His lips turned upwards. 'There is no need to discuss it. I live in the present.'

'You see my past all around me, but you don't want to speak of your childhood. Childhood shapes you.' Edith brushed her lips against his cheek. 'Indulge me. I'm curious.'

'Why the sudden interest?'

Edith pressed her lips together. She could hardly confess to seeking an answer for her problem.

Edith took a deep breath. 'I want to know if the rumour is true. Did your mother try to have you hung?'

'My father was a jaarl, one of the old Viken king's most trusted advisers.'

'Then why aren't you there?'

'Because my mother was his concubine.' He fingered the scar on his neck. 'My father's wife had other plans about who should inherit my father's wealth. She did not want to follow our custom of providing for all children.'

She drew in her breath swiftly. 'She did this to you? Not your mother, but your father's wife? She caused you to be hanged!'

'And charged no one to help me on pain of death.' His mouth twisted. 'I had made the mistake of loving the woman intended for my half-brother as well as daring to beat him in swordplay. She claimed I had stolen the sword.'

'But someone took the risk?'

'One of my father's servant's. I think he was in love with my mother. He arranged for the fake hanging. There was barely life in me when I was cut down. He spirited me away and it was a long time before I returned to Norway.'

'Where is he now?'

'Dead. His son Sven was my comrade-in-arms. We rose together. He was a far better man than I could ever hope to be and my father dismissed him as a thrall.'

'How old were you?'

'Fourteen. I sailed for Byzantium and made my name there. I suspect one of the reasons I was taken on initially was because I sported the scar.' He gave a half-smile. 'Her intention went awry.'

Edith pressed her hands together. His story gave her hope. He knew what it was like to be an outcast. She might be able to use that to save Athelstan if it came down to it. 'Why did you leave Byzantium?'

'There was nothing there for me.' A muscle jumped in his cheek. 'I trusted the wrong woman and was dismissed. Halfdan and his brothers conceived of the plan to invade England and it gave me a purpose. Halfdan has proved true to his word—he promised me land so that I could marry the woman of my dreams.'

'Is that as rare in Norsemen politics as it is in Northumbrian?' Edith asked lightly as a pain shot through her. There was someone he was in love with.

'Yes. I value a man who keeps his word. Once my path is chosen I do not deviate.'

'Even if a better way appears?'

He shook his head. 'There has never been a need. I find it important to keep my main goal in sight at all times.'

'And what is that?'

He gestured about him. 'To have my own patch of earth where I can sow and farm without fear. Here I will put down my roots. The wanderer has found a place to lay his head.'

'And is that all?'

He sighed. 'Where is this conversation leading, Edith? If you must know, I intend eventually to send to Norway for a bride. I told Halfdan I would do so once I had land when I entered his service.'

Her stomach churned. 'Then you have an intended?'

'In a manner of speaking. There is a woman with whom I had an understanding. Her father gave me leave to ask if I ever became a jaarl. I suspect he never believed it would happen, but everyone knew my intention.'

Everyone but her. The small fantasy that he might come to love her and want to marry her died. She hadn't even realised that she had had that dream until it was gone. She raised her chin and refused to show how much his words hurt her. 'And when were you planning on telling me?'

'Why should I? It has nothing to do with us.'

Edith clenched her hands together so tightly that her knuckles went white. 'You should have said something. It would have made a difference.'

'Why?' He seemed genuinely astonished.

'Because I could never do to another woman what was done to me.' Edith fought against the urge to weep. She never cried. 'That's why.'

'I intend to look after you. I never shirk my responsibilities.' He frowned. 'I know what it is like to be the son of a concubine.'

Each word tore into her soul. She had been living in some sort of dream. She had thought after the passionate night that he was bound to ask her to marry him. It was the most sensible solution. Now she discovered that she was someone of no consequence to him, a warm body in the night. His heart already belonged to someone else. It shouldn't bother her but it did. Once in her life, she wanted to be loved.

That she even had feelings for him was such a new and raw thing to her. It wasn't love, she told herself. Love was supposed to be comfortable like what her parents had with each other. This was completely unsettling.

'But you still intend to send for her despite what has passed between us? You intend to treat me like your father treated your mother. Why? To humble me?'

His eyes flashed fire. 'Do not equate the two.'

'I see.' Edith gathered as much dignity about her as she could. She wanted to sink to the ground in despair, but that would only be fuelling his masculine pride.

'You were not living with some false hope that I would marry you?'

She pressed her lips together, counted to ten and regained control over her temper. She'd been so foolish. 'I hardly know how to answer that.'

'I was clear before we began, Edith. You are my concubine for a year. After we are done, I will give you and your baggage train safe passage to wherever you want to go. I gave in to your sensibilities and wooed you.'

'And men don't marry such women?' The words escaped from her lips before she had a chance to think.

'You are being impossible, Edith. First you question me closely about what I want from life and then you react badly when I tell you. If you don't want to know the answer, refrain from asking the question. You should be pleased that I was honest.'

That sort of honesty she had little need of. She'd been living in a fool's paradise.

'And you are seeking to dismiss me, like you dismiss a child? What precisely did you have planned?'

'I hadn't thought that far ahead. I like to live each day at a time.'

'But you were going to make the decision soon.'

'You are being unreasonable.' He reached for her. 'It is the shock.'

Edith twisted out of his embrace. A kiss now would make matters worse. She had her pride. 'Unreasonable? You treated me like a brainless child.'

'A jaarl has to marry, Edith,' he said slowly, his accent becoming thicker with each word. 'That is beyond question. It has to be someone who will enhance his standing. Halfdan must approve the marriage. He wants his earls to marry well. You should hear him on the subject. For Halfdan, the ideal wife is from Norway.'

With each damning word, she felt smaller and smaller. Of course she no longer had standing or position—the failed rebellion had seen to that. There was no reason for him to marry her. He desired her, but didn't want to marry her. He didn't even want her to stay after the year was done.

She hadn't even realised that she had hoped for something like a loving marriage. She had been so naive in building dreams. Somehow, she thought they'd go on this like this for ever when all along he'd been planning this to be a short-term thing. She felt used and betrayed. She had thought what they shared was special and unique and that he felt it in the same manner that she had.

'Thank you for making your position clear,' she choked out around the increasing lump in her throat.

'I didn't want you to harbour any false hope.'

'That is my concern.' She kept her head up and her face a careful mask. Silently she was pleased that she'd had so many years of dealing with Egbert and knew how to conceal her emotions. Right now, she wanted to scream and shout at him that he was being unfair. He had demeaned her and what they shared.

'And you need not worry. I would hardly install a wife here while you are in residence.'

Edith drew in her breath sharply and counted to ten before she trusted her voice. Install a wife? He made it sound like he was offering her a huge favour. She'd hope that as a courtesy to this unknown woman, she'd be gone. 'That is supposed to keep me sweet? You will make sure we have ended before you marry.'

'It is the best I can offer. I will see you have nothing to fear for the future either.'

She winced as if he had slapped her.

Brand frowned. What did she want? His head

on a silver platter? He had behaved honourably. He could have allowed her to have illusions, but it was better to have the truth. It was hardly his fault that some day he would have to marry and produce an heir. He would never humiliate her in the way his mother had been humiliated. 'You will do as I say, Edith.'

'We have an agreement, Brand, and I will honour it. I expect to be released when my year is up.' Each word was clearly enunciated.

'So where will you go?' he asked through clenched teeth. 'Where will you find refuge? Who will take you? I will see you safe and settled. You can have a small cottage with a little land. I intend to be generous, Edith.'

'That is my concern!' Edith glared back at him, her hands balled into fists. 'When I go, I'll no longer be your problem or in need of your *generosity*. Perhaps I will go to Wessex. I have some distant relations there. Or maybe to a nunnery on the coast where my second cousin twice removed is the abbess. But I won't stay here, hanging around like a bad smell.'

Brand raised an eyebrow. 'Two places at once?'

'I haven't decided.' Edith's cheeks flushed. 'It depends on many things. When the time is right,

I will know where I will go. You never said that I had to decide immediately. You are seeking to change the terms. That is not allowed, Brand.'

'I should have some input,' he said with icy politeness. 'There might be other considerations— a child.'

'You should have nothing! The trouble with you is that you want everything and give nothing in return.'

With great difficulty, Brand swallowed his inclination to shout. If he gave vent to his anger, Edith would have won. He concentrated on taking slow even breaths. Edith was impossible. When she had calmed down, she'd see that he had offered her the truth, rather than the pap of a lie. She should see that he respected her enough to give her honesty rather than sweet meaningless nothings.

He was in no hurry to marry and he'd never have a situation like his father had. But he'd not offer false hope. A year was a long time. Brand refused to think about how empty his life would be without her and how much he looked forward to waking up with her by his side or sparring with her with words. The solution would come to him. Edith would listen to reason.

'When the time comes, I will lead the party that

provides you with safe passage,' he said when he trusted himself to speak reasonably. 'You will have to tell me some time.'

'When that day comes, I will inform you of my destination, but it will be far from here.' She turned on her heel and started to stride away.

'I didn't give you permission to go.'

'Do I have to ask?' She stopped and made a mocking curtsy. 'Very well, may I go, your lordship?'

'You are impossible. Go. Get out of my sight. I don't care where you go. Just go!'

Chapter Ten

Edith stood silently in Brand's chamber, listening to the sound of heavy drinking filter in from the hall. Tonight, she'd pleaded a headache and had retired to bed. The message was curt and she thought designed to provoke a reaction, particularly as one of the serving women breathlessly confided that the king's messenger had arrived.

Brand had not bothered to check on her, but instead sent word through one of the serving women that this was acceptable. He understood that she was not feeling her best.

Acceptable? Understood? Who was he to dictate if what she did was acceptable or not? Even now, her blood fizzed at the thought. She wanted to storm down and shout at him. She refused to be dictated to. She might have agreed to stay as his concubine because she'd no choice, but that did not mean she was his slave!

When she'd returned earlier that evening, Hilda had reported in a hurried whisper that Athelstan had refused to see her, but declared his intention through Mary of staying. This was his home, where his forefathers were buried. He would remain as long as he had breath in his body.

He had also heard of her liaison with Brand and did not approve. Hilda reported in breathless tones that everyone was speaking of how she'd become the Norseman's whore. The entire village.

Edith stared over at the bed. One of the reasons she had stayed, rather than protecting her modesty through retirement to a convent, was to ensure the safety of her people. She'd known some would point their fingers and judge, but she hadn't expected it to hurt so much.

She had to do something to help Athelstan and his family, something solid, rather than paying lip service to the ideal.

'A man is judged by the quality of his actions, rather than the words he mutters,' Edith whispered. 'I've always proclaimed it and now it is time to prove it.'

She made her way onto the stone wall at the

back of the room and counted in the darkness seven stones along. Her fingers curled about the edges of the stones and she pulled. The stone refused to yield. She redoubled her efforts and there was a great scraping noise.

Instantly Edith froze. Listened. The noise from the hall grew louder. The strains of the saga of Ivar the Scarred echoed in the room. She had first heard the saga two nights ago and thought it fantastical then. It seemed even more so now. Sweat poured down her back.

She spat on her hands and tried again. The stone suddenly gave way and she fell back onto her bottom with a deafening thump.

She sat on the ground, listening. The hall had gone deadly silent. Her heartbeat resounded in her ears. When she thought all was lost she heard a great roar of laughter and the music of the harp started again. Safe.

Placing the stone to one side, she reached back into the cavity. Rather than the quantity of silver and jewels she'd expected, a single silver cup remained. One solitary cup, pushed to the back and lying on its side. She thrust her hand in the space again and felt around more, desperately searching.

Her mother's jewels, including the brooch of

the hare with sapphire eyes that she'd loved seeing her mother wear, had to be there. She'd put
everything there the afternoon after Egbert departed. Nothing remained except the cup.

Edith tapped her finger against her mouth and
tried to keep the great hollow from opening inside
her. That hoard was supposed to see her through
if anything dire happened.

Egbert would have taken the entire lot if he had
discovered the hiding place. Edith made a face. He
couldn't be the one. She'd waited until he was gone
before she retrieved everything and placed it here.

There was only one conclusion—Brand had discovered it, but had left her a message so she'd
know. Asking him about it would be impossible
as then she'd have to explain why she had been
in the hiding place. She had to assume that he'd
left the cup, in case she wanted to flee.

She gave a small laugh as she weighed the cup
in her hand. 'I don't quit, Brand. I never have and
I don't intend to now. This cup will have another
use.'

'Why did you return, Athelstan?' Edith asked the
man who lay on the rough bed the next morning.

When first light came she had slipped out of

her lonely bed, dressed and made her way to Athelstan's cottage. Mary had let her in and shown her to the back room where the injured man hid, more of a cow byre than the resting place for a warrior of his repute.

Each step of the way as the cup hit her hip, her resolve to do right by Athelstan had hardened. The only thing she could do was to see Athelstan and have him leave. Every moment he stayed on these lands put everyone in danger.

The bearded man hauled himself to standing. He swayed slightly and despite his wife's entreating look stood stubbornly at attention. 'My lady, it is an unexpected visit.'

'My cousin implied you would refuse to see me. I wanted to know the truth.'

'Why would Athelstan ever refuse you, my lady, when you come in person?' Mary said pointedly, giving her husband a stern look. 'My husband knows the good you have done.

Edith concentrated on the man who had served her family so well. He shifted from foot to foot and refused to meet her eye.

'Aye,' he said. 'I would never refuse to see my Lady Edith when she troubles to call on me in person.'

'Has Mary explained about the danger?' Edith asked, ignoring the strong undercurrent of disapproval. 'There is no place for you here, Athelstan. You have a price on your head, but your family can still have a life. Your family has served mine for generations and I'm not about to abandon you.'

'I know the Norsemen are here and you have been dishonoured.' Athelstan waved an impatient hand. 'The entire countryside is talking about it. You had no choice. I understand that, my lady, but it was not what your father or mother would have wished for you.'

'I suppose I can thank Father Wilfrid for that piece of gossip-mongering.' Edith gave a wry smile. She refused to apologise for what she'd done. 'He seemed to be particularly shocked with the arrangement, but then what is new with him being shocked at my behaviour? You must know that I have the best interests of everyone at heart.'

'I know you did what you had to, my lady. There was no one left to defend this place or you.' He hung his head. 'I deeply regret this. I mean to put it right. You will always have a champion in me.'

Edith clenched her fist. She couldn't have Athelstan suddenly deciding to put things right. She had to convince him to go. 'We don't have time for regrets. The new lord wants to foster Godwin. It is a huge chance for your son. We live in a new world with new masters.'

Mary gasped behind her. 'He wants to take an interest in Godwin? That is wonderful!'

'Hush, woman!' Athelstan frowned. 'If you had your way, he'd be fostered with the devil himself.'

'Brand Bjornson is hardly the devil, husband.'

'It is a great opportunity, but Brand must not learn Athelstan is here. You will need to go to see him, Mary, rather than waiting for him to arrive here. When Athelstan is well enough, he must go to Wessex. There he can make a new life.' Edith brought the silver cup out from under her cloak. 'This should give you the start you need, Athelstan. It belonged to my grandfather. He would… he would want you to have it.'

Mary gave a slight nod. 'I understand, my lady, what you are trying to do, but you should keep it in case you need it. It wouldn't be right.'

'Wife,' Athelstan rumbled, 'I remain the head of this house. I should have a say. And I say no. It is not going to happen. You must keep that cup, Lady Edith, and use it when you need it. Some day, you may have the greater need.'

'It is a good opportunity, Athelstan.' Edith held

out the cup and willed Athelstan to understand what was being offered. He might not have a future here, but his family would be looked after always. And she could look after herself, whatever came. She refused to think about a time when she might need silver. 'Why do you want to throw it away? It is a chance to rebuild your life. You know there is a price on your head.'

He took the cup and placed it down on the bed. Edith heaved a little sigh of relief. All would be well. She, with Mary's help, would get him to start a new life elsewhere.

'Do you believe this Brand Bjornson an honourable man?' he asked, turning towards her with a fierce expression.

Edith started. She had not really considered it before, but she thought about all the small incidents of kindnesses as well as how he'd behaved over the straw man. A lesser man would have found a reason to protect his friend. 'He is true to his code.'

'Can't you see, husband? Her ladyship blooms. Brand Bjornson brought roses to her cheeks. If her ladyship is happy, that is enough for me. He is repairing various buildings and has provided corn planting. He is a better lord than the last one.'

'That is because you are a woman and know naught.'

Edith crossed her arms, counted to ten and tried to keep her temper. Athelstan had no right to speak to his wife that way. Neither did he have a right to pass judgement on her, but losing her temper and storming out would hardly solve her immediate problem of how to get rid of him without endangering everyone else.

'Athelstan,' she began, making a supreme effort to keep her voice even and steady. She made sure it contained her most commanding tone. 'I have very little time. What is between Brand and me is private, but it benefits everyone on these lands. You must trust my judgement on this. You have not been here. You have not seen the improvements he has made. This estate must have an overlord and he should do right by it.'

'Any man can repair a building or plant corn.' Athelstan scowled. 'I want to know the measure of him. He must prove himself worthy. Nothing I have seen or heard of him makes me think he has one ounce of honour in his body.'

'In what manner should he prove himself?' Edith asked. 'What do you want him to do?'

'He should do the decent thing and marry you,'

Mary burst out. 'Then I will say to everyone what an honourable man he is! And my husband will as well.'

'How many times do I have to tell you to be silent, wife?'

'Mary is entitled to her opinion.' Edith shook her head and started for the door. 'Brand Bjornson's decision to marry will be based on his king's wishes, not his own. I will have no more said.'

Athelstan raised his hands in supplication. 'I deserve my say, your ladyship. Simply because you dislike the words is no call for them to remain unsaid.'

Edith halted. She was behaving worse than Hilda. Unlike Hilda, she didn't have the luxury of giving in to impulsive behaviour. How often had her parents scolded her for doing that? 'Very well, speak your piece.'

'Your father was well respected. Unlike the man who now calls himself our jaarl, he never brought dishonour to the name of lord in these parts. Brand Bjornson's name is used to terrify children. Nurses whisper that he will come to get them. Have you ever asked him why he has that scar? It is a hanging scar.'

'You are overly harsh.' Edith tapped her fingers

together. She'd forgotten that Athelstan considered himself her protector. Neither did it give her the right to break Brand's confidences. 'Brand Bjornson has not done anything dishonourable. Give me one example, one thing other than his liaison with me that makes him unworthy in your eyes. Rumours and tales told around a campfire only show that he was a warrior. Warriors have all manner of scars.'

Athelstan raised an eyebrow. 'Do you know how your husband died? He was foully murdered under a parlay by the man who sits in the hall, stuffing his face on honest food. I know that for a fact. I was there. I saw your husband's body and the bodies of his guard. Dismembered. Even now they haunt my dreams. I stood there, saying a prayer when I heard voices, Norsemen. I hid myself, waiting for them to go, but I overheard one of them, the largest one, bragging how he'd caused the truce to be broken.'

'And you are sure that this was Brand Bjornson?'

'How could it be any other? He carried a bloody axe.' He clenched his fist. 'I'd run him through if I had the chance.'

Edith put her hand over her mouth. Brand had

killed Egbert in cold blood, rather than in battle? It seemed out of character for him to do anything like that.

Her stomach churned. However, it was not out of character for Egbert to break a truce. She wished Brand had told her the full circumstances of the final battle, but it made sense now why he'd been given this particular earldom.

'Are you sure of your facts?' she asked when she could control her voice.

'Aye, I'm sure, my lady.' Athelstan made an ironic bow. 'I was there or near enough. Six of them went out on a winter's morning and none of them returned. The Norsemen fell on us like ravenous wolves afterwards. We had been sitting about the fire, eating our porridge, waiting for Lord Egbert to return. We were all unprepared for the attack. I took a blow to my shoulder and then to my head. I thought I was a goner for sure and feigned death. I must have passed out, but came around later. Everyone had departed, save the corpses and the crows.'

'And how do you know how my husband was killed, if you were not with him?'

'I saw the bodies afterwards. Hacked to pieces, they were. I heard it whispered that the great

Brand Bjornson was there. Then he gets these lands and I knew I had to come back and do something. Such a man could not be allowed to hold sway of these lands.'

'I had no idea,' Edith confessed. Of all the important things they had shared, Brand had not bothered to share with her something so vitally important such as the fact that he had personally killed her husband. Or had at least been there when Egbert died.

'I thought you ought to know.' Athelstan hung his head. 'It was a terrible business. They had discarded the bodies like worthless criminals. I made sure the bodies were buried.'

'That was good of you.'

Athelstan reached for the cup and thrust it back into Edith's hand. 'You can understand why I can't take this either. You will need it more than I. I have my sword arm and you—'

'You have a family,' Edith interrupted.

'They are my concern. Begging your ladyship's pardon, but what do you have? How well do you know your lover if he didn't even tell you the manner of your husband's death?'

Edith swallowed hard and desperately tried to figure out an answer which would satisfy Athelstan. All the while her brain kept hammering the words—what else hadn't Brand shared? Could she truly trust him to be the man she hoped he was?

After they had made love the first time, when he held her after she confessed about losing her baby, she'd felt so connected to him, but now she knew that she had shared things, yet he had shared very little about the battle. He'd kept the manner of her husband's death from her. He'd even gone so far as to say that he wished he'd killed him. Why say that? Someone was not telling the full truth and she knew she had to trust her instinct. Only lately, it had not kept her safe.

'Thank you for telling me, Athelstan,' she said quietly, tightening her grip on the cup. 'I will keep your words on advisement.'

'What are you going to do, my lady?' Mary said, bringing her back the present. 'Are you going to go back to him, knowing what he is like?'

'My reasons for becoming his concubine remain the same. I can hardly depart simply because something went wrong with a parlay. Athelstan, for all his talk about being there, wasn't. He saw the aftermath, not what truly happened. I do know my late husband and what he could be like.'

'You are being a fool.' Athelstan made a grimace. 'But then you are a woman. Your grand-mother was the same—always wanting to believe the best of the people.'

Mary wrung her hands. 'I can't allow our son to be fostered by a monster, but neither can I refuse my current lord's request without causing friction. If he is as bad as you say, husband, it would be very wrong to anger him.'

'This changes nothing—the fact remains that Athelstan cannot stay here. The risk is far too great. He puts everyone in danger.' Edith concentrated on the wall behind Athelstan, rather than meeting Mary's eyes. Brand was no monster. Egbert had been. It bothered her that Athelstan was so insistent, but she refused to argue with him. Now was the time for solving problems, rather than debating someone's merits or lack of them. 'You have said your piece, Athelstan, and I allowed it for the sake of our long friendship. Now, you allow me to protect you and your family. You will take this cup and go from here. You may take all your family with you, if that is what you prefer, but I remain here. I've given my word. My word is worth something.'

Athelstan grunted. 'Not the cup.'

'And what will become of us? Are we to become beggars?' Mary persisted.

'You may go with him if you like, but the road will be treacherous. You have a baby daughter. Go slowly and travel at night.' Edith pointed towards the door. 'But it is far too dangerous for Athelstan to remain here. I'm sorry, Athelstan. You can't put everyone at risk to pursue some private vendetta. I refuse to allow that. I have more than just your family to think about.'

Brand's head ached like Thor personally had taken his hammer and driven it straight into his skull. His mouth tasted of ash and sour ale. A faint groan escaped his throat as he lay face down on the cold stone floor of the stable. He rolled onto his back, willed the world to stop spinning and gazed directly up at Edith's horse. He could not remember the last time he'd voluntarily done something like this. Possibly in Byzantium when he'd learnt his desire for a woman had nearly cost his emperor his life.

He had drunk far more than was good for him, but he'd wanted to blot out Edith's face. She was an incredibly stubborn person. He had no intention of marrying anyone. He could not marry without Halfdan's leave, but it would have to be someone suitable. The more he thought about it, the worse he felt. He refused to become like his father, marrying for dynastic reasons and betraying the woman he had feelings for.

Halfdan's messenger had provided the excuse he needed to drink his disgust away at the way he'd treated Edith. It made it easier somehow that Edith had refused to come down. He had toyed with physically carrying her into the hall, but decided that lacked dignity. He'd ignore her instead. Only now, he had a thick head to deal with.

His stomach roiled. He'd forgotten the morning after the night before. He shook his head. Over two decades a warrior and still capable of such folly.

He slowly stood, swayed and focused on the horse's manger until there was only one. He brushed the straw from his trousers. He needed his bed, preferably with Edith in it, rather than punishing himself on the practice yard.

He strode across the yard, trying not to blink in the spring sunshine. When he reached his bedchamber, the room was empty and the bed tidily made.

His eyes immediately flew to the stone wall.

The loose stone he'd uncovered on the second night had been slightly moved. The scrap of cloth he'd wedged in lay unnoticed on the floor.

Cold sweat broke out on his brow.

Headache forgotten, he crossed the room in three steps and pulled it out. The solitary cup it had contained was gone. He reached back in the cavity. Nothing else.

He placed his hands on the stone. It made no sense. She had given her word to stay. It bothered him that he'd have been prepared to stake his life on her keeping her word. He slammed his fists into the stone. 'You gave your word. Not you as well. I would have protected you!'

The empty room echoed the words back to him, mocking him. He'd been prepared to forget the hard-learnt lessons about trusting women with her.

He turned on his heel and went out of the room. Suddenly the entire hall and surrounds seemed empty of its beating heart. Edith wasn't there. He found himself listening for the slightest sound or movement that might mean his fears were for nothing.

'Edith!' Silence and stillness except for a grey

cat which paused in its pursuit of a mouse to look at him strangely.

He continued on through the kitchens and the physic garden, but there was no tall black-haired lady.

'Where might I find your cousin?' he asked Hilda when he spied her sitting half-concealed near the fish pond.

'My cousin has gone out,' the overly obvious blonde cousin said, instantly jumping to her feet and dropping a curtsy as her cheeks flamed scarlet. 'I expect she will return soon. Is there anything I can do for you? I hadn't expected anyone to come to this place. I…I like to think here.'

She batted her lashes and wet her lips.

Brand's breath came easier and relief trickled down the back of his neck. Edith would never abandon her cousin. She had risked everything for this woman when he first arrived. It was simply the panic associated with drinking far too much sour ale. 'Do you know where she has gone? I've been looking for her. There are things I wish to discuss with her.'

'To see Godwin's mother, I believe.' The woman fluttered her long lashes, reminding Brand of some large docile cow. He could not see how anyone in his right mind could prefer such a creature to Edith. 'My cousin wanted to make sure that she was aware of the great honour you wish to bestow on her son. She expected only to be gone a short time. I'm certain she'll be back directly.'

It all sounded plausible enough, but it didn't explain about the cup. He clenched his fist. He would discover the answer from Edith when she returned.

'So early?'

'My cousin is an early riser. She believes she does her best work in the morning when everything is peaceful.'

'I wish to speak to her. She is supposed to be my adviser. She should inform me before she does anything or goes anywhere.'

'That is not how Edith behaves,' Hilda said, colouring an even brighter shade of pink. 'She is used to getting her own way and doing what she wants.'

'She will learn.'

'Is everything all right between you two? Has she done something you object to? It will be all her own idea if she has. She hates interference in her plans.'

'Everything is fine.' Brand concentrated on

keeping his voice calm. He wanted to run to where Edith was and make demands, but that would be revealing too much. He hated that he needed her.

Hilda curtsied again. 'I had wondered, that is all. My cousin is headstrong and impetuous, but her heart is good. She always means well. But she has a temper and can be impossible.'

Brand tilted his head. 'Is there something I should know? Has Edith confided in you?'

She shook her head far too quickly. 'Nothing, nothing at all. Everything is absolutely fine. She simply wasn't at the feast. I've never known Edith to miss something like that. Even when she had a raging fever last Michaelmas, she insisted on being there.'

'But if anything should change and she should become unhappy, you would tell me if I asked?'

She fingered her neckline. 'I'm not sure I understand. Edith is more than capable of making her feelings known.'

'I believe you do. I am interested in everything that happens on my land. I want everyone to feel that they can confide in me.'

'If something goes amiss, I'm sure Edith will shout it from the rooftops.' She gave her first genuine smile. 'She says that you like to argue and don't mind if you lose. If so, then you are well matched. Her late husband hated losing.'

'I always win, in the end…most times.' Brand pursed his lips. If Edith was prepared to rise early to make something happen for Godwin, he should be prepared to meet her halfway and show her that their quarrel had no good purpose. It was foolish to look beyond tomorrow.

When Edith returned, he'd clearly demonstrate the benefits of being his mistress and give her a reason to confide in him. All he knew was that he wanted her by his side. He wanted to hear her counsel.

The entire household was awake by the time Edith returned. The cup clanked against her side. Despite her urging, Athelstan had refused to take it. He had agreed to consider leaving with his family once his wounds had healed. A small concession, but an important one.

Edith's shoulders relaxed slightly when the doors of the hall came into view. The weather-beaten lintels always cheered her, but here and there she could already notice the changes Brand and his men had wrought. This was her home, but no longer hers entirely any more.

'There you are, Edith.' Brand strode out from one of the storage houses. His golden-brown hair gleamed in the sunlight and his shoulders appeared far too big for his tunic. Was he truly the cold-blooded murderer Athelstan claimed? 'I've been searching for you.'

Edith froze. Brand was the last person she wanted to encounter, particularly after her conversation with Athelstan and while she carried the cup. She wanted to get it back to its hiding place in the bedroom. It should be safe there until she could convince Athelstan or Mary to take it.

'What did you need from me?' she asked cautiously. She forced her hands to stay at her side and not clutch the cup.

'There is something I want to show you.' He smiled as if the quarrel had never happened.

'I've been to see Godwin's mother. I believe she would rather come to see you. The prospect of her lord visiting her house sent her into a fair state. She feels it is far from adequate.'

Brand's lips curved upwards. 'I can imagine. I've no wish to cause difficulties. She may attend me here.'

'She is aware of the great honour that you are about to do to Godwin.'

'It will be good for everyone to see that all have a chance of favour. I promote on merit, rather than old allegiance.' He inclined his head. 'Your cousin told me where you had gone.'

'Hilda did?' Her voice went up an octave and the sweat pooled at the back of her neck. The pleasant spring day suddenly seemed icy cold. 'She told you why I had gone there?'

'Did you want it to be a surprise?' He came over to her and gathered her in his arms. 'You can be foolish. I'm grateful you wanted to inform Godwin's mother of my offer, but I wanted to speak to you. Halfdan's messenger gave me all the gossip in Jorvik. I thought you would have been interested to hear it.'

She breathed in deeply; his masculine scent was at once comforting and exciting. She'd missed his arms last night, more than she had wanted to admit. She wanted to lean her head against his chest and draw from his strength, but that was impossible.

'It is behind us,' she said instead. 'We both understand the situation now.'

He rested his chin on her head. 'It is amazing how the early morning air can clarify your mind. You must know, Edith, I will never hurt you intentionally. I, better than most, know the pitfalls. There are things in my life that have been constant for many years. They will remain so.'

'We won't speak of it again. We have a bargain, you and I, and I shall keep it.'

'What do you want to speak of?'

She swallowed hard and knew she had to ask. She leant back against his arms and regarded his scarred face. 'Were you there when the rebellion ended?'

'Yes,' he said shortly, his arms tightening about her and holding her in place. 'I was there. I escaped with my life, but it was one of the few times in my life I can say that I looked death in the eye. My best friend died because of rebel treachery. They broke the truce. They came with concealed weapons.'

'Did you have your axe that day?'

'No, I used my sword. I normally use a sword. An axe takes no skill.'

'You were wielding an axe the first time I met you!'

'The axe I used to break down the door belonged to Hrearek.' He ran his hands through his hair. 'Where is this leading, Edith?'

Edith's heart hammered. Egbert and treachery.

That failed to surprise her. She trusted Brand's version. 'You swear this? You will give your sacred oath on this?'

'Ask any of my men. An axe lacks the refinement of a broadsword.' Brand put his hand on her shoulder. 'Edith, I know your husband died that day. Had I known what he did to you, his death would not have been so swift. I can't even say that it was my sword which slew him. Everything went crazy when the rebels broke the truce. Sven was the first to fall. He'd been prepared to accept the terms of surrender when concealed swords were pulled out. His death was avenged. Sven Odd was hugely admired. We had been closer than brothers.'

'I'm glad you didn't know,' she whispered and concentrated on the place where his tunic gaped open. 'It makes things easier somehow. What happened, happened because of war rather than some sort of revenge.'

His fingers raised her chin. 'You must believe me, Edith. I did not break the truce. I would never break a truce. No true warrior would. Without his bond and code, a warrior becomes little better than a wild beast.'

Edith nodded. It bothered her that she wanted

to believe him. If he was near, all doubts vanished under her desire for him. 'There is no point in dwelling in the past, but I believe you. I know my late husband and his casual disregard for the niceties.'

'What brought this about?'

'A rumour Godwin's mother heard. It upset her dreadfully.'

'What did you say to her?'

'That I would ask you. I could hardly do more than that. She will accept my assurance.'

His lips twisted. 'She didn't want her son fostered with a monster?'

'Your name is infamous. Godwin is her only son.' Edith breathed slightly easier. She could keep from mentioning Athelstan and his accusation.

'She should trust me. I like the boy. He reminds me of myself when I was that age. I want to be a good lord to everyone who lives on my lands and who upholds the king's laws. But it is her choice. I make the offer once and once only. It depends on what sort of life she wants for her son.'

'I will let her know.' Edith balanced on her toes.

'Good, but it can wait for another day,' he said, putting an arm about her shoulders. 'I want to show you something first, the reason I've been searching for you.'

'What?' She kept herself completely still. Was he going to confess about the silver and the jewels, taunt her with it? 'What have you found?'

He dropped a kiss on her forehead. 'Our new bath house. It is a huge improvement. I was right. Your priest was wrong.'

'And you like being right?'

'It is the best way.' He led her to a stone building. 'Have a peek in. You don't have to go in.'

Edith peered into the room. A blast of heat hit her face. Blissful.

'Do you want to use it now?'

She hesitated. The cup weighed heavy on her waist. She needed to put it in a safe place. Athelstan might not want it now, but some day…and then there was the question of her mother's jewels. Where had Brand hidden them? And, more important, why had he left the cup except as a taunt and tease?

'I'm not sure. People might talk. Allow me some time to think about it. Taking a bath like this is a huge step.' She backed cautiously away from the door. With every step, the cup clunked against her hip. She had to hope that he hadn't noticed it or suspected. It would be impossible to explain away and she knew Athelstan's death would be for ever seared on her conscience.

'Then again, perhaps you wish to return the cup to its proper storage place before I learn it is missing.'

Chapter Eleven

Brand knew about the missing cup and that she had it. Edith struggled to breathe in the unfamiliar heat of the bath house. Had he guessed why she'd gone to see Mary as well?

After one gulp of air, she calmed. He couldn't know about Athelstan or she'd not be in the bath house. She'd be standing, shivering in the yard, having been beaten within an inch of her life.

Brand would have summoned everyone to watch her punishment and he would have hauled Athelstan from his hiding place. He would not be gently probing about the cup.

Athelstan remained safe and she had to do everything in her power not to betray him. She refused to be the one to send the loyal servant to his death.

Right now, she needed time and opportunity to

confront Athelstan again. Somehow with her new-found knowledge about what had truly happened when Egbert died, she would convince him to go before more damage was done. But always she needed to keep in mind what a good tafl player Brand was and how he thought several moves ahead.

'Do you have an answer for me, Edith? Why is the cup hanging from your waist, rather than where it had been kept, safe in my bedroom?'

Her eyes flew to his face. He was watching her much as a cat might watch a mouse. Her heart thudded. 'You know I have the cup.'

'I know. You took it out last night after we quarrelled.'

'How do you know? How could you possibly know that?' Despite the heat of the bath house, a chill entered her soul. She had been very careful.

'I found the hiding place on my second night here.' He gave a superior smile. 'It made sense that there would be a storage place. I had a look and then left a marker in case you decided to open it.'

'A marker? I didn't see anything."

'That, my dear Edith, was the whole point of my scheme. You were not supposed to notice. The small piece of cloth was on the ground and you had not replaced the stone the same way. The graining of the stone was tilted the other way. Little things can save lives, Edith. It pays to plan ahead.'

Edith winced. So simple and straightforward, marking the position with a piece of cloth as well as the grain of stone. She should have considered that he'd create a trap for her. Once she discovered that the jewels and silver were missing, she should have backed away from the idea of taking the cup. Or at least considered that he might have a scheme like this. But he still did not know her reasons.

'The cup belonged to my grandfather. It belongs to me. Everything in that cavity belonged to me.' She stuck her chin in the air. 'You had no right.'

'You had no right to conceal it.'

'You would have me a beggar?'

'I shan't steal it away. You may take it with you when you depart.' Brand inclined his head. 'Openly, rather than as a thief in the night. You deserve something and the estate can spare a single silver cup.'

Edith rolled her eyes. 'Your charity overwhelms me.'

'Sarcasm does you few favours.' He put a hand

on her shoulder. The simple touch made her insides turn over. 'I know how much your family meant to you. If you feel you can't live without the cup, then so be it. Some things are precious for what they represent, rather than their metal.'

The words made her heart knock. Brand understood. She knew she had to ask. She wanted to know what had happened to her mother's jewels. 'And the rest?'

'The rest?' His brows drew together and he took a step backwards. 'All that hiding place contained was the single cup, pushed far to the back. I thought it empty to begin with, but I reached back to make sure nothing was concealed behind a hidden door and the cup rolled out.'

Edith's heart thudded. Empty? Impossible. 'My mother's jewels were there and other pieces of silver. It was where I'd placed them after Egbert left. I struggled to get the stone back in because it was so full. It seemed the safest place in case… in case we were overrun by Norseman.'

He shook his head. 'No great quantity of jewels or silver. Only a single cup was there when I first looked. I'm sorry. I didn't see any point in taking anything. I didn't want to alert you that I had discovered one of your hiding places. It would have spoilt my plan.'

The sincerity of his voice convinced her. If he'd wanted to know, he'd have confronted her with it, much as he'd done with the salt cod.

She closed her eyes, thinking back to when Egbert had left. The first thing she had done was to move the jewels and silver in there. She had not slept there until Brand appeared. It was possible that Egbert had returned and emptied it. It had taken three more days before she had thought to block the tunnel. How Egbert must have laughed that the jewels and silver she had denied him were used to fund his rebellion. She had wondered where he received the funding. Now she knew. She'd been naive.

'I thought they were safe. I truly thought they were.' She wrapped her arms about her waist, hating that Egbert had practised one last deceit on her. 'I stored everything that was precious to me in that cavity. It was surrounded by stone and I thought if the worst happened and we burned to the ground… It was all in vain.'

'Who else knew?' His hard voice broke through her misery. 'Who else knew about the cavity?

Were you the only one? Did you have help to fill it?'

'I presume Egbert must have known. My father made sure he knew all of the hall's secrets. But I never moved anything in there until after he left.' She put her hand to her head, trying to think. 'It was something passed from father to son. My father only told me because he had no son.'

'It is a mystery then, but I will swear wherever you want that the cavity only held that cup when I first opened it.'

'He could have returned,' Edith said slowly. 'It is unlikely, but it could have happened. About a week after Egbert left, Godwin told me his story about bad men coming through the tunnel. I thought it was a story, but I did arrange for that tunnel to be blocked.'

'Godwin sees much. You should have checked your hidden wealth at the time.'

She sank down on a stone bench. 'It is not so much the wealth, but the sentiment. The jewellery belonged to my mother and her mother before that, going back generations. It was my link to the past. It was one of the reasons I refused to give them to Egbert. I wish I had something, no matter how small.'

He dug his hand into his pouch and held out the circlet of keys. 'I wronged you before. You should wear these while you remain here. You are far better at looking after this house than I could ever be.'

Edith stared at the circlet without taking them. He was returning them to her. He might never marry her, but he was allowing her to be in charge. Would he do that if he knew where she'd been? 'My mother always held the keys.'

'Take them.' He placed them in her palm. 'Unless there is some reason you can't.'

She traced the emblem of the running hare that adorned the circlet, torn. She couldn't confess now. She'd give Athelstan more time to recover. It was what her mother would have done. 'You can see my mother's crest. I should give you back the keys.'

'I trust you, Edith.'

Edith swallowed hard. 'I will endeavour to live up to that trust.'

'Good. Don't disappear on me again. Tell me when you go. I worried.'

'How did you guess I was coming back?'

'You'd never leave Hilda to face my wrath. She doesn't deserve you as a cousin, but you're loyal.'

'You're right.' Edith closed her hand about the keys. 'I'd never leave her to face you alone.'

Her throat worked up and down as she traced the lines of the hare. She conjured up an early memory of her mother wearing the hare and confiding that seeing a hare always meant that good fortune was sure to follow. Finally everything would work out. She could do her duty and find a measure of happiness.

'Thank you,' she whispered finally, knowing the words were inadequate.

'My pleasure.' He took a step closer to her. 'I do want to give you pleasure, Edith. Remember that.'

She glanced about the stone room, suddenly aware of what her mother might have thought about her being here. 'I should go. There will be things that need to be done. Not the least of which is putting the cup back where it belongs. You needn't worry. I won't take it again without your leave. I'm no thief.'

He put his hands at her waist and gently undid her belt, taking off the pouch that held the cup. He laid it on a bench. 'I will keep it safe for now. When you require it, you may have it back. I hope you trust me like I trust you.'

A single tear trickled down her face. She'd been

angry with him and now he had done the most un-expected thing—he'd given her back some of her heritage. He wasn't seeking to have everything.

'They were part of my dowry. They were what I had left of her. That and my mirror.' She brushed the tears away with impatient fingers. 'You must not mind me. I'm obviously overtired. There is so much to be done as well. This time of year is busy. I've taken too much time for myself today.'

He pulled her to him. His hand tangled in her hair, gently pulling out the pins until it tumbled down about her shoulder. 'Not too tired, I hope?'

A warm tingle circled her insides, driving all thoughts of the things she ought be doing away. She had missed sleeping in his arms and waking up to his lovemaking. 'Last night was fraught.'

'There is no need to explain. Some day, you will have more jewels. Promise me that you won't run away.'

Edith swallowed hard. 'When I leave, I shall leave by the front gate and you can travel with me until I reach my destination…wherever that is. But I've no plans to go. I keep my word, Brand, and I don't want to think beyond tomorrow. My future will take care of itself.'

'I'm sorry.' His lips touched her forehead. The gentle touch undid her.

'It is not their value in money or what they can buy but what they represented.' Edith attempted to explain why the gesture meant so much to her. 'My mother used to tell me stories of how they came into her family. After I grew up, I never believed the stories, but when I was little, they were wondrous.'

'I'm sorry about that loss, but I'm sorry we quarrelled about something which neither of us can change.'

She glanced up into his eyes and knew her thoughts about keeping her heart safe were an illusion. She had feelings for this man. She had been so wrong about him being a barbarian. He had finer feelings than any man she'd ever met. The trouble was that some day he would go out of her life and her heart would break. She knew instinctively that it would be easier if she didn't say anything.

She touched the brooch. 'My mother used to tell me to concentrate on changing the thing I could change. I found it hard to listen. I'm sorry we quarrelled as well.'

'My mother used to tell me stories about grow-

ing up in Ireland. She claimed to have been a nobleman's wife and daughter. How true it was, I
will never know. But she used to say it whenever I
was in trouble. I had reasons to be proud.' His lips
travelled down the side of her face. 'You should
know that I intend to look after you. I wouldn't
abandon any woman to the fate my mother suffered. I will see you safe. Always.'

Edith found she was too tired to fight. She
wanted to have his arms about her and feel his
skin slide under the palms of her hands. Her feelings for him were far too new and too deep. 'I
missed you.'

She lifted her mouth and met his. The kiss
quickly became deep and long, lighting the dark
reaches of her soul. His tongue moved against
hers and she pressed her body against his, letting
it do the talking. The kiss rapidly deepened and
Edith knew she needed far more. She wrenched
her lips from his.

'Are you tired?' she murmured when she could
breathe again.

His eyes twinkled. 'Sleeping on a stable floor
is not the most comfortable way to pass the night.
You will probably say that I deserved it for the
asinine way I behaved.'

She gave a soft laugh. 'I would never have mentioned it, but it is an appropriate place.'

'It is far better to sleep in your arms.'

'I think so as well.' She licked her lips. 'Shall we retire there and catch up on our sleep?'

'I have a better idea.' He drew her to him so that their groins touched, his hands cupping her bottom. The sensation caused her breath to come faster. 'Shall I play your maid? Show you how to bathe properly? You will enjoy it once you get the hang of it.'

'I'm sure I shall.'

'You don't need to move a muscle. Allow me to look after you.' His hot breath caressed her ear, doing strange things to her insides.

She knew then that she needed to take the lead. For too long she'd played the passive partner allowing him to do things to her. Today he'd given her something precious back and she wanted to show him that she appreciated him. She wanted to be his equal in this at least.

'Will we be alone here?' she asked, pretending to consider.

'Nobody would dare disturb us, but I'll bolt the door if it makes you feel better.' He went over to the door and slid the bolt home.

The simple sound gave her courage. What happened here would remain here. She didn't have to worry about interruptions.

'Good. I'm new to this, but I'm willing to learn.' She tapped her finger against her mouth, pretending to consider. 'I assume first you need to be naked in order to enjoy the benefits of bathing.'

'That's right.'

Her hands tugged at his tunic and raised it slowly inch by inch revealing his bare skin. She leant forwards and tasted.

'Patience,' he growled. 'I'm the one who knows what to do.'

'I'm a fast learner,' she murmured and returned her exploration of his body. Despite the many indentations and scars, his skin was silky soft. It held a fresh clean scent. 'What comes next?'

'You naked,' he growled. 'The proper way.'

He removed her shawl and quickly undid her gown, pushing it down until it pooled at her feet. She stepped out of the gown and stood before him in her tunic. He dipped his head and his tongue drew small circles, wetting the fine linen, turning it translucent so that her dusky-rose nipples showed through.

As his tongue lapped ever closer to her nipples,

they contracted to hardened points. She moaned slightly in the back of her throat, enjoying the exquisite torture. He captured each nipple in turn and suckled through the cloth. The wetness of the cloth rasped against her breast, driving the aching between her legs to new heights. Finally, he lifted the undertunic and divested her of the rest of her garments until she stood before him, naked. His hands ran over her bottom, kneading and stroking.

'This is how you get someone ready for a bath,' he purred in her ear. 'You were going too quickly.'

'I want to try.' She placed her hand on his chest and pushed him back to the bench.

He looked at her quizzically, but allowed her to ease him back on the bench.

Mimicking him, she slowly moved her mouth down his torso, stopping to lap his nipples. His chest hair was rough against her tongue. She continued southwards, making a trail with her lips, following the line of hair until she reached his trousers.

She ran her hand down the front and felt the hard muscle underneath. Her body ached to know that he wanted her as much as she wanted him.

Her hands worked at his trousers, undoing the leather ties. She eased them over his hips and his desire for her sprang free. She put her hand on him and he pulsed silky hot. She cupped his balls, tracing the outline of each. He groaned and his hands clenched her shoulders.

He moved as if to flip her onto her back, but she shook her head. This time she wanted to be on top and she wanted to give him pleasure. It gave her a heady sense of power. This powerful Norseman was hers. He wanted her and was ready for her and her alone.

She lowered her mouth. 'You need to be washed all over. I wanted to make sure that everywhere is clean.'

She captured him and felt him grow even harder. She glanced up and saw his eyes were half-shut with pleasure. His hands gripped her shoulders and urged her upwards. She climbed on the bench and slowly impaled her body on him.

Her body opened and took all of him. She marvelled how natural this had become and how easy it was to know precisely what to do. Slowly she tilted her hips back and forth. Each rock drove him deeper in until the climax came over them both.

Brand crushed her body to his and felt the final shuddering of her climax. There had been an added depth in their passion today. She was fast becoming as necessary to him as breathing. He knew he wanted to bind her to him and the very thought frightened him. Dependency only led to heartache in his experience.

'I think we are sweaty enough,' he rumbled against her ear, pushing the thought away. He refused to look beyond the moment with Edith. Always in the past when he had, things had gone awry.

She raised herself up on one elbow while her other hand played in his chest hair. Even though he thought himself completely spent a few heartbeats ago, his body craved more of her.

'What happens next?' she asked, giving a slight stretch and exposing the curve of her breast. Her dusky-rose nipple dangled tantalisingly in front of his mouth, reminding him of the delights they had just experienced.

He knew if he gave in to his passion, he'd be tempted to go too far and deep.

'We plunge,' he said, putting her from him. The air rushed around him and his body protested.

Her mouth dropped open. 'In the lake?'

'You are worried?' he teased. It had been one of the great finds. Starkad spoke the truth when he said that this was a proper bath house, like the ones in Constantinople, rather than the sweat houses back in Norway. In Norway, they would have had to plunge into the lake. The Byzantines had a more sophisticated approach, inherited from the Romans. He had to assume that this estate was far more ancient than Edith had guessed.

'I have never tried,' she admitted, her cheeks flaming. 'But I doubt I have any more of my reputation to lose. Shall we do it and truly shock everyone?'

'Come with me,' he said, relenting. 'There is no need to shock anyone. But you will have to admit that you didn't know everything about this estate.'

'I find that difficult to believe.'

He took her hand and led her into the next room where his men had uncovered the pool and the mosaics. The water softly glinted.

Her eyes gleamed with pure joy. All the time and trouble it had taken was nothing compared to seeing Edith in rapture. All of his early fears were groundless. Edith was a woman who kept her word. A slight unease came over Brand. She had agreed to a year and that was all he was going to get. He forced his mind from the unwelcome thought. There were other ways besides marriage to bind Edith to him. Right now, he didn't want to think about the future. He wanted to enjoy the present. 'How? How did you do this? How could you create this so quickly? I've never seen anything like it.'

'It was full of rubble and easy to clean. The men worked hard, but you and I have the honour of being the first to use it.'

Edith went immediately in. Her indrawn breath echoed around the chamber.

'Do you like it?' he asked.

'It is magical. Something out of a dream.'

She walked into the pool and sank down. 'After the heat of the first room, this feels heavenly. Are you going to come in?'

She held out her arms, her dark hair floated about her and he could see the paleness of skin in the depths of the water.

'Are you a siren now, seeking to make me forget my duty?'

'Sirens are dangerous creatures who lure men to their death,' she said, laughing. 'I'm not trying to lure you anywhere but into this pool. Come join me. You'll feel better for it.'

'Is that all you want?'

'Yes, that's all.' She gave a little splash of water.

'Surely you have time for that. After all, it was your suggestion that we bathe. All I'm doing is following orders.'

He smiled and decided that it was well she did not know her power. If she asked him to marry her looking like that, if she had asked for anything, he'd have given it to her.

'There are times when I'm happy to obey.'

Chapter Twelve

'Is there something I can do for you, Father Wilfrid?' Edith asked the priest later in the afternoon. The spring sun had dried her hair. Being thoroughly clean caused her worries to ease. There would be a solution to everything. She even felt strong enough to deal with the priest.

The priest's thin lips frowned. 'There is nothing a woman like you can do for me except repent. I am looking for the heathen who calls himself lord of this place.'

'How do you know he is a heathen?' she asked, provoked.

'All Norsemen are and he deliberately provokes me.'

'Brand Bjornson served in Constantinople for the very Christian Emperor of Byzantium. Have you ever asked him how he prays? Or why he wears a Byzantine cross about his neck?'

'Why has he not appeared in my church, then?'

'Has he once stopped you from preaching?'

'You should not use that tone with me.'

'Or what?' Edith crossed her arms. Always before she'd respected his right to speak but now she could see that he enjoyed making matters worse. 'What will you do to me? There is a new master here. I would suggest you find a way to get on with him, rather than stirring up trouble.'

The priest stared at her, mouth open. 'I had best see to some of my parishioners. You have changed, Lady Edith. I used to think you considered the souls of these people more important, but now I see you only consider your pride. I will pray for you.'

He slunk off.

Edith sank down onto the bench and buried her face in her hands. She found she didn't know the woman she was rapidly becoming. She wanted to take a breath and return to the old certainties.

She had made love to Brand in broad daylight in the bath house and then bathed with him, after which they had made love again. When they had emerged from the building several of Brand's men were standing around with huge smiles on their faces. Brand had ostentatiously kissed her before departing.

She fingered the circlet. She hated to think what her mother might say. Her mother never put her hand on her father, much less kissed him in public. She wanted to think she was doing it for the hall and the people, but she knew she was also doing it for herself and the way he made her feel. She liked feeling like a desirable woman who was cherished, rather than someone who didn't fit anywhere and who was more comfortable with ledgers and quantities of wool.

A small sigh escaped her throat. The old Edith would never have kissed in public. She was worried, though, how long she would be able to be this way, how long before she reverted to the old Edith?

'There you are, Edith,' Hilda said. 'I was wondering if you had gone to Godwin's house?'

Edith firmed her mouth. 'No, but I will go and see them tomorrow and explain the situation.'

'You know you are far prettier when you smile. Right now you look fierce enough to turn people to stone.'

Edith stood up. Trust Hilda to thoroughly deflate her well-being. 'I will take that as a compliment. There are times when I have to be fierce, but I enjoy smiling more. I trust there is nothing else amiss?'

'Did you find out what the messenger wanted?'

'I forgot to ask.'

'Halfdan has sent a decree.' Hilda put her hands to her head. 'Anyone harbouring or aiding the rebels will be severely punished. Edith, you know what this means. You and I will be punished if we are caught. You must give Athelstan up.'

'How did you learn about this?'

'They were talking about it in the kitchen. I went to see about the bread.' Hilda shivered. 'I'm beginning to get a bad feeling. Why did he have to come back?'

'The proclamation changes nothing. It merely confirms what I suspected. The king will not forgive readily and Brand will have no choice but to follow orders.' She took a deep breath. 'He owes everything to his king.'

'But what about us?' Hilda's voice rose an octave. 'What will happen? It is bound to come out. You must protect me, Edith.'

'Your part is finished,' Edith said, covering

Hilda's hand with hers. 'I will not ask any more of you.'

Hilda crossed her arms and then she tilted her head. 'You have washed your hair.'

'The sun is drying it. I had a bath.'

'The one thing I will say for the Norsemen is that they smell better than the Northumbrians.' Hilda's laugh was a little too loud.

A shadow fell over her. Edith felt a distinct tingle. Brand. He put his hand on her shoulder. Hilda rapidly made her excuses and departed.

'She seemed awfully nervous about something.'

'She wants to look her best for the feast this evening.' She leant forwards and dropped her voice. 'I suspect secretly she wants to have a bath.'

'There won't be a feast tonight. The king's messenger has returned to Jorvik. I gave him a full accounting of what passed with Hrearek.'

'Surely it will be up to the king to decide now?'

Brand's mouth twisted. 'Hrearek escaped, rather than face Halfdan.'

A distinct shiver went down Edith's spine. Hrearek had escaped and probably blamed her for what had happened to him. 'But there is no danger here.'

'He'd be unwise to try his luck here. The men

know what he is about. I suspect he will go to Ireland and try for a position there. His sword arm is second to none. You have nothing to fear if that is what you are worried about.'

Edith forced a laugh and tried to ignore her churning guts. Hrearek had given her such a look when he left. 'Am I worried?'

'You wore a distinct frown when I spied you sitting with your cousin. I'd wondered if that was the gossip—that he wanted revenge. Hrearek is not like that.'

'Hilda feared you remained angry with me. I assured her that our breach was healed,' Edith said and carefully composed her face. Every time she thought about it, her heart gave a little pang, but she knew what she was doing was right for everyone and when the time came, she'd confess.

'Is there anything else?'

'Hilda explained anyone helping the rebels is to be punished. Surely the rebellion has finished? All the rebels are dead or at least the ones from here are.' Edith clenched her fists. Athelstan had only gone because she insisted. He hadn't precisely rebelled against the king. He had followed her orders.

'A formality. I've assured Erik that all the rebels from here are dead.'

'You were there,' she said lightly. She knew it should make her heart easier, but it only served to twist the knife. Brand would not go searching for any rebel, but there would come a day when she'd have to confess.

'Yes, I was.' He gave her a curious look. 'Know this, Edith, even if Halfdan had not given that order, I would have done precisely the same thing. We are like-minded on this. The rebels abused our trust. Good men died that day because of your late husband and all his men.'

'Is your world always so black and white?'

'What do you mean?'

'Many of the men who died were good men. They had a bad leader. There is a difference.' She concentrated, trying to pick the right words. 'I'm not seeking to excuse Egbert, but do you seriously think the men who followed him had a choice, once he'd decided on treachery?'

He shook his head. 'I don't see the difference. Many of them stood by and allowed him to treat you horribly.'

'You wouldn't.' Edith stood up. It did her heart good to know that he remained outraged at her treatment, but what sort of man interferes when a man chastises his wife, particularly when the man in question is the master? 'There is little point in discussing this as it is something which won't happen. They all died. A dead man's reputation means nothing to a corpse.'

'That's obvious.'

Edith stopped. Her entire being trembled. She suddenly realised that she might have found a solution to her problem. So simple. If everyone believed that Athelstan was dead then he could take another name. As quickly as the thought came, she rejected it. Such deceptions were always found out. Her best course remained convincing Athelstan to leave before he was discovered.

'Searching for dead men is a waste of time.'

Brand stroked his chin. 'Are you trying to tell me something? Should I be hunting for ghosts?'

'No!' Edith regarded her hands. This was much harder than playing tafl. Real lives were at stake. 'I simply wondered why Halfdan had sent the message.'

'He likes to be thorough. After your husband's rebellion, he refuses to take any more chances. He also requests my presence in Jorvik.'

'So you will be leaving.'

Brand placed his hand on her shoulder. 'I thought to take you with me. You should see the city now that it has been rebuilt.'

Edith's heart knocked against her chest. He wanted her to go to Jorvik with him. 'You want me to go with you?'

'I can leave Starkad in charge for the few weeks in which we will be gone.'

'When do you want to depart?'

'In a few days, once the planting is well under way. Halfdan can wait for a bit, but kings grow restless if they think their wishes are being ignored. I want you with me, Edith. You may look on it as an order or an invitation, whichever you prefer, but you will be coming with me.'

Edith frowned. This time she wasn't going to spin dreams. He wasn't offering marriage or anything permanent, simply an excursion to Jorvik. But it was hard to stop her heart from leaping. He wanted her with him, rather than finding an excuse to leave her behind. She just wished that the offer had come after she sorted Athelstan out, rather than before. Without her here, the possibilities that Athelstan would be discovered increased. She had only a few days to solve the problem.

'Why are you telling me this now? Instead of when we bathed?' she asked.

'I had other things on my mind.' His hand went down her back. 'Is it so wrong of me to want you by my side? You are far from indispensable here.'

'You keep reminding me of that.' She looked up at him and put all her worries to one side. Anything that happened she would find a way of dealing with—right now she wanted to be with him. 'I am happy to go. Delighted to be asked. The last time I was in Jorvik was before the Norsemen arrived.'

He gave an amused laugh.

'What is so funny about that?'

'You called it Jorvik.' He gave a crooked smile. 'Progress.'

'I am being practical. The name has changed. Everything has changed. There is little point living in the past.' She had to hope that the shadows from the past didn't reach out and spoil this happiness. 'Did the king say why he wished to see you?'

Brand rested his chin on the top of her head. 'He will make his wishes known in due course, but it is never good to keep a king waiting.'

A distinct chill went through her. She wanted to ask if the reason he was being summoned had to do with his unmarried state, but she also remembered the row. She'd accepted that he wasn't going to marry her, but she knew if he had to marry anyone else, she'd be desolate. She wasn't ready for things to end. 'Did he mention me?'

'Why would he?'

'No reason. I merely wondered.' The words stuck in her throat.

Brand's gaze narrowed. 'Halfdan has set ideas about things. I doubt your paths will cross.'

'I know my place, Brand. You need not remind me. I was curious.' She gave a quick smile to hide the hurt. 'Curiosity can lead to heartache. I've learnt my lesson. There is no need to repeat it.'

'I always knew you were a quick learner.' He raised her hand to his lips. 'I do want you by my side, Edith. I want your company.'

She knew it should be enough, but somehow she longed for more.

'Everything will be well, Hilda,' Edith said a week later. Brand had ordered their departure for the next day and Edith had spent most of the day getting ready, making sure the covered cart was full, while, after Edith's suggestion, Brand decided to get a day of hunting in. Although she would have liked to ride Meera, she thought it best not to shock people. Brand had agreed.

'Who are you trying to convince? The estate will be here when you get back. Your little problem will be as well. Have you considered that? Each day Athelstan remains, he puts everyone in danger.'

'I won't be gone long. Mary is capable.' Edith gave her keys a little pat. 'It makes it easier without Brand being here to supervise the packing. I do like having things packed the way I like them packed. Knowing Brand, he would be giving me advice about the proper way.'

'Does that bother you?'

'Most of the time, no, but I didn't want him to take over with packing.' Over the past few days, she'd noticed how he took her ideas and improved on them. Most of the time this was fine, but Edith wanted to make sure that there were no awkward questions or helpful suggestions. Everything about this trip needed to be perfect. She wanted to demonstrate to Halfdan that he need not suggest Brand take a wife. Edith knew she wasn't ready for their affair to end, but it would have to, if the king insisted.

'I'm worried, Edith. You are playing a dangerous game. Think about the consequences. Other people depend on you.'

Edith grasped Hilda's cold hands between hers. 'No one is hunting for ghosts. If Athelstan travels now, it would kill him. The last thing I want is his death on my conscience.'

'Is there anything you want me to do?'

Edith slowly shook her head. 'I believe everything is under control. Shall I bring you back a present? Perhaps some ribbon or something for your hair? The merchants are well regarded. It is one of the benefits of the Norsemen. We do get more goods now or so I'm told.'

Hilda gave an envious sigh. 'I hear the metalworking is superb. But I would love some ribbon. A pretty red one if you can find it, it always flatters my complexion.'

Edith raised an eyebrow. She did notice that Hilda seemed to be taking extra pains with her dress. 'So you are no longer adverse to the Norsemen? Is that a new hairstyle?'

'The old one kept getting in the way of spinning. I find this one more practical.'

Edith was tempted to ask how a more elaborate hairstyle with curls hanging about her face was going to help with the spinning, but she made a non-committal noise. 'And the Norsemen? Should I worry about any more incidents with you or have you learnt your lesson about encouraging men?'

Hilda dipped her head and her cheeks flamed. 'Starkad is very pleasant. We talk occasionally. He has travelled all over the world. Some day I would like to see the world beyond Northumbria.'

Edith laughed, trying to picture the big Norseman as being shy. 'Do you think?'

Hilda shrugged. 'He has not said anything yet and I have let him know that I might enjoy a kiss or two, but he does nothing. It is most aggravating.'

'That makes a change. I thought all men were in love with you.'

'You are teasing me now, Edith. I know he likes me. I simply wish he would refrain from treating me like I might break.'

'Lady Edith! Lady Edith!' Godwin hurried up. 'Me mam asked me to find you. It is important. You must come at once.'

'Her ladyship is busy,' Hilda answered and clutched Edith's hand. 'You won't have time. Other things are more important. You need to finish this packing. You going to Jorvik could be the making of everyone. You could see the king and maybe convince him that Brand should marry you. The king could make him marry anyone. Starkad told me. Think about what you could do before you throw it all away, Edith.'

'Who is spinning dreams?' Edith whispered back and slipped out of Hilda's restraining hand. She knelt down. 'Godwin, what is wrong? Slowly. Count to ten first, then tell me. Why do I need to go to the cottage?'

The boy gulped air and she could see him mentally counting to ten.

'Godwin,' Brand's voice boomed out. 'It is good to see you. I trust your sister's health has improved.'

Edith froze. 'Brand, I wasn't expecting to see you. I thought you were out hunting.'

'The game proved elusive and there are a thousand things which I need to do here. You didn't think I'd leave the packing all to you, did you?'

'I'd hopes.'

Brand put his hands on Godwin's shoulders. 'Has your mother decided to allow you to foster here?'

Godwin flushed. 'My…mother has been very busy lately. We have…have sickness in our house.

We haven't discussed it, but I would like to be a warrior.'

'Lady Edith told me.' Brand looked over Godwin's head. 'I would like to visit his mother, Edith.'

'Right now?' Edith put her hand to her throat and kept her gaze from Hilda's. The faint gasp told her all she needed to know.

'Yes. No one else has fallen ill in the village. We may safely assume the illness is not contagious.'

'I feel certain that Mary will come to you when she can.'

'We will be in Jorvik. I wish to have this matter settled. Godwin should come and take up his duties.'

Godwin's face lit up, then quickly fell. 'My mother will never allow it.'

'You think she will refuse her lord?' Brand thundered. 'What sort of woman is she?'

'We will go together and see your mother, Godwin,' Edith said quickly. 'Do you wish to run on ahead and tell her that we are coming?'

'There is no need for that. I've no wish for her to stand on ceremony. I always enjoy my talks with Godwin.'

'Yes, I do as well.'

The pit of Edith's stomach sank. There was nothing she could do to prevent this disaster. She gave one last look at the cart piled high with its trunks and silently bid the dream of Jorvik good-bye. All she could do was pray for a miracle and they had been thin on the ground recently. 'Shall we go? It is best that I come with you.'

The cottage stood on its own, a little way from the other houses in the village. The garden was well turned over and the young plants had started to push through. Brand's scar itched and he instinctively checked for his sword.

What wasn't Edith telling him? Her mouth had become more and more pinched the closer they came to the cottage. And her cousin had gone positively white at the thought of them going together to the cottage. Or perhaps it had another cause. Maybe they had quarrelled because Edith was going to Jorvik.

'Is everything all right, Edith?' he asked. 'What do you want to tell me? Your face always has that expression when you fear you are going to lose at tafl.'

Edith stopped. 'Godwin, run on ahead and tell your mother that Brand Bjornson is also coming.'

'There is no need. Why don't we surprise her?'

'I doubt she likes surprises. It is a major honour for the lord to visit.'

'It is how I want it done.' Brand put a hand on Godwin's shoulder, restraining him. 'I want to find out the true reason why Godwin's mother has avoided sending him to me. The boy should become a warrior. You want to be a warrior, don't you, Godwin?'

The boy glanced at Edith, who gave an almost imperceptible nod. 'Yes. I want to carry a big axe and fight bad men. My mother worries about me getting hurt.'

'Good lad.' Brand turned towards Edith. 'You see, you are worrying for naught. The boy and I will convince his mother.'

'If that is what you want...'

'You don't approve?' He lifted his brow. 'Pray, what is wrong with my plan?'

She gazed away from him and a gentle breeze moulded her skirts to her legs. 'I would like Godwin to become a warrior,' she said finally. 'He will make a good one.'

'Trust me to make him into one.' He leant over and allowed his breath to caress her ear. 'I am a good teacher.'

He was rewarded by her cheeks turning a deep crimson. It amused him that she still blushed. Later he intended on showing her exactly what a good instructor he was when he had an apt pupil, but first he was going to ensure that Godwin had a good future.

'My lady, my lady.' Godwin's mother rushed out of the cottage and then stopped. The colour drained from her face and she dropped into a deep curtsy. 'Your lordship, you are here as well. A most…unexpected pleasure.'

'You appear to have recovered.' Brand frowned. Something was very wrong. Edith appeared more uncomfortable than ever as the woman paled.

'It is…is my daughter, your lordship. I haven't dared to leave her.' The woman toyed with her apron, not quite meeting his eyes.

Brand's gaze narrowed. Whatever was going on, Edith knew about it. Had she kept it from him, hoping not to embarrass the woman? He could understand why she might be apprehensive as a warrior's training was far from easy, but the boy deserved a better fate than being a farm labourer.

'I sent word that I wished to speak with you.'

'I apologise.' The woman refused to meet his eye. 'I know the great honour you wish to do my son, but my daughter occupies all my attention. I wanted to honour you with my full attention.'

'Is there no one who could have looked after your daughter? I understood people around here looked after each óther.'

'Mary is most particular about who looks after her daughter,' Edith said, stepping between him and the woman. 'It was an unintentional slight. I told you, Mary, that Lord Bjornson was most determined to give Godwin this honour. You would be wise to think about it.'

'I…I…' The woman went beet-red and started stammering. 'I've no idea what to say. Your coming is most unexpected. We're far from ready.'

'Come, come, what is the problem?' Brand moved towards the door. 'I want to advance the boy, not eat him for dinner!'

'Mary! Has Lady Edith arrived yet?' a man's voice boomed from the cottage. 'I need to see her. There are things we must discuss before…before I leave this place.'

Brand reached for his sword. 'Who is this man?' he shouted. Instinctively he looked for ways to escape.

The guilty pair regarded each other and Brand knew without a doubt that Edith had been a party to the deception. A great hollow opened up inside him. She had betrayed him and he'd been prepared to trust her with his life.

Chapter Thirteen

Everything slowed down. Edith heard a great rushing noise in her ears and saw Brand's terrible expression as he gripped his sword. He knew. The absolute worst thing in the world had happened. He knew what she had done and he would never forgive her for it. He would also exact the punishment Halfdan decreed from Athelstan. Blood would be spilt today. Rather than saving Athelstan, she'd ensured his death.

All the happiness she'd experienced over the past week was never going to be repeated. They were enemies once again. She could see it from the way he regarded her. They were enemies and she knew she loved him. She had to hope that he'd listen before he acted and that he would understand.

'Put away the sword, Brand. Allow me to explain,' she said into that terrible stillness.

'Who is there?' he thundered, gesturing with his sword and his face growing darker with every breath he took. 'What man resides in that cottage? What sort of trap have you led me into, Edith? Quick about it before the carnage starts. Tell me the truth and you might be spared.'

Mary gave a muffled shriek and a single tear ran down Godwin's face. Silently Edith prayed for a miracle. Then she took another breath and knew there would be no miracle. There was only her to stop a boy being for ever scarred.

'Godwin's father,' Edith answered as steadily as she could.

'The rebel.'

Her heart shattered. He had already made up his mind about Athelstan's guilt.

'This is no trap, Brand.' Edith made her voice gentle and held out a coaxing hand. 'You're safe here. Put away the sword. Listen. You were never supposed to find out. He is a ghost who will melt away.'

The sword stayed in his hand, but he made no move towards the cottage. Silently Edith prayed that Athelstan would stay put as well. Somehow she had to diffuse the situation before it led to bloodshed. Even if he was uninjured, Athelstan would never be able to match Brand.

'Will you listen for once? Listen and find it in your heart to forgive?' she pleaded.

He stood as if carved from stone. 'I am listening but all I hear is the sound of the breeze in the trees. You have not told me anything, Edith. Start explaining now!'

'Godwin's father is in there. He has come home. He means you no harm.' Silently she prayed the last was true. Although she'd told Athelstan and Mary the tale as Brand had related it, she wasn't entirely sure how much they had believed. Athelstan still repeated his tale, insisting it was Brand who had broken the truce before Egbert.

Athelstan had promised that he would not harm Brand as long as Brand treated her properly. Edith had rolled her eyes. Mary had agreed, but neither of them had sent Godwin to Brand. 'He means you no harm, Brand. All he wants to do is be with his family. When he is well enough, he will go.'

'His father is dead. He died in the battle. You told me.' Brand shook his head. 'I trusted your word. What else have you been hiding from me, Edith? Who?'

Edith drew herself up to her full height. 'I told you what I believed to be the truth at the time, but I was wrong. Perhaps I should have informed you straight away, but you must trust I had my reasons. I am willing to vouch for him, but I was wrong about his death.'

'Amazing, you admitting that you were wrong.'

'It happens.' Edith ignored the sarcasm and concentrated on keeping her voice steady. He had to see that her duty came before everything. Her only crime was to selfishly want a tiny piece of happiness. 'Athelstan has returned. He wanted to come home to his family and the people he loves. What is wrong with that?'

Edith prayed Brand would understand the need to return home. She had to wonder if Brand knew the feeling and the deep peace of homecoming. For so many years, he had lived the life of a wanderer. His only home was the battlefield.

Brand stood completely still as if rooted to the spot, his face giving away nothing. He had become the fearsome warrior of the first day, rather than the tender lover who had held her all last night.

'He wanted to see his children,' she continued, trying to reach the man who had held her so lovingly rather than confronting the warrior. 'This is where his blood is and where his ancestors are buried. Surely you can understand what drove him? He knows there is a price on his head, but he still had to come.'

'He is incapable of finer feelings!' Athelstan suddenly shouted. 'The Norsemen do not understand such things.'

'You have no idea, Athelstan.' Edith retorted. Her blood boiled on Brand's behalf. 'Brand Bjornson is no barbarian. How many times must I tell you that?'

'How long? How long has he been back?' Brand demanded, his face turning even more thunderous. It was all Edith could do to stand there and face him. The man had gone and only the warrior remained. 'How long, Edith? How long have you been defying me over this? How long have you been hiding a rebel?'

'My husband returned, your lordship. It is why I sent for her ladyship.' Mary gave a low curtsy. 'You must believe that. Lady Edith had nothing to do with it. She is innocent of any blame, except the knowing. If you must blame someone, blame me.'

'Is this true, Edith?'

'Over a week.' Edith bowed her head. 'I've known ever since we came back from Owen the Plough's. Hilda informed me of the rumour. I went to see him as soon as I could leave the hall without causing upset. It is why I took the cup. I wanted to convince him to go and thought if he had money, he might leave and everything could be as it was.'

An expression of extreme hurt and betrayal crossed his face, but was instantly masked. His eyes grew colder than ice.

'Were you going to tell me? Or did you hope that by keeping my bed warm, I'd forgive you everything?'

'I hoped never to have to tell you.' Edith pressed her hands together. Her chest ached as if it had been stabbed. He didn't understand. 'I saw no need. And it had nothing to do with keeping your bed warm.'

She kept her head up and refused to beg. The words—keeping his bed warm—seemed so inadequate and cheap for what had passed between them. For her, certainly, it had been so much more.

'Why?'

'For you, he is a ghost. For Godwin and his mother, he is the most important person in the world. I had hoped to convince him to go south either with or without his family, but as yet that had not happened. The injuries he received haven't healed. You must believe me that his arrival had nothing to do with what passed between us.'

She went forwards and touched his sleeve. He turned from her, rejecting her.

'Was he on his own? Or was there some other plan? Why precisely did you take the cup?'

Each word lashed through her.

'My original thought was to have him go south to Wessex and take the cup to provide some funds. He has been a good and loyal servant to my family.' Edith shook her head. Every time she opened her mouth, she made the situation worse. 'He refused to even countenance taking the cup, saying I needed it more than he did.'

'Why did you need it? What did he think you would do with it?'

'Your reputation precedes you. Athelstan feels uncomfortable about fostering his son with you.'

'Does he now?'

The back of her neck prickled and she readied herself for an attack. If he should move towards Athelstan, Edith knew she'd have to physically throw herself in front of him. She could not let him do something in temper that he'd regret later, and knowing Brand the way she did, she had to hope that he would see the sense in what she'd done, even if he couldn't forgive her for it.

'Yes, despite my reassurance.' Edith forced a smile. 'There is a rumour that you killed Egbert in cold blood. That you were the one to break the truce. All ill-founded rumour. I explained.'

He turned his head sharply to her. 'Do you believe it? Do you believe I am capable of such a thing?'

'Why would I? I knew my late husband and what he was capable of. He was a man who would cheat at tafl even when there were no stakes. You never cheat.' She held out her hands and gave Athelstan a hard look. 'I believe it makes it easier for your enemies to believe otherwise.'

Athelstan stood impassively in the doorway. 'I judge a man by his deeds.'

'I would trust you with my life, Brand,' Edith said. 'This is what I told Athelstan. I wanted you to foster Godwin as I know you'd mould him into the sort of honourable warrior both his parents want him to be.'

Silence fell as the two warriors regarded each

other. Edith knew if it came to it, Brand would win. He was the fitter, but nothing was ever certain.

'You know the penalty for helping this man,' Brand said in a terrible voice. 'There are no exceptions to this. Man, woman or child. The king has decreed.'

'I could not live with myself if I didn't help him.' Edith put her hands on her hips. He hadn't listened to her plea. She had thought he might. 'What would you have done if it had been you?'

'I would have done the right and proper thing. And I will do it. The king's decree will be fulfilled.'

Edith's heart sunk. Athelstan and his family were dead. Everyone who had helped from the kitchen boy who'd supplied the bread to Hilda who had carried the basket. They had all helped on her say so. Any blood split would be on her hands.

'And what is the proper thing?' she forced out around the lump in her throat.

'You should have informed me immediately. Any loyal subject would have done.'

'Why? Athelstan might yet perish. I had assumed that I could get him away. He was not going to harm you. He'd only gone with Egbert because I begged him to.'

'You went behind my back.'

'Because I had to.' Edith attempted to be reasonable. 'You were the one who received the order from the king, not me. I wouldn't be me if I had done otherwise.'

'That fails to signify. It covered the entire estate. Just as you feel responsibility for these people, I bear responsibility. Halfdan will judge me on what happens here.'

'What is going to happen now? Are you going to take your sword and mete out the king's punishment?'

His winter-smile chilled her to the bone. 'I am going to do what you did to Hrearek. Athelstan will come with us to Jorvik as my prisoner. The king can deal with him.'

Mary fell to her knees and raised her arms in supplication.

'You won't take my father!' Godwin cried and started to race towards Brand.

'He must, Godwin,' Edith answered, catching the little boy about the waist. She held him tight as his feet hit her shins. 'Don't you see? He has no choice. The king has decreed and you must always obey your overlord.'

As she said the words, she desperately hoped that Brand would contradict her. Surely he had to see that Athelstan's death would change nothing? And Halfdan was not known for his merciful qualities. She shuddered to remember how Aella had been made into a blood eagle after the failed attack to regain control of Eoferwic.

'Even if he is wrong?' Godwin asked.

'Even then,' Brand said, eliminating any small remaining hope. 'I have pledged my obedience to Halfdan. It was wrong of Lady Edith to offer false hope. In this case, I do not believe Halfdan was wrong. People who rebel against their rightful lord must be punished.'

'I don't want to be a warrior now.'

Edith knelt down beside Godwin. 'You must be brave for your mother and baby sister.'

The boy gave a great sniff and slowly nodded.

'You will get your things,' Brand said to Athelstan. 'And I will escort you back to the hall. You are my prisoner as you should have been from the start.'

'You will leave my wife and children here?'

'I see no reason to involve them. You are the one the king wants.'

Edith let out a breath. Godwin along with his mother and baby sister would be spared if Athelstan agreed to come quietly.

Athelstan gave a nod. 'All I wanted to do was to ensure my family were safe and well looked after. Will you give me your word?'

'I give my word that they will be as long as they stay on my land.' Brand banged his sword on the ground. 'You have my solemn oath.'

'Lady Edith speaks highly of you and I will accept your word.' Athelstan paused and glanced over his shoulder. 'Will you give me time to say my goodbyes in private?'

Brand shook his head. 'Too many men have tried that ruse. You may say them in front of me.'

Athelstan pursed his lips together before making a low bow. 'It was worth a try.'

'My lady.' Mary came over to Edith. 'He was going to go south today on his own. He'd decided his shoulder was well enough. He wanted to tell you himself.'

Edith clutched Mary's hand. 'I wish I could figure out a way to allow him to go free.'

'He was only doing his duty.'

'They both are.'

Edith went over to where Brand stood. 'I suppose you will wish me to stay here, rather than go to Jorvik.'

He raised an eyebrow. 'You underestimate me, Edith. You are going to go to Jorvik and you will be the one to explain to Halfdan what happened. He will be the one to decide your fate.'

Brand clung on to his temper until they returned to the hall through sheer will power. He wanted to do something and fight, not be lumbered with this dilemma.

Athelstan had gone willingly enough, but Brand knew he'd been deceived. It was fine for Edith to pontificate about her duty, but she had deliberately misled him—more than that, she'd lied to him. A lie by omission rather than actively telling him a falsehood, but a lie none the less. Edith was cut from the same cloth as his father's wife after all. He loathed himself for caring.

How many other people were aware? Was the entire hall laughing at him? The gullible Norseman taken in by a fine pair of eyes and a shapely turned calf. So intent on slaking his lust that he failed to notice what was happening under his nose!

He'd given Halfdan his word. And Edith expected him to break it. He refused to do that. This man, Athelstan, was his enemy. Halfdan's order made that clear. He knew where his loyalty and duty lay.

The thought that Edith considered that she could change his mind and make him forget his duty made his blood boil. He had wanted to believe that she was better than that and that she understood.

'Keep this prisoner in the yard!' Brand barked as they entered the stables. Two of his warriors leapt into action.

'One of the rebels escaped, but he has been found. He will be dealt with, properly,' Brand said at their shocked glances.

'What shall become of me?' Edith asked in a small voice. 'Am I to stand in the yard as well?'

'You are to retire to your room and await my pleasure.' He made a bow. 'Lars and Helgi will escort you there and ensure you stay there. I have no wish for you to go missing.'

The colour drained from her face. 'I never wanted it to be like this.'

'Then why did you do it? Why did you destroy what we shared? Why did you use me?'

'I had no choice.'

'I refuse to believe that. You always have a choice. You chose to place your loyalty with your manservant rather than with me where it belonged.'

'I'm sorry, Brand.' She held out her hands and Brand had the uncomfortable memory of Constantinople and the aftermath of the plot against the emperor. Teresa had come to him with tears in her eyes and blood on her hands. He'd refused to believe her guilt and had nearly died for it.

'Sorry for what? That you were found out or that you lied to me? You are like a thief who has been caught with his hand on the chicken and wants to avoid the punishment.'

A muscle jumped in her cheek. Brand willed her to say the truth. He concentrated on breathing easily, rather than roaring with rage.

'I will retire to my bedchamber and hope you calm down. When you reflect on what happened, you will see that I acted in your best interests. Think about how the people here will judge you and your mercy.'

'No, you acted in yours.' Summoning the last ounce of his self-control, he made a low bow. 'Now, will you go or do I need to get my men to drag you away?'

'I remain capable of walking.' She stalked off.

Brand silently cursed his fate. Why did he always have to become involved with black-hearted women? When was he going to learn? His heart ached more than it had with Teresa in Byzantium. His mouth twisted. He had thought Edith different.

Brand pushed the thought away. Later he'd take time to grieve for what could have been; now he had to see the full extent of his folly.

The shocked look on the servants' faces when he summoned the household to see the prisoner told him that the vast majority of them had had no idea. It was simply Edith and her cousin who knew.

Of the pair, Brand blamed Edith. The cousin had thrown herself sobbing and wailing on the floor. Starkad had intervened for her and Brand left the couple.

Edith stood in the middle of the bedchamber. Silent tears streamed down her face. She wiped them away with fierce fingers, but still they fell.

All her clothes were packed for Jorvik, even the bed hangings had been taken down. Silent reminders of how much her life had changed in a few heartbeats. Once she thought to be going and enjoying the splendours, maybe even convincing the king that she was the right person to marry Brand, and now she would be going as a prisoner. She was never going to return to her home.

'I had to do what I did,' Edith whispered. 'Why can't he see that? I wanted to protect him and us.'

The door crashed open and Brand stood there, glowering at her.

She knew she had to tell him. 'What we shared was too new. I wanted to keep some happiness. I hated that Athelstan returned, but I had a duty towards him. I was selfish, but I hoped you might share my desire.'

His mouth turned down. 'Why would I have feelings for you?'

The words cut her far more than any of Egbert's heavy blows had done. She staggered backwards. She might have feelings for him, but he only saw her as a warm body in the night.

'I thought we shared something special. You made me feel like I was the most important person in the world. I wanted to remake the world for you. Athelstan and his family had nothing to do with our future. I thought I was protecting you.'

'When I need that sort of protection I will ask.'

He gave a cynical smile. 'You were a pleasant bed partner, Edith. Untried but enthusiastic. I suppose I should be grateful that you didn't attempt to seduce me when I came in just now.'

Edith's cheeks burnt. Pleasant and untried? She had thought him so much more. 'Why would I do that?'

'Next time remember, Edith, I prefer honesty. Faithless women mean nothing to me.'

He turned on his heel and left the room.

Brand rode his horse slowly, keeping pace with the covered cart. The prisoner, Athelstan, walked behind with his hands tied and Edith rode within.

'Why did you do it, Edith?' he muttered. 'Why did you abuse my trust in this fashion?'

He'd gone over and over it in his mind. Despite what had passed between them, Edith wanted everything her way. She could have confessed and asked for help when it first happened.

He'd have listened sympathetically, but he had no choice to act otherwise. Edith would have saved herself though. She would have shown where her loyalties lay. The worst thing was the knowledge that what they had shared had been tainted. It had been a lie from start to finish. He had thought she was turning to him. In reality, she had been trying to deflect attention away from her servant.

He had longed for her to say those words about sharing something special and now he wished that she had left them unsaid.

Halfdan's orders were clear. He could not challenge something like that. It did not make it any easier to know that Athelstan was Godwin's father and probably a good man who had been caught on the losing side of a fight. For Edith he refused to have any pity. She had made her choice long ago.

'We halt here for this evening,' he said, pulling his horse up. 'Make a camp. There is water near here. I rested here on the way out to Breckon.'

Edith stumbled out of the cart. Despite the jolting she must have had, she managed to look as if she had stepped straight from the bath. His loins tightened. Despite everything, he still wanted her. And he would have her. Only, he would know not to trust her with his heart. He had considered it. Going to Jorvik had been devised as a test. There was always the remote possibility that Halfdan had forgotten about Edith's existence and that, once he knew, Brand would be ordered to marry her.

Brand shook his head. He'd come very close,

but he would never come that close again. When they got to Jorvik, he would send for a bride from back home, someone who would provide the right sort of loyalty.

'Why have we stopped?'

'It is best to make camp early. There have been reports of bands of outlaws. I camped here on the way to the hall. It has a good aspect.'

'It seems strange to think of outlaws and bandits roaming the countryside. Northumbria used to be such a peaceful place when I grew up.'

'Why? Men like Athelstan have survived and they have nowhere to go, nothing except to prey on innocent travellers. Halfdan is intent on having his peace kept. They will be brought to justice in time.'

She pressed her lips together. 'You are attempting to frighten me.'

'On the contrary, I am telling you the truth, rather than treating you like a child to be kept in the dark about matters.' As her face did not clear, he added, 'You must not be concerned as you will be protected. I will deliver you to Halfdan for his judgement safe and sound.'

'Brand, I'm sorry.' She raised her bound hands. 'I never meant for it to happen like this. You have to know that. I have been thinking in the cart and I wanted you to know that this had nothing to do with my feelings for you. I meant what I said in the bedchamber. I love you. I wanted to…to protect you. But I also had a duty to the people who had served my family. What passed between you and me was beyond all imagining. I didn't want to jeopardise that. I didn't explain it very well.'

'You have deep feelings for me? Funny you can only tell me about them after your little deception is discovered.' Brand forced his lips to turn up into a cynical smile. He'd heard those sorts of lying words before and made the mistake of believing them in Constantinople. He'd wanted to believe them in the bedchamber but the small sane spark of him refused. It had taken every ounce of will power to turn on his heel and leave. 'One might even call them self-serving.'

She visibly flinched. 'I knew before then. I was simply afraid to say something. I do have deep feelings for you Brand. I want what is best for you.'

'You have a strange way of showing it. You never showed me the slightest regard.' Brand stopped and regained control of his temper. 'Do you know what you did to me? What could have happened?'

She wet her lips and her hips swayed. 'If there was anything I could do to make it up to you, I would.'

She came closer to him and brushed her body against his. His body responded instantly. He pushed her away from him. Disgusted at her and, more important, disgusted with himself for wanting to believe in her. When was he going to learn that whenever a woman was in difficulties she resorted to seduction?

'Are you worried about your punishment?' he asked, making his voice drip with scorn. 'Do you think I would make it easier for you? Maybe allow you and Athelstan to escape if you kissed me or pretended that you might have feelings for me?'

Her eyes widened. 'I had hoped to persuade you about Athelstan—but for myself, I expect the punishment. I simply wanted to let you know I admire you. I hoped you might have feelings for me and want to understand why I felt compelled to do it.'

He shook his head. 'You lied to me and you expect me to think you have great feelings for me? It is far too convenient, Edith.'

'I never lied.' She stood up straighter. 'I omitted to tell you of Athelstan, that much is true. But then what punishment did the man who saved you when you were younger risk? Did he ever confess to your father's wife?'

'You have no right to bring that up!' White-hot anger surged through Brand. Odd had refused to come with him, sending his son Sven instead. Years later, Brand heard he'd died after his father's wife had turned her fury on him. He would have saved him if he could, but the two situations were not the same. Odd had not been in love with that woman.

'I've every right. Your friend risked his life to save yours, disobeying orders.' Edith glared at him. 'Why should I do any less for a man who has shown me and my family great loyalty and personal courage?'

Anger shot through Brand. How dare she use something private? He knew the sacrifice Odd had made. 'Do not compare the two. They are not the same!'

'Why?' she persisted.

'Because they are not.' Brand stared up at the sky and watched the clouds as he sought to control his temper. She had wronged him because she always thought of others, not herself or him or them. 'You like to pretend that you are doing it for the good of others, but really you do these things so that you can be lauded as being good. Why should one man's life matter more than anyone else's? You destroyed everything between us.'

'If I did, then there wasn't much to destroy.' She held out her hands with tears streaming down her face. 'Please tell me there was more between us than just desire.'

Brand's stomach knotted. Even now Edith sought to use him. It reminded him so much of when he had faced Teresa in Constantinople with the information that she had plotted against the emperor. He had believed her and men had died. He refused to make that mistake again. But he could not bear the thought of one hair on her head being harmed.

'Get out of my sight. Run and don't come back if you must. Or face up to the punishment you deserve. But don't ever expect me to understand what you did. Or try to dress it up as feelings for me. You used me! You used what we had and I can never forgive you for that.'

Chapter Fourteen

Edith dropped her hand to her side and allowed the tears to flow unhindered. Much of what Brand shouted was true and she had no defence. Not one he'd accept. She knew she'd destroyed any chance she had of happiness with him but she had hoped he could begin to understand.

All about her she was aware of the stillness of the glade and the various men pretending to go about their jobs rather than listening to her argument with Brand. She wanted to curl up in a ball and die. She had confessed her feelings for him, wept in public when she never wept and he'd thrown it back in her face. She was only thankful that there appeared to be far fewer men in the group—but by nightfall everyone would know.

No doubt there would be jokes and back slaps. All at her expense. Deep anger and resentment filled her. She didn't need to hear it. She would take his advice and go.

With Brand's words ringing in her ears about leaving, Edith marched out of the camp, expecting someone to stop her. No one did. With each step she took, a steady calm descended. It was better that she had discovered about Brand's lack of feeling now rather than building up any expectation about a long life with him.

She put her hands on her knees and drew a deep breath. She was sick of putting her duty before herself. No one thanked her for it. She wanted to have her dreams, rather than living for someone else. But was this the right way to go about it?

Running away would mean others would suffer for something she had done. She had to face the consequences of her actions. Maybe Halfdan would listen and spare lives when Brand would not. She had to do something to fight.

Straightening her shoulders, she started back towards the camp.

The sound of a snapping twig made Edith freeze and press back against a tree. From the opposite side of the camp, men advanced stealthily towards the camp, but the men in the camp seemed un-awares.

Horror flooded through Edith. Brand and all his men were in danger. She attempted to scream, but no sound came out. She swallowed hard and tried again.

'Brand!' she shouted. 'We are under attack! To arms! To arms!'

Brand and his men instantly had their swords out, but the others rushed forwards, shouting their battle cry in Norse. She saw the first Norseman fall and knew that this was no ordinary attack. It had been planned.

When she caught a glimpse of a great hulking shadow she knew. Hrearek had not made his way to Ireland, but had gathered men here, intent on revenge. Edith remembered what Brand had said the first time they played tafl—Hrearek was a formidable opponent. Brand could not know if anyone was loyal or not.

She had unwittingly provided Hrearek with the opportunity. He must have guessed that she'd react that way. Had Halfdan's messenger even been from him?

She grabbed a knife from the fallen Norseman.

She ran towards where Athelstan stood, with his bound hands, and started to saw away.

'What are you doing, my lady? Hide! Save yourself!'

'Freeing you to fight.'

'Why? We should run. The Norseman brought the trouble on his own head.'

'It is a trap. Brand is in danger. I know the outlaws' leader.'

'Why should I lift a finger to help him? He wanted to kill us both.'

'Because I ask it, Athelstan.' Edith made one final swipe with the knife and tried to think of a reason which would appeal to Athelstan's better nature. 'He is a good man, the best. If he dies, we both die.'

'I die anyway. Keep your head down, my lady, and hope for the best. We may yet escape.'

Edith's shout had given Brand that instant of warning. Silently he cursed his folly. It had been too easy for the attackers.

He had been too distracted with his problems with Edith to notice the obvious signs. He'd been set up, but by whom? Was that why Athelstan had been so complacent? Was this the start of renewed hostilities? 'To me, men!'

He drew his sword and pivoted with metal meeting metal. The bone-jarring crash reverberated up his arm and he knew the attackers were not Northumbrians, but Norsemen. But which ones? His jaw dropped as a man emerged from the thicket. Hrearek. He'd been played. The messenger from Halfdan was false. He'd come from Hrearek. Hrearek knew of Brand's past and had used it. Brand ground his teeth, furious with himself.

His sword dispatched the first attacker and he turned to meet another.

Brand redoubled his efforts to reach Hrearek, his sword flashing and men falling.

Finally he met Hrearek. The great warrior stood with his fellow countrymen's blood on his axe.

'You false worm!' Brand ground out. 'You do challenge!'

'At a time and place of my choosing. You know I always play the game until the end.' Hrearek made a mocking flourish with his sword. 'You were always predictable, Brand. Your lust blinded you. I knew you'd doubt her and I would find a chance to strike.'

Their swords clashed and Brand circled Hrearek,

probing and jabbing, countering each stroke of Hrearek's sword with one of his own.

'Why?' Brand ground out.

'I want what you have and I will finally have it.' Hrearek gave a little smile as spittle bubbled in the corner of his mouth. 'When you are dead, I will enjoy your woman and then I will kill her slowly. Afterwards, I will take your bodies to Halfdan and he will proclaim me as the jaarl as he should have done after I arranged for the truce to be broken. You were supposed to die that day.'

Brand half-checked his sword. Hrearek breathed evil. 'You will not prevail.'

'Where are your men, Brand? Who will be your saviour…this time? You are alone as you always have been.'

Sweat dripped down Brand's back as the swords clashed and clashed again. Always moving about the glade. Closer to the trees and then further away. They were well matched. Each knowing the other's strength because of the years of practice, both watched for the tiniest hint of an opening. Hrearek feinted to the left. Brand blocked it and moved to his right. His left foot twisted on a tree root. He stumbled, hitting his knee on the ground. Hrearek's sudden swipe with his sword resulted in the sword spinning out of his hand, landing on the other side of Hrearek.

'The great Brand Bjornson felled by a tree.' Hrearek laughed, raising his sword for the killing blow. 'You should have known I would return. I do not forget those who have done me wrong. Look on me and despair.'

'You will not succeed, Hrearek!' Edith shouted from where she stood, paralysed with fear. Her stomach knotted and she found it impossible to turn away from the horrific spectacle. One after another the men had stopped fighting and stood watching the two Norseman warriors battling it out. It was a fight to the death. She clenched her fists. Brand had to win, but how? In the next heartbeat he'd be dead.

She started forwards but Athelstan grabbed her arm. 'It is not your fight. One Norseman is like another.'

'Let me go!' She fought against his hold. 'This is my fight. I refuse to allow Brand Bjornson to be killed. I love him. Help me, Athelstan.'

Hrearek turned towards her and made a slight salute with his sword. He raised it above his head and prepared to strike the final killing blow, but as he brought it down Brand twisted out the way.

'Please,' she whispered. 'I beg you.'

'No! I can't allow you.' Athelstan twisted her arm so that the knife fell to the ground. He stood straight, far straighter than he had since he'd returned. 'I'll do it. I know that man. We have a score to settle. He is the one I overheard boasting about how he broke the truce. You were right. Your lord is innocent. I should have gone when you first asked, my lady.'

He grabbed the fallen knife and started forwards. Edith fell to her knees, hand stuffed in her mouth, unable to turn her head.

Everything happened in slow motion—the slice of Hrearek's sword towards Brand, Athelstan's cry as he ran with his knife, Hrearek's sudden pivot as he sought to fend off Athelstan, Athelstan's one desperate stab forwards.

Hrearek blocked the attack. Easily. Almost lazily, he swiped the knife away before jabbing his sword. Even before he withdrew the blade, Edith knew it was deep, potentially fatal. In that instant Brand twisted to the right and drove his sword upwards, connecting with Hrearek

The Norseman toppled to the ground dead. Brand retrieved his sword and cleaned it on the spring grass before replacing it in its hilt, the studied action of a man who had performed the same task a hundred times before. The tight expression of his lips showed Edith how shaken and upset he was. She sat back on her heels and waited, understanding that Brand needed time to finish his rituals.

The other warriors started to round up the remaining attackers and started to lay out their fallen in preparation for a pyre. Hrearek, Edith noticed, had no attention paid to him.

'I owe you a life-debt, Edith,' Brand said, coming up to her and raising her up. 'Your shout saved my life and many of my men's lives. And you caused Hrearek's death.'

'Not me,' Edith replied. Her legs trembled so much that she doubted they could hold her. She wanted to throw her arms about Brand and check that every particle of him was unharmed, but after what had passed between them, she didn't dare. 'You owe Athelstan one. He wielded the knife.'

Brand glanced over to where the man lay. Blood bubbled out of Athelstan's mouth and Brand knew what that meant. Death would come within a few heartbeats. He turned back to Edith and wondered if she guessed what this man's future was?

'Indeed I owe him a life-debt,' Brand said, bowing his head. 'I will honour it to the best of my abilities.'

'Will you allow him to go free now?' Tears shimmered in her eyes. 'He is a ghost to you. He could take a different name and serve as your loyal subject.'

'Alas, I would if I could,' he said, shaking his head.

'You and your stupid honour! There are things which are more important.'

'Edith,' Brand said, laying his hand on her shoulder. He had never expected her to defend him like that. She was completely different to any other woman he'd ever known. He had wronged her in thought, word and deed. He did not deserve her. 'He is dying. He gave his life for yours. He did what you asked.'

'For mine?' Her eyes widened. 'He saved you.'

'You would have rushed Hrearek yourself and died. He knew this as I do. You are many things, Edith, but you are no warrior. You've never been trained. You would not have stood a chance.'

She did not reply, but instead went over to her servant and raised his head up so that he rested on her lap

'Lady Edith, I wanted to tell you before…' the man croaked.

'Hush, don't try to speak.' She put two fingers against his lips. 'Save your strength. Save your breath. Your family needs you.'

'I'm dying, my lady. I've known that for days. My other wound, the one in my shoulder, is putrid.'

'Athelstan, these things are never certain.'

He raised his hand and reached towards where Brand stood. 'I made a mistake. Lord Bjornson was not who I thought he was. All Norsemen look alike to me. The other one, the one who attacked, was…he was the one with the axe. The one who broke the truce.'

'Thank you for telling me.' Edith bowed her head. 'I already knew Lord Bjornson was innocent. I'm pleased you know it as well. All this was caused by one man—Hrearek. I know this in my heart.'

'I owe you my life,' Brand said, kneeling beside the pair. Without Edith's quick thinking and Athelstan's help, he would be the one on the ground dead. In his blindness and jealousy, he had blamed them for using him. He'd been afraid of what he felt for Edith and had used her actions as the wedge to drive them apart. 'Are you sure of your intelligence?'

'I watched...' Athelstan gave a hard cough which prevented him from speaking.

Brand knew the end was near and that there were things which were far more important than who did what on a distant battlefield. This man had returned because of his family. 'I promise you to look after your son as if he was my own. He will want for nothing. I will make him a brave warrior.'

The former rebel gave a ghost of a smile. 'I could not ask for better payment of a life-debt. You do that and it will be paid.'

His eyes rolled back and his body convulsed sharply before lying still. Brand leant over and closed Athelstan's unseeing eyes.

'Edith?' Brand laid a gentle hand on her shoulder. 'It is done and finished. You need to get cleaned up.'

A single tear rolled down her face. 'What happens next? Will we be able to bury him back on the estate? Athelstan should have a proper place with his ancestors.'

Brand lifted the body off Edith's lap and laid him out with arms folded. The warrior looked oddly at peace. Brand knew that in another time and place they could have been friends.

'Shall we return to Breckon, Edith?' he asked softly. 'Forget this ever happened? We can take him back ourselves.'

She stood up and walked away from him with hunched shoulders. He knew it had to be her choice, but silently he willed her to understand what he was offering.

'No,' she said, turning. With her shoulders back and her head erect, she looked beautiful despite the dirt smudges. 'I can never forget this day. We must go to Jorvik. The king must know what happened, but Athelstan should be buried in the churchyard where his son can visit. Can this be done?'

Brand's heart sank. She had chosen a warrior's path, the same one he would have done, but it did not mean it would be easy.

'Very well. Enough of my men remain standing. I will send a detail with Athelstan's body back to Breckon. The outlaws will not have a stomach for a fight now that their leader is dead. Are you sure you want to do this? You could return.'

She shook her head. 'Halfdan needs to hear the

full story and see the proof with his eyes. I want to make sure the truth is known.'

He gathered her in his arms. 'I will tell Halfdan the truth.'

'Will you tell him about me and my part?' she asked, giving him a strange look.

'I could hardly lie about it.' Silently he vowed to keep her out of things.

She gazed up at him. Her eyes shimmered. 'He needs to know, Brand. I can't have you lie on my part.'

'Halfdan is not without feeling,' Brand sought to explain. The order about wanting to punish all the rebels might have come from Hrearek, but Brand knew Halfdan had expressed such wishes in the past. 'I have never heard it said that he harms women. His heart may yet soften.'

'And that is supposed to comfort me? I made my choice long ago.'

He willed her to relax, but she stood stiffly away from him. It was as if he were hugging a statue. He took his arm away. He'd been wrong to hope that her feelings went deeper than saving Athelstan. He knew now that he loved her and had wronged her. He had to hope that she would find it in her heart to love him, properly and without reservation. He knew he had to give her a reason to love him. But just as she had tried to tell him that she had feelings for him and he could not believe, he knew she would not believe him. He had to show her. Maybe over time, she would see that he needed her.

'I promise not to allow anything to happen to you. I owe you a life-debt. Is that better?'

'It will have to be.' She moved away from him, her arms hugging her waist. 'I would like to return to my cart. I want time alone to grieve. I want to learn my fate as soon as possible. If it is to be death, I want it done quickly. Know, Brand, I could not do anything differently.'

'I will do all in my power to protect you. You must know that. Search your heart.'

Edith shook her head. 'You would never go against your king. You were right in what you said before, Brand. There is nothing between us but desire and even that is gone now. Please leave me alone to grieve.'

Brand forced his hands to stay at his side. He had deeply wronged her and now he had to pay the price. He and he alone had destroyed the fragile flowering of their relationship. Silently he thanked his lucky stars that Edith had agreed to remain his concubine for a year. He had time to mend the relationship. He would bind her irrevocably to him.

'We have not finished, Edith,' he muttered. 'I will find a way to show you that I am worthy of you.'

Chapter Fifteen

Jorvik teemed with life. Edith peered out of the narrow slit in the jolting cart. The next time she went to Jorvik, she would ride. Next time? She gave a wry smile. She doubted that she would get out of Jorvik alive.

The best she could hope for was that Halfdan would allow her to retire to some windswept convent. Her entire body seemed to be numb, encased in ice ever since Athelstan's death. She was grateful that Brand had not tried to touch or hold her, but had left her strictly alone. The last thing she wanted was to feel alive.

The wooden buildings were larger and more numerous than she had remembered. There were far more people than she thought possible, thronging the streets and going about their business. Everywhere there was an air of peaceful prosperity.

Edith shivered slightly, remembering the last time she'd seen this city with its burnt-out buildings. She'd never have considered in a few short years all that misery would be swept away. The market appeared to hold all manner of objects. Edith wished she had time to properly explore and find red ribbons for Hilda. She needed to remember to ask Brand to look after Hilda.

'We've arrived.' Brand appeared at the door of the cart.

They had barely spoken since the aftermath of the attack. Edith hated that her body leapt every time she saw him. She wanted to sink into his arms and ask him to take away this terrible fear about what was going to happen to her.

'Will Halfdan see us today?' she asked in a small voice.

'I'll arrange an audience. There is an order to such things. Hrearek's body will have to be laid out in the palace's yard for him to inspect.'

Edith nodded. Her entire body felt numb. This was probably the last time she'd be able to speak to Brand in private. 'Once you have returned home to Breckon, I trust you to make sure the appropriate number of masses are said for Athelstan. Father Wilfrid might be tempted to skimp, but don't allow him to. He must say them all.' She paused, hating how her voice broke on the word home. She swallowed hard. 'When you see Godwin and his mother again, I know you will tell them in the appropriate way of Athelstan's heroism. You gave your word.'

Half of her waited for him to give some easy answer about her going back there as well.

'I will be sure to do that.'

She peered out of the cart. 'Where are we?'

He lifted an eyebrow. 'At my house.'

'You have a house here?'

'Where else would I live?' He tilted his head. 'There have been times when I haven't been out campaigning. I wanted somewhere to lay my head which isn't infected with palace intrigue. Halfdan understands.'

'I hadn't thought about it,' Edith confessed. Her senses spun. They were going to his house, rather than having her endure proper captivity. He was true to his word. But that added to the danger. She couldn't bear it if he took the punishment for her wrongdoing.

'I see no point in sending a message when I can tell him the full story, refreshed and the dust from the road washed off. Sometimes stories need to be told face to face. Once he knows, you have nothing to fear.'

It was easy for him to say, but she knew the stories. Her limbs trembled.

'Do you think he will believe it?'

'He will. Hrearek's challenge to me was also a challenge to Halfdan's kingship. Halfdan is now more secure than ever on the throne. I will put it in the right way. They will be cheering you from the streets when I am done.'

'You are going to lie.'

He gave a small smile. 'I prefer to call it—telling the story in the correct light.'

'I will take your word for that.'

'It is a start.'

'What?'

'You believing me on this.' He lifted her chin and looked her in the eyes. The ice that had been around her heart melted and all the desire she thought she'd never feel again came flooding back. 'After tomorrow, I hope you will believe me that I intend to protect you for as long as I can.'

Edith knew that she wanted to walk into his arms and lay her head against his chest. And that would be the worst thing in the world to do. He only felt an obligation towards her because she had saved his life, rather than this overwhelming need to be with her. He had been quite clear on that. 'I have done a fair job thus far.'

'And I haven't appreciated you enough.' He reached out and pulled her into his arms.

He put his mouth on hers and Edith allowed herself to sink into his embrace. She knew it was wrong, but she needed to use the passion to forget about her future.

'I won't regret this,' she whispered against his chest. 'Ever. You taught me there was more to life than duty.'

He recaptured her lips. 'No more talking, Edith. Kiss me.'

Norseman in their resplendent furs, along with a few exotic women, crowded the palace yard. It seemed the rumours had already circulated around Jorvik and everyone wanted a glimpse of the woman who had defied the king.

Edith looked neither to the right or left, but kept her gaze focused on the grey-haired man who sat on the throne. Even his pointed beard bristled with importance. This was the man who would decide her fate.

Edith found she was more than calm. The peace

had descended some time in the middle of the night. She'd lain in Brand's arms and she knew that whatever happened, she discovered there was more to living than simply existing to serve others.

'Who do you bring, Brand Bjornson?' the king boomed out.

'Lady Edith of Breckon. I believe you knew her father. Her husband was one of the leaders of the recent rebellion.'

'I understood Lady Edith died in childbirth two years ago. I sent money in condolences. I understood her husband was far too grief-stricken to remarry.'

Edith stared at him. Egbert had lied. It made sense now why he had refused to allow her to go to Jorvik with him. She had been a fool not to question the order. It seemed far easier to stay on the estate and oversee everything. 'I am Lady Edith of Breckon. We met many years ago when you first gained the throne. You told me that I had a very stubborn chin.'

'Ah, I remember the encounter,' the king said and tugged at his pointed beard. 'I can see your father in you. You have his chin and nose and your chin remains stubborn.'

Edith inclined her head. 'I take that as a compliment as my father was regarded as a handsome man in his youth.'

'What brings you to Jorvik after all this time?' His face grew stern. 'I will not countenance giving you back your lands. They belong to Brand Bjornson.'

Edith glanced at Brand. 'I know that.'

'Lady Edith is here to support my claim that Hrearek wronged me and was killed in lawful combat when he challenged for the leadership of the felag. No tribute is owed to his relatives and he died a traitor and a coward.'

'I saw Hrearek's body.' The king's blue eyes seemed to peer deep into her soul. 'I would ask Lady Edith to tell her story. I wish to verify everything and then I will pronounce my judgement, Brand Bjornson.'

Brand frowned, but fell silent.

Edith rapidly explained about what had happened, leaving out nothing including how she had sought to help Athelstan and how Brand decided to take them both to Jorvik. Brand started to splutter when she mentioned this, but Halfdan silenced him with a look. Brand was right when he said that Halfdan deserved to know the full truth. Finally she finished with Athelstan's death and Brand's promise to him to look after Godwin.

Halfdan was silent for a long while, but Edith kept her head up. She had nothing to fear. Brand laid his hand on her shoulder and squeezed.

'Leave us, Brand Bjornson.' Halfdan clapped his hands. 'Leave us, everyone. I would speak to Lady Edith alone before I give my judgement.'

Brand glanced at her. 'I will go if Lady Edith wishes me to go.'

'I will not have you defy your king,' Edith said in an undertone.

'You should have allowed me to speak. You did not have to say half the things you said. But I am proud of you, Edith.'

'No, you were right.' Edith put two fingers over his mouth to keep him from saying anything more. 'Halfdan needed to know the full truth. Now obey your king and go.'

Brand looked annoyed, but he obeyed her request.

'What am I to do with you, Lady Edith?' the king asked when all had departed.

'Do, your Majesty?' she said.

'There were those who might say I should punish you as you aided one of the rebels.'

'He was my man. I kept him hidden from everyone, but I had no intention of allowing him to stay in this realm.'

'I understand why you helped him. I did not say that as king I approved, but as a man who has a heart, I know why you did this.'

Edith frowned. 'Then I appeal to the man, rather than the king. Please make my punishment lenient. I promise to be a faithful subject as much as I can.'

'Well said.' The king smiled. 'Your father kept the peace well. If I had known you were alive, I would have ordered Brand to marry you.'

Edith gulped. He would have ordered Brand to marry her. It would have been as she thought it might be when he first arrived. 'Please don't order him now.'

'I understand you are his concubine. Do you wish to remain as such?' The king's eyes narrowed. 'Or did he force you to take the position and you wish to retire to a convent? Your heart is as strong as any Norsewoman's. You should have the privilege of choosing your lover.'

'I wish Brand to be able to marry the woman he chooses, rather than having it forced on him.'

His eyes assessed her. 'Even if that woman isn't you?'

'I doubt he wants to marry me.'

'Then the man is a fool.'

'You will tell him.' Edith kept her head up. Inside her heart broke into a thousand shards. Last night, Brand had made tender love to her, but no words of love were spoken. She knew she needed more than that. She had no wish to spin dreams again. It was better to have the pain now, rather than see him grow to hate her. 'I know the lands are in good hands with Brand Bjornson.'

'Where will you go?'

She shrugged. 'I had not thought about that. Perhaps I should retire to a convent.'

'You may stay at court until I say you can go.' The king nodded. 'It is the best place for you. Now let me speak to Brand Bjornson. Alone.'

Edith's throat closed and she could only nod.

'You are going to stay *where*?' Brand burst into the room. His eyes were wild and his hair askew. Little remained of the polished courtier who had escorted her to the palace and, in his place, Brand had become the warrior again.

'The king has informed you?' Edith closed the book she had been pretending to read while she waited in the antechamber and folded her hands in her lap. The waiting time was over. All she wanted was for this interview to be finished. It was best to break quickly and cleanly.

'You are to remain at court under the king's protection. Why is this necessary?' His eyes blazed. 'How do you think you will advance your people by being here rather than back at home? You belong at Breckon, Edith.'

Edith's heart did a queer leap. He spoke of the estate as home. It would always be that for her, even if she could only visit it in her dreams.

'The king asked me to remain at court.' She gave a light laugh. The sound held a false note. 'Apparently I impressed him. There is no need for me to return to Breckon. I can stay in this bustling city and really learn what it is like to be at the centre of politics. The king has promised me a place based on the respect he held for my father.'

She hoped he would not question her further. With each passing breath, this act became harder to maintain. Already she could feel the tears pooling at the back of her throat.

His lips turned down. 'You promised to be my concubine for a year. You never break promises, Edith. Ever.'

Her throat became far too tight. She struggled to breathe. All he cared about was slaking his lust. The closeness she had felt after making love was illusory. He had told her that before. Last night didn't make a difference to him. She took several life-giving breaths. Brand must not guess exactly how much she wanted to be in his arms. There were so many reasons why it would be wrong. Today was about getting her life back, but right now it felt like she was being sentenced to a life of unhappiness. In many ways it was a far worse punishment than losing her life.

'Are you going to hold me to the promise?' she whispered, concentrating on the whiteness of her knuckles.

Brand made a disgusted noise. 'I never thought you would give up on your promise. I never thought you were a quitter.'

'The king thought it best. It might cause difficulties if I stayed your acknowledged concubine.

He expects his earls to marry.' Edith dug her nails into her palm. He had to understand why she was doing this. It was far better to have a clean break. Waiting for him to summon whichever lady from Norway was too dreadful to contemplate. And she couldn't have had the king force Brand to marry her. She had her pride and she'd already experienced a forced marriage. This was the best solution even if her heart ached like the very devil. 'Did you want me to refuse the king? He was already very charitable towards me.'

'No.' Brand stood up straighter. He made no move to gather Edith into his arms. He wanted to haul her away and keep her a captive until she agreed to marry him. But he also knew that she had to be happy. He had this one last chance and he would take it. Of all the women he'd ever met, Edith was the one who was worth fighting for. But he hadn't anticipated this move by her.

He had planned on spending the rest of the time they had convincing her to stay. Now she had neatly sidestepped the issue. Once again he was going to be left alone. Only this time it was worse as he knew the one person he wanted was forbidden. At least he knew she would be looked after, whatever happened.

Her face closed and took on a mulish expression. 'I'm pleased you are being so understanding.'

'I, too, had a conversation with the king.'

'Did you?' She raised a brow. 'How good of you. I'm sure you are very relieved to get it out of the way. You need to get your life in order.'

'He agrees with me that for the sake of the estate, it would be best if we married.'

Edith's jaw dropped. 'Why are you doing this? You want to have a Norsewoman for a wife.'

Brand waved a hand. 'You have a duty towards your people. I am allowing you to do that duty.'

'You had no compunction before.'

'I didn't know you then. I didn't know how much people depended on you.' Brand reached for her hand. 'It is the right thing to do.'

'And will the king force me to marry you as a result of your actions?' she asked, drawing her hand to her side and ignoring him. 'I don't want a forced marriage.'

'Halfdan will do as he pleases,' Brand admitted with a frown. He had to hope his plan worked. When he'd learned from Halfdan that her request for a reward was that he marry any woman that he wanted, he had known what he had to do. He'd asked for the king's help in marrying the woman he loved. 'For now, he is content that you should have the estate as a dowry to attract the right husband.'

'I don't want a husband who is only interested in my dowry or who marries me out of duty. I had one of those before. It doesn't work. It is a cold, lifeless thing.'

'Doesn't it work?' he asked. 'How could a marriage with you in it ever be cold or lifeless? You have more heart than anyone I have ever met and you have shown a hardened warrior what loyalty is truly about. You have shown the true essence of caring for people.'

'I have no wish to take a husband simply because people say I must,' Edith retorted cautiously. Her heart began to hammer. She didn't dare think about what he was saying. She'd been so wrong before.

'What do you want to do, Edith?' he asked quietly.

'I am not sure what I want any more. I thought I knew, but lately everything has been muddled.' She resisted the urge to lay her head on his chest.

'I want you to be happy. I want you to have your most cherished dreams.'

'I know the feeling. You can give that to me.'

'How?'

He dropped to one knee. 'Edith, I want to spend the rest of my life with you. I want to marry you. I want you to bear my children if we are so blessed or, if we are not, I want to grow old with you.'

Edith started shaking. Brand was on one knee, proposing to her. He had convinced Halfdan to give her back the estate. But she knew she needed more.

'Why?'

'Because I love you with all of my soul. I want you in my life and in my bed. I have no desire for any other woman. I want to know that you want me for me, not because it will benefit the estate. Selfishly, utterly and completely.'

With each word, Edith's heart grew lighter. 'I want you to be happy, Brand. I love you. Not because you are an earl or because you hold the power of life and death over people I care about, but because you are you.'

'I have no wish for some faraway maid, all I want I hold in my arms. Your love is my most cherished dream. Will you marry me?'

Edith threw her arms about his neck. 'Yes, yes, I will.'

'I have come home at last,' he whispered against her hair.

'As have I.'

* * * * *

Discover more romance at

www.millsandboon.co.uk

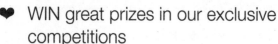